School
STORIES

Kingfisher Books, Grisewood & Dempsey Ltd,
Elsley House, 24–30 Great Titchfield Street,
London W1P 7AD

First published in paperback in 1992 by Kingfisher Books
10   9   8   7   6   5   4   3
Originally published in hardback in 1989 by Kingfisher Books

BRITISH LIBRARY CATALOGUING IN PUBLICATION DATA
A catalogue record for this book is available
from the British Library

ISBN 0 86272 875 4

Designed by Penny and Tony Mills
Cover design by The Pinpoint Design Company
Phototypeset by Waveney Typesetters, Norwich
Printed and bound in Great Britain by
BPCC Hazell Books
Aylesbury, Bucks, England
Member of BPCC Ltd.

·STORY LIBRARY·

School

STORIES

CHOSEN BY
JAN MARK

ILLUSTRATED BY
DAVID PARKINS

Kingfisher Books

CONTENTS

Acknowledgements   6

THE BALACLAVA STORY   7
George Layton

A PRINCE IN ANOTHER PLACE   16
Philippa Pearce

AMY'S VALLEY OF HUMILIATION   27
Louisa May Alcott (from *Little Women*)

THE CONVENT OF THE BLESSED LIMIT   36
Andrew Davies (from *Educating Marmalade*)

A NICE OLD-FASHIONED ROMANCE WITH LOVE   45
LYRICS AND EVERYTHING
William Saroyan (from *My Name Is Aram*)

COUSINS   55
Noel Streatfeild (from *Curtain Up*)

M.13 IN FORM ONCE MORE   67
Gene Kemp

THE DAY POSY BATES MADE HISTORY   74
Helen Cresswell

THE WOOLLEN BANK FORGERIES   84
Keith Waterhouse

GREEN GRAVEL   97
Jill Paton Walsh

THE PRIZE POEM   107
P. G. Wodehouse (from *Tales of St Austin's*)

THE EIGHTEENTH EMERGENCY – an extract   116
Betsy Byars

BILLY THE KID   128
William Golding

MAM'ZELLE'S 'TREEK'   136
Enid Blyton (from *In the Fifth at Malory Towers*)

MIDGE PROVOKES HYSTERIA   143
Winifred Holtby (from *South Riding*)

FRIDAY   156
Susan Cooper

THE EXERCISE   161
Bernard MacLaverty

THE LEFT OUTSIDE   170
Beryl C. Lawley

A SCHOOL STORY   181
M. R. James

A NEW BOY   190
Talbot Baines Reed (from *The Fifth Form at St Dominic's*)

THE CHOICE IS YOURS   202
Jan Mark

THE FALL OF THE IDOL   213
Richmal Crompton (from *Just William*)

JANE EYRE – an extract   226
Charlotte Brontë

TOM SAWYER – an extract   237
Mark Twain

I AM GOING TO BE GOOD   243
Geoffrey Willans (from *The Compleet Molesworth*)

Acknowledgements

For permission to reproduce copyright material,
acknowledgement and thanks are due to the following:

Longman Group UK Ltd for 'The Balaclava Story' from
A Northern Childhood: The Balaclava Story and other stories
(Knockout series) by George Layton;
Laura Cecil on behalf of the author for 'A Prince in Another
Place' from *Whose Afraid?* © Philippa Pearce 1980, published by
Puffin Books (UK) and Greenwillow Books, a division of
William Morrow (USA);
Blackie & Son Ltd for 'The Convent of the Blessed Limit' from
Educating Marmalade by Andrew Davies;
Harcourt Brace Jovanovich for 'A Nice Old-Fashioned Romance
with Love Lyrics and Everything' from *My Name Is Aram*
by William Saroyan;
the author's estate and J. M. Dent & Sons Ltd for 'Cousins' from
Curtain Up by Noel Streatfeild;
Laurence Pollinger Ltd on behalf of the author for 'M.13 In Form
Once More' by Gene Kemp from *Hundreds and Hundreds*
published by Puffin Books;
the author for 'The Day Posy Bates Made History' by Helen
Cresswell from *Jubilee Jackanory* published by BBC
Enterprises Ltd;
David Higham Associates Ltd on behalf of the authors for 'The
Woollen Bank Forgeries' by Keith Waterhouse from *Voices*, and
for 'Green Gravel' by Jill Paton Walsh from *A Quiver of Ghosts*
published by The Bodley Head;
Souvenir Press Ltd for 'The Prize Poem' from *Tales of St Austin's*
by P. G. Wodehouse;
The Bodley Head for an extract from *The Eighteenth Emergency* by
Betsy Byars; and for 'Friday' from *Dawn of Fear* by Susan Cooper;
Faber & Faber Ltd for 'Billy the Kid' from *The Hot Gates*
by William Golding;
Methuen Children's Books for 'Mam'zelle's "Treek" ' from *In the
Fifth at Malory Towers* by Enid Blyton;
The Blackstaff Press for 'The Exercise' from *Secrets and other stories*
by Bernard MacLaverty;
Penguin Books Ltd for 'The Choice is Yours' from *Nothing to be
Afraid of* by Jan Mark;
Mrs Richmal Crompton and Macmillan, London and
Basingstoke, for 'The Fall of the Idol' from *Just William*
by Richmal Crompton;
and Tessa Sayle Agency for 'I am Going to be Good', copyright
© 1958 by Geoffrey Willans, from *The Compleet Molesworth* by
Geoffrey Willans and Ronald Searle published by Pavilion Books.

While every effort has been made to obtain permission, there
may still be cases in which we have failed to trace a copyright
holder, and we would like to apologize for any apparent
negligence.

THE BALACLAVA STORY

GEORGE LAYTON

Tony and Barry both had one. I reckon half the kids in our class had one. But I didn't. My mum wouldn't even listen to me.

"You're not having a balaclava! What do you want a balaclava for in the middle of summer?"

I must've told her about ten times why I wanted a balaclava.

"I want one so's I can join the Balaclava Boys . . ."

"Go and wash your hands for tea, and don't be so silly."

She turned away from me to lay the table, so I put the curse of the middle finger on her. This was pointing both your middle fingers at somebody when they weren't looking. Tony had started it when Miss Taylor gave him a hundred lines for flicking paper pellets at Jennifer Greenwood. He had to write out a hundred times: "I must not fire missiles because it is dangerous and liable to cause damage to someone's eye."

Tony tried to tell Miss Taylor that he hadn't fired a missile, he'd just flicked a paper pellet, but she threw a piece of chalk at him and told him to shut up.

"Don't just stand there – wash your hands."

"Eh?"

"Don't say 'eh', say 'pardon'."

"What?"

"Just hurry up, and make sure the dirt comes off in the water, and not on the towel, do you hear?"

Ooh, my mum. She didn't half go on sometimes.

"I don't know what you get up to at school. How do you get so dirty?"

I knew exactly the kind of balaclava I wanted. One just like Tony's, a sort of yellowy-brown. His dad had given it to him because of his earache. Mind you, he didn't like wearing it at first. At school he'd given it to Barry to wear and got it back before home-time. But, all the other lads started asking if they could have a wear of it, so Tony took it back and said from then on nobody but him could wear it, not even Barry. Barry told him he wasn't bothered because he was going to get a balaclava of his own, and so did some of the other lads. And that's how it started – the Balaclava Boys.

It wasn't a gang really. I mean they didn't have meetings or anything like that. They just went around together wearing their balaclavas, and if you didn't have one you couldn't go around with them. Tony and Barry were my best friends, but because I didn't have a balaclava, they wouldn't let me go round with them. I tried.

"Aw, go on, Barry, let us walk round with you."

"No, you can't. You're not a Balaclava Boy."

"Aw, go on."

"No."

"Please."

I don't know why I wanted to walk round with them anyway. All they did was wander up and down the playground dressed in their rotten balaclavas. It was daft.

"Go on, Barry, be a sport."

"I've told you. You're not a Balaclava Boy. You've got to have a balaclava. If you get one, you can join."

"But I can't, Barry. My mum won't let me have one."

"Hard luck."

"You're rotten."

Then he went off with the others. I wasn't half fed up. All my friends were in the Balaclava Boys. All the lads in my class except me. Wasn't fair. The bell went for the next lesson – ooh heck, handicraft with the Miseryguts Garnett – then it was home-time. All the Balaclava Boys were going in and I followed them.

"Hey, Tony, do you want to go down the woods after school?"

"No, I'm going round with the Balaclava Boys."

"Oh."

Blooming Balaclava Boys. Why wouldn't *my mum* buy *me* a *balaclava*? Didn't she realize that I was losing all my friends, and just because she wouldn't buy me one?

"Eh, Tony, we can go goose-gogging – you know, by those great gooseberry bushes at the other end of the woods."

"I've told you, I can't."

"Yes, I know, but I thought you might want to go goose-gogging."

"Well, I would, but I can't."

I wondered if Barry would be going as well.

"Is Barry going round with the Balaclava Boys an' all?"

"Course he is."

"Oh."

Blooming balaclavas. I wish they'd never been invented.

"Why won't your mum get you one?"

"I don't know. She says it's daft wearing a balaclava in the middle of summer. She won't let me have one."

"I found mine at home up in our attic."

Tony unwrapped some chewing-gum and asked me if I wanted a piece.

"No thanks." I'd've only had to wrap it in my handkerchief once we got in the classroom. You couldn't get away with anything with Mr Garnett.

"Hey, maybe you could find one in your attic."

For a minute I wasn't sure what he was talking about.

"Find what?"

"A balaclava."

"No, we haven't even got an attic."

I didn't half find handicraft class boring. All that mucking about with compasses and rulers. Or else it was weaving, and you got all tangled up with balls of wool. I was just no good at handicraft and Mr Garnett agreed with me. Today was worse than ever. We were painting pictures and we had to call it 'My favourite story'. Tony was painting *Noddy in*

Toyland. I told him he'd get into trouble.

"Garnett'll do you."

"Why? It's my favourite story."

"Yes, but I don't think he'll believe you."

Tony looked ever so hurt.

"But honest. It's my favourite story. Anyway what are you doing?"

He leaned over to have a look at my favourite story.

"Have you read it, Tony?"

"I don't know. What is it?"

"It's *Robinson Crusoe*, what do you think it is?"

He just looked at my painting.

"Oh, I see it now. Oh yes, I get it now. I couldn't make it out for a minute. Oh yes, there's Man Friday behind him."

"Get your finger off, it's still wet. And that isn't Man Friday, it's a coconut tree. And you've smudged it."

We were using some stuff called poster paint, and I got covered in it. I was getting it everywhere, so I asked Mr Garnett if I could go for a wash. He gets annoyed when you ask to be excused, but he could see I'd got it all over my hands, so he said I could go, but told me to be quick.

The washbasins were in the boys' cloakroom just outside the main hall. I got most of the paint off and as I was drying my hands, that's when it happened. I don't know what came over me. As soon as I saw that balaclava lying there on the floor, I decided to pinch it. I couldn't help it. I just knew that this was my only chance. I've never pinched anything before – I don't think I have – but I didn't think of this as . . . well . . . I don't even like saying it, but . . . well, stealing. I just did it.

I picked it up, went to my coat, and put it in the pocket. At least I tried to put it in the pocket but it bulged out, so I pushed it down the inside of the sleeve. My head was throbbing, and even though I'd just dried my hands, they were all wet from sweating. If only I'd thought a bit first. But it all happened so quickly. I went back to the classroom, and as I was going in I began to realize what I'd done. I'd *stolen* a

11

balaclava. I didn't even know whose it was, but as I stood in the doorway I couldn't believe I'd done it. If only I could go back. In fact I thought I would but then Mr Garnett told me to hurry up and sit down. As I was going back to my desk I felt as if all the lads knew what I'd done. How could they? Maybe somebody had seen me. No! Yes! How *could* they? They could. Of course they couldn't. No, course not. What if they did though? Oh heck.

I thought home-time would never come but when the bell did ring I got out as quick as I could. I was going to put the balaclava back before anybody noticed; but as I got to the cloakroom I heard Norbert Lightowler shout out that someone had pinched his balaclava. Nobody took much notice, thank goodness, and I heard Tony say to him that he'd most likely lost it. Norbert said he hadn't but he went off to make sure it wasn't in the classroom.

I tried to be all casual and took my coat, but I didn't dare put it on in case the balaclava popped out of the sleeve. I said tarah to Tony.

"Tarah, Tony, see you tomorrow."

"Yeh, tarah."

Oh, it was good to get out in the open air. I couldn't wait to get home and get rid of that blooming balaclava. Why had I gone and done a stupid thing like that? Norbert Lightowler was sure to report it to the Headmaster, and there'd be an announcement about it at morning assembly and the culprit would be asked to own up. I was running home as fast as I' could. I wanted to stop and take out the balaclava and chuck it away, but I didn't dare. The faster I ran, the faster my head was filled with thoughts. I could give it back to Norbert. You know, say I'd taken it by mistake. No, he'd never believe me. None of the lads would believe me. Everybody knew how much I wanted to be a Balaclava Boy. I'd have to get rid of the blooming thing as fast as I could.

My mum wasn't back from work when I got home, thank goodness, so as soon as I shut the front door, I put my hand down the sleeve of my coat for the balaclava. There was nothing there. That was funny, I was sure I'd put it down that sleeve. I tried down the other sleeve, and there was still nothing there. Maybe I'd got the wrong coat. No, it was my coat all right. Oh, blimey, I must've lost it while I was running home. I was glad in a way. I was going to have to get rid of it, now it was gone. I only hoped nobody had seen it drop out, but, oh, I was glad to be rid of it. Mind you, I was dreading going to school next morning. Norbert'll probably have reported it by now. Well, I wasn't going to own up. I didn't mind the cane, it wasn't that, but if you owned up, you had to go up on the stage in front of the whole school. Well I was going to forget about it now and nobody would ever know that I'd pinched that blooming lousy balaclava.

I started to do my homework, but I couldn't concentrate. I kept thinking about assembly next morning. What if I went all red and everybody else noticed? They'd know I'd pinched it then. I tried to think about other things, nice things. I thought about bed. I just wanted to go to sleep. To go to bed and sleep. Then I thought about my mum; what she'd say if she knew I'd been stealing. But I still couldn't forget about assembly next day. I went into the kitchen and peeled some potatoes for my mum. She was ever so pleased when she came in from work and said I must've known she'd brought me a present.

"Oh, thanks. What've you got me?"

She gave me a paper bag and when I opened it I couldn't believe my eyes – a blooming balaclava.

"There you are, now you won't be left out and you can stop making my life a misery."

"Thanks, Mum."

If only my mum knew she was making *my* life a misery. The balaclava she'd bought me was just like the one I'd pinched. I felt sick. I didn't want it. I couldn't wear it now. If I did, everybody would say it was Norbert Lightowler's. Even if they didn't, I just couldn't wear it. I wouldn't feel it was mine. I had to get rid of it. I went outside and put it down the lavatory. I had to pull the chain three times before it went away. It's a good job we've got an outside lavatory or else my mum would have wondered what was wrong with me.

I could hardly eat my tea.

"What's wrong with you? Aren't you hungry?"

"No, not much."

"What've you been eating? You've been eating sweets haven't you?"

"No, I don't feel hungry."

"Don't you feel well?"

"I'm all right."

I wasn't, I felt terrible. I told my mum I was going upstairs to work on my model aeroplane.

"Well, it's my bingo night, so make yourself some cocoa before you go to bed."

I went upstairs to bed, and after a while I fell asleep. The last thing I remember was a big balaclava, with a smiling face, and it was the Headmaster's face.

I was scared stiff when I went to school next morning. In assembly it seemed different. All the boys were looking at me. Norbert Lightowler pushed past and didn't say anything. When prayers finished I just stood there waiting for the Headmaster to ask for the culprit to own up, but he was talking about the school fete. And then he said he had something very important to announce and I could feel myself going red. My ears were burning like anything and I was going hot and cold both at the same time.

"I'm very pleased to announce that the school football team has won the inter-league cup . . ."

And that was the end of assembly, except that we were told to go and play in the schoolyard until we were called in, because there was a teachers' meeting. I couldn't understand why I hadn't been found out yet, but I still didn't feel any better. I'd probably be called to the Headmaster's room later on.

I went out into the yard. Everybody was happy because we were having extra playtime. I could see all the Balaclava Boys going round together. Then I saw Norbert Lightowler was one of them. I couldn't be sure it was Norbert because he had a balaclava on, so I had to go up close to him. Yes, it was Norbert. He must have bought a new balaclava that morning.

"Have you bought a new one then, Norbert?"

"Y' what?"

"You've bought a new balaclava, have you?"

"What are you talking about?"

"Your balaclava. You've got a new balaclava, haven't you?"

"No, I never lost it at all. Some fool had shoved it down the sleeve of my raincoat."

A PRINCE
IN ANOTHER PLACE

PHILIPPA PEARCE

I WAS CARETAKER at our school at the time; but I was not –
I repeat, *not* – responsible for the damage done to the
school playground. People said the asphalt looked as if it
had boiled up under extraordinary heat: how could I be held
responsible for that?

I'll begin at the beginning, and the beginning was when
poor young Mr Hartley hanged himself.

Mr Hartley was one of the three teachers at Little Pawley
Church of England Primary School; the other two were Mr
Ezra Bryce, the headmaster, and Mrs Salt, in charge of
Infants. The Vicar, old Mr Widdington, came into school
sometimes to help with Assembly and Religious Instruction.

Mr Hartley was very young, very timid, and very
inexperienced – and he had just recovered from an illness, I
believe. This was his first teaching job, and – as it turned out
– his last. Mr Bryce did for him. Mr Bryce bullied him and
harried him and sneered at him and jeered at him and
altogether made Mr Hartley's life so appalling (as only Mr
Bryce knew how) that the poor young man decided to leave
it. He committed suicide in his lodgings on the second day
of his second term at the school.

Of course, anyone in the village could make a good guess at what lay behind that death; but Bully Bryce was sly as well as a bully, and he could always cover up after himself. At different times the police and the Education people came round asking questions, but he was able to explain everything. He said that poor young Hartley had been far too highly strung to be a teacher – and he had previously been so ill, too. So, in spite of all the fatherly support that he – Mr Bryce – had tried to give him, the young man had cracked under the strain. Such a pity! said Mr Bryce. (I can imagine the tears coming to his eyes as he spoke.)

After the inquest, the funeral took place far away, in Mr Hartley's home parish. His only family was a widowed mother and an elder brother, who came home from abroad. That seemed to be the end of Mr Hartley.

The day after the funeral, a new teacher turned up at the school, to take over Mr Hartley's work there. This was Mr Dickins. He was just a stop-gap, of course – a supply teacher sent by the Education people; he wouldn't be staying long, he said. For a teacher, he was rather a remarkable-looking man. He had a head of flaming red hair. He smiled to himself a good deal, and, when he laughed, you saw he had excellent teeth, strong-looking and rather pointed, almost sharp. He had very small feet. I must have said something about them to him once – he was an easy chap, and often had a word with me. I remember he said he had the greatest difficulty in getting shoes to fit – "The trouble is my odd shaped feet, Mr Jackson," he said. But at least he was nimble enough, as far as I could see.

At first, everyone wondered how the new teacher would stand up to his headmaster. For it was possible to stand up to Bully Bryce. Mrs Salt, of Infants, had been doing it for years, by being deaf as a post whenever her headmaster addressed her; and she defended her Infants as a tigress defends her cubs. And the Juniors were able to look after themselves, chiefly by banding together in self-defence. I've heard them chanting outside the headmaster's window:

Bully B, Bully B,
My dad will come
If you touch me!

As for myself, I could stand up to Mr Bryce – or I wouldn't have been school caretaker for so long. But if I'd been young and frightened, like poor Mr Hartley – oh! there's no doubt of it: Mr Bryce knew how to pick his victims.

But it was soon plain that Mr Dickins wouldn't need to stand up to Mr Bryce: he became his friend instead – his bosom friend. They were always together: in school hours they consulted together, and took their cups of tea and their dinners together. In the evening, they would go for a drink together in the pub.

For some reason, old Mr Widdington became very much upset at this friendship. He was worrying about it one day when he met me in the village street. "And there's another thing, Mr Jackson," he said. "Is this Mr Dickins suitable as a teacher, even for a short time? You've a grandchild in the Juniors: what does she say?"

"Well, Vicar," I said, "I think Susie quite enjoys being taught by him."

"We must look for more than *pleasure*," he says, shaking his reverend grey locks. He was an old-fashioned chap in his ideas. "What does he *teach* them?"

"The usual things, I suppose," I said, "even if he teaches them in these unusual, funny ways they do nowadays."

"Unusual? Funny?" Mr Widdington said quite sharply. "What do you mean?"

"Well, Susie says her class were doing number-work, and Mr Dickins wanted to show them five-and-five. So he lit all the fingers and thumb of one hand, like candles. And then, with his flaming fingers and thumb, he lit all the fingers and thumb of his other hand, so that he had five-and-five – ten candles."

After a little pause, Mr Widdington said: "That was a conjuring trick."

18

"I suppose it must have been," I said.

"Anything else?" asked Mr Widdington.

"Well, Susie says he's told them that he's really a Prince in another place."

"Where?"

"He didn't say. In another place. Those were his words, according to Susie. But I said to Susie: 'He can't be one of our Princes, from Buckingham Palace; and there aren't as many princes about elsewhere as there used to be, even abroad.'"

"I don't like it," said Mr Widdington. "'A Prince in another place' – I don't like it at all. I shall get in touch with the Education Authority to check up on the man's background and qualifications." (I thought to myself, And a nice long time that'll take!) "And in the meantime," said Mr Widdington, "I shall make a pint of having a private word with Mr Bryce about his Mr Dickins."

"You'll be lucky, Vicar," I said. "You'll find it hard to get Bryce without Dickins – it's like a man and his shadow, nowadays."

"I'll get Bryce to come into the church for a chat," says the Vicar. The church and the churchyard are right next to the school, with only a wall between them, and a door in the wall.

19

I didn't know why the Vicar thought he could get Mr Bryce into the church without Mr Dickins: the plan didn't seem a particularly good one to me. But the Vicar thought it was, and – oddly – he was proved right.

The next day, after school, the Vicar caught Mr Bryce and asked him to come into the church to look at some arrangements there that might affect the next Children's Harvest Festival. Mr Bryce could be very obliging, if it suited him, and he agreed to go at once. "Coming, Nick?" he said over his shoulder to Mr Dickins. Mr Dickins hesitated for a moment, then followed them through the door into the churchyard.

I pretended to be clearing rubbish, so that I could watch the three of them, over the wall.

They were going through the churchyard by a path so narrow that you could only walk single file. Mr Widdington led the way, and Mr Dickins came last; and Mr Bryce was in the middle, between the two of them. They rounded the corner of the church and so came to the main south door. Mr Widdington was just leading the way into the church, and Mr Bryce following, when I heard Mr Dickins give a cry of pain; and they turned back to him. I couldn't hear what was said, but it was plain from the tones of voice and the gestures that Mr Dickins had twisted his ankle or hurt it in some way. He wanted to rest it for a few moments, while the other two went into the church. So they went in, and he stayed outside, sitting on one tombstone with his foot up on another.

I was watching Mr Dickins, but I didn't realize that he was also watching me. Now he waved to me in a very cheery way from his tombstone. I had a feeling that if I'd been near enough, I should have seen him wink.

Mr Widdington and Mr Bryce were a long time talking in the church. When they came out, they didn't come out together. Mr Bryce burst out first and rushed up to Mr Dickins as if he'd been longing to get back to him. He seized him by the hand and hauled him to his feet, paying no attention to the hurt done to Mr Dickins's ankle – and really it didn't seem as if there could have been much wrong with it, anyway. They went striding off together, the two of them, arm in arm; and, a little later, the Vicar came shuffling out of the church, by himself. He looked his age then – old, feeble, dejected.

And now Mr Bryce and Mr Dickins seemed closer than ever. They took to staying on at the school, after the children and Mrs Salt had gone, and Mr Dickins would play his fiddle. He may have played well, but his tunes were strange, and I didn't like to hear them.

And now I noticed that Susie and her friends had a new little ditty for playtime. They'd dance in a ring and chant:

> Bully B, Bully B,
> Where are you going, and what do you see?

It wasn't just a few children, either. That nonsense chant became a kind of craze. All the children were singing the same song in playtime, dancing round in rings of five or six or seven. The playground was giddy with the whirling and the singing. Once I saw Mr Bryce at his window looking out on it all, and, at his elbow, just behind him, Mr Dickins smiling quietly to himself as usual.

All this was in the summer term. The weather was fine, dry; but there was no sultriness, no hint of storms building up. Yet perhaps there was a strange feeling in the air – or was I just imagining it? Certainly old Mr Widdington was fussing more than usual. He dropped into the school almost every day now, on one excuse or another. The dancing and singing of the children in the playground worried him. Why did they do it? he asked. He got me to ask Susie that – where the words and the dancing came from, who started it, or who had taught them all. But Susie didn't know. She said they had all just begun doing it; that was all.

I told Mr Widdington what Susie had said, and he looked even more upset.

I said: "Well, have you had an answer to that letter you

wrote to the Education Office, about Mr Dickins?"

"Not yet. But I've also written to – to someone else."

I didn't want to seem inquisitive. As it turned out, I learnt soon enough who *someone else* was.

Playtime was just over that day. The rings of dancing, singing children had broken up; they were all going back to their classrooms. I had been by the school gate, watching them. I heard footsteps coming up behind me, but I paid no attention. Then a voice: "Excuse me. Is Mr Widdington about?"

And the voice was the voice of poor young Mr Hartley, that killed himself . . .

I turned round, because I was too frightened not to, if you see what I mean; and there was Mr Hartley looking at me! For two awful seconds, that's what I thought, and then I realized that this man was very like our Mr Hartley, but older, more solid-looking, and sunburnt from foreign lands. He could see what I had been thinking. He said: "I am the brother of Timothy Hartley, who used to teach here; and you must be Mr Jackson." We shook hands. He explained that the Vicar had asked him to meet him there; he was a little early. Then he said: "Mr Widdington has asked me to see Mr Bryce, to talk to him."

I said: "If it's for the sake of your poor brother, Mr Hartley, it'll be a waste of your breath. It will, really."

"It's not for his sake; it's for Mr Bryce's own sake."

I could only stare at him. He went on: "Mr Jackson, I would never, never have consented to come, except that your Mr Widdington asked me to – implored me to. He said the matter was very urgent indeed." I still stared at Mr Hartley; and now he looked aside in an embarrassed way, and said: "Mr Widdington mentioned Mr Bryce's immortal soul."

From the school, the fiddle-playing of Mr Dickins had started up: Mr Dickins had never played his tunes in school hours before.

The elder Mr Hartley heard the fiddling. He said: "I'm not

22

waiting for Mr Widdington, after all. I'm going to Mr Bryce now. Now."

"Through that door," I said, and pointed across the playground.

When he had gone into the school, everything was very quiet and still, except for the fiddling: that went on for a while. Then the door from the churchyard into the playground clicked, and I looked that way and saw the Vicar coming through. He hesitated on the edge of the playground, looking round him. I was just going to go over to him, when things began to happen.

The school door through which Mr Hartley had gone opened again, and he came out. He had not looked to me a man to be easily frightened, but now his face was chalk-white; his eyes were staring, and he walked altogether like a sleepwalker in a nightmare. He came across the deserted playground towards the gate; and I came forward a little to meet him.

Behind him, in the doorway, appeared Mr Bryce. His face was dark, and he was shouting foul abuse after Mr Hartley – abuse not only of him, but of the poor young man who had hanged himself. And behind Mr Bryce smiled the face of Mr Dickins.

Mr Bryce stood in the doorway, nearly filling it, for he was a big man. I've not yet told you what he looked like. Bullies

23

can be fat or thin or medium size: Bully Bryce was the heavy, bull-like kind. He filled his clothes almost to bursting, and his head seemed to have burst up out of his collar, and his eyes seemed to be bursting from his head. They were bloodshot eyes, as well as bulging, and they glared now; and when he bellowed his abuse across the playground, the spittle flew from his mouth at every word.

Mr Hartley had reached me, and I was partly supporting him, while he tried to recover himself. So we stood on the edge of the playground, and I was facing it. Mr Hartley had his back to it at first, but pretty soon he turned his head to see what was fixing my attention. And the Vicar, too, also on the edge of the playground, was staring; and Mrs Salt, of the Infants, now stood in her doorway to the playground, gazing distractedly and crying: "Children! Children! Stop, stop!"

For all the children of the school were coming out of it, on to the playground. The Infants were climbing out of the low windows of their classroom, one after another, and holding hands as they danced away across the playground, while Mrs Salt called to them in vain: "Whatever are you doing? Stop, stop!" The Juniors, too, had come streaming out of the building and, hand in hand, ran and danced and joined up with the Infants in one long skein of children that moved to and fro in ceaseless meander over the playground.

Now Mr Bryce was advancing into the playground. At first, I thought he was coming to put a stop to what was going on; but this was not so. He had stopped storming and shouting; he was quite silent. He walked slowly, perhaps reluctantly, step after slow step, into the middle of the playground, and the skein of dancing children kept clear of him as he moved. I saw that Mr Dickins had tucked his fiddle under one arm, and had the other hooked into Mr Bryce's. They were arm in arm, as so often, but this time they were not walking equally – Mr Dickins was urging Mr Bryce forward, positively pulling him along. They reached the middle of the playground, and went no further. And the children were running mazily about them, chanting now:

> Bully B, Bully B,
> Where are you going, and what do you see?

The long line of children wavered about the playground until the two ends came together. Suddenly there was one irregularly shaped ring of children, with Mr Dickins and Mr Bryce in the middle of it.

As they ran, the children pulled outwards – outwards – to form a proper circle round the two men; and, when they had achieved this, more or less, they began dancing on the spot, still chanting as they danced:

> Bully B, Bully B,
> Where are you going, and what do you see?

And the air in the playground seemed to tighten, so that there was hardly room to breathe; and we, the witnesses – the Vicar, Mr Hartley, Mrs Salt and myself – stood stock still and staring –

> Bully B, Bully B,
> Where are you going, and what –

– and there was a sound such as I hope never to hear again: a CRACK! and at the same time an upward burst of flaming light against which – instantaneously – my eyes closed. But, against the inside of my eyelids was printed off the image of Mr Dickins and Mr Bryce, entwined, and they seemed to be all on fire, inside my eyelids; and I heard a howl that was more than any human being could make, and yet it was human, and I knew that it had been made by Mr Bryce.

I put my hands up to my shut eyes, as though I had been blinded, and I fell to my knees.

When I opened my eyes again, the playground was in confusion. The children were no longer holding hands, or dancing, or chanting; they ran aimlessly, or stood, or sat, some sobbing or weeping, others laughing hysterically. Mrs Salt was trying to control them and get them back to their classrooms. The Vicar was leaning against the wall of the churchyard, as though he had been flattened there by the blast of an explosion. Mr Hartley was lying on the ground beside me, half out of his senses for the time being.

The middle of the playground was empty: no Mr Bryce, no Mr Dickins. Where they had stood, there was a huge bubbled scar in the asphalt, like two lips that had opened widely once – perhaps to swallow some tasty morsel – and then closed again in a dreadful sneer.

That's really all. Mr Bryce and Mr Dickins were never seen again. Nobody knew where they'd gone. Mrs Salt said they couldn't just have vanished, as we seemed to think: that was against commonsense and reason. She was sure they'd slipped away, under our very noses, and escaped abroad to an Enemy Power, for whom they had been spying in this country.

"An Enemy Power . . ." Mr Widdington said thoughtfully.

We had trouble with the Education people. They had never answered Mr Widdington's letter because they hadn't been able to trace Mr Dickins in their records. Certainly, they had never sent us a Mr Dickins as a supply teacher. They denounced Mr Dickins as an imposter.

When they heard of the mysterious disappearance of two of our staff – well, one, because, of course, they wouldn't count Mr Dickins – they went so far as to send an official in person to make inquiries. He found out no more than I've already told you; but, just before he was leaving, he noticed the damage in the playground. He said to me: "What the Hell's been going on here?"

I didn't answer him. I didn't think that kind of language was suitable for an Education person, in a primary school playground; I wouldn't like Susie to have heard him.

AMY'S
VALLEY OF HUMILIATION

LOUISA MAY ALCOTT

from Little Women

Louisa M. Alcott's most famous book tells how the four March sisters and their mother coped at home while their father was away during the American Civil War. The girls regularly made life difficult for themselves and in this story Amy, the youngest, is in trouble at school.

"THAT BOY IS a perfect Cyclops, isn't he?" said Amy, one day, as Laurie clattered by on horseback, with a flourish of his whip as he passed.

"How dare you say so, when he's got both his eyes, and very handsome ones they are, too," cried Jo, who resented any slighting remarks about her friend.

"I didn't say anything about his eyes, and I don't see why you need fire up when I admire his riding."

"Oh, my goodness! That little goose means a centaur, and she called him a Cyclops," exclaimed Jo, with a burst of laughter.

"You needn't be so rude, it's only a 'lapse of lingy', as Mr Davis says," retorted Amy, finishing Jo with her Latin. "I just wish I had a little of the money Laurie spends on that horse," she added, as if to herself, yet hoping her sisters would hear.

"Why?" asked Meg kindly, for Jo had gone off in another laugh at Amy's second blunder.

"I need it so much; I'm dreadfully in debt, and it won't be my turn to have the rag-money for a month."

"In debt, Amy? What do you mean?" and Meg looked sober.

"Why, I owe at least a dozen pickled limes, and I can't pay them, you know, till I have money, for Marmee forbade my having anything charged at the shop."

"Tell me all about it. Are limes the fashion now? It used to be pricking bits of rubber to make balls"; and Meg tried to keep her countenance, Amy looked so grave and important.

"Why, you see, the girls are always buying them, and unless you want to be thought mean, you must do it too. It's nothing but limes now, for every one is sucking them in their desks in school-time, and trading them off for pencils, bead-rings, paper dolls, or something else, at recess. If one girl likes another, she gives her a lime; if she's mad with her, she eats one before her face, and don't offer even a suck. They treat by turns; and I've had ever so many, but haven't returned them, and I ought, for they are debts of honour, you know."

"How much will pay them off, and restore your credit?" asked Meg, taking out her purse.

"A quarter would more than do it, and leave a few cents over for a treat for you. Don't you like limes?"

"Not much; you may have my share. Here's the money. Make it last as long as you can, for it isn't very plenty, you know."

"Oh, thank you! It must be so nice to have pocket-money! I'll have a grand feast, for I haven't tasted a lime this week. I felt delicate about taking any, as I couldn't return them, and I'm actually suffering for one."

Next day Amy was rather late at school; but could not

28

resist the temptation of displaying, with pardonable pride, a moist brown-paper parcel, before she consigned it to the inmost recesses of her desk. During the next few minutes the rumour that Amy March had got twenty-four delicious limes (she ate one on the way), and was going to treat, circulated through her 'set', and the attentions of her friends became quite overwhelming. Katy Brown invited her to her next party on the spot; Mary Kingsley insisted on lending her her watch till recess; and Jenny Snow, a satirical young lady, who had basely twitted Amy upon her limeless state, promptly buried the hatchet, and offered to furnish answers to certain appalling sums. But Amy had not forgotten Miss Snow's cutting remarks about 'some persons whose noses were not too flat to smell other people's limes, and stuck-up people, who were not too proud to ask for them'; and she instantly crushed 'that Snow girl's' hopes by the withering telegram: "You needn't be so polite all of a sudden, for you won't get any."

A distinguished personage happened to visit the school that morning, and Amy's beautifully drawn maps received praise, which honour to her foe rankled in the soul of Miss Snow, and caused Miss March to assume the airs of a studious young peacock. But, alas, alas! pride goes before a fall, and the revengeful Snow turned the tables with disastrous success. No sooner had the guest paid the usual stale compliments, and bowed himself out, than Jenny, under pretence of asking an important question, informed Mr Davis, the teacher, that Amy March had pickled limes in her desk.

Now Mr Davis had declared limes a contraband article, and solemnly vowed to publicly ferrule the first person who was found breaking the law. This much-enduring man had succeeded in banishing chewing-gum after a long and stormy war, had made a bonfire of the confiscated novels and newspapers, had suppressed a private post office, had forbidden distortions of the face, nicknames, and caricatures, and done all that one man could do to keep half a hundred rebellious girls in order. Boys are trying enough to human patience, goodness knows! but girls are infinitely more so, especially to nervous gentlemen, with tyrannical tempers, and no more talent for teaching than Dr Blimber. Mr Davis knew any quantity of Greek, Latin, Algebra, and ologies of all sorts, so he was called a fine teacher; and manners, morals, feelings, and examples were not considered of any particular importance. It was a most unfortunate moment for denouncing Amy, and Jenny knew it. Mr Davis had evidently taken his coffee too strong that morning; there was an east wind, which always affected his neuralgia, and his pupils had not done him the credit which he felt he deserved: therefore, to use the expressive, if not elegant, language of a schoolgirl, 'he was as nervous as a witch and as cross as a bear'. The word 'limes' was like fire to powder; his yellow face flushed, and he rapped on his desk with an energy which made Jenny skip to her seat with unusual rapidity.

"Young ladies, attention, if you please!"

At the stern order the buzz ceased, and fifty pairs of blue, black, grey, and brown eyes were obediently fixed upon his awful countenance.

"Miss March, come to the desk."

Amy rose to comply with outward composure, but a secret fear oppressed her, for the limes weighed upon her conscience.

"Bring with you the limes you have in your desk," was the unexpected command which arrested her before she got out of her seat.

"Don't take all," whispered her neighbour, a young lady of great presence of mind.

Amy hastily shook out half a dozen, and laid the rest down before Mr Davis, feeling that any man possessing a human heart would relent when that delicious perfume met his nose. Unfortunately Mr Davis particularly detested the odour of the fashionable pickle, and disgust added to his wrath.

30

"Is that all?"

"Not quite," stammered Amy.

"Bring the rest immediately."

With a despairing glance at her set she obeyed.

"You are sure there are no more?"

"I never lie, sir."

"So I see. Now take these disgusting things two by two, and throw them out of the window."

There was a simultaneous sigh, which created quite a little gust as the last hope fled, and the treat was ravished from their longing lips. Scarlet with shame and anger, Amy went to and fro six dreadful times; and as each doomed couple – looking, oh, so plump and juicy! – fell from her reluctant hands, a shout from the street completed the anguish of the girls, for it told them that their feast was being exulted over by the little Irish children, who were their sworn foes. This – this was too much; all flashed indignant or appealing glances at the inexorable Davis, and one passionate lime-lover burst into tears.

As Amy returned from her last trip, Mr Davis gave a portentous 'Hem!' and said, in his most impressive manner:

"Young ladies, you remember what I said to you a week ago. I am sorry this has happened; but I never allow my rules to be infringed, and I *never* break my word. Miss March, hold out your hand."

Amy started, and put both hands behind her, turning on him an imploring look which pleaded for her better than the words she could not utter. She was rather a favourite with 'old Davis', as, of course, he was called, and it's my private belief that he *would* have broken his word if the indignation of one irrepressible young lady had not found vent in a hiss. That hiss, faint as it was, irritated the irascible gentleman, and sealed the culprit's fate.

"Your hand, Miss March!" was the only answer her mute appeal received; and, too proud to cry or beseech, Amy set her teeth, threw back her head defiantly, and bore without

flinching several tingling blows on her little palm. They were neither many nor heavy, but that made no difference to her. For the first time in her life she had been struck; and the disgrace, in her eyes, was as deep as if he had knocked her down.

"You will now stand on the platform till recess," said Mr Davis, resolved to do the thing thoroughly, since he had begun.

That was dreadful. It would have been bad enough to go to her seat and see the pitying faces of her friends, or the satisfied ones of her few enemies; but to face the whole school, with that shame fresh upon her, seemed impossible,

32

and for a second she felt as if she could only drop down where she stood, and break her heart with crying. A bitter sense of wrong, and the thought of Jenny Snow, helped her to bear it; and, taking the ignominious place, she fixed her eyes on the stove-funnel above what now seemed a sea of faces, and stood there, so motionless and white that the girls found it very hard to study, with that pathetic figure before them.

During the fifteen minutes that followed, the proud and sensitive little girl suffered a shame and pain which she never forgot. To others it might seem a ludicrous or trivial affair, but to her it was a hard experience; for during the twelve years of her life she had been governed by love alone, and a blow of that sort had never touched her before. The smart of her hand and the ache of her heart were forgotten in the sting of the thought:

"I shall have to tell at home, and they will be so disappointed in me!"

The fifteen minutes seemed an hour; but they came to an end at last, and the word 'Recess!' had never seemed so welcome to her before.

"You can go, Miss March," said Mr Davis, looking, as he felt, uncomfortable.

He did not soon forget the reproachful glance Amy gave him, as she went, without a word to any one, straight into the ante-room, snatched her things, and left the place 'for ever', as she passionately declared to herself. She was in a sad state when she got home; and when the older girls arrived, some time later, an indignation meeting was held at once. Mrs March did not say much, but looked disturbed, and comforted her afflicted little daughter in her tenderest manner. Meg bathed the insulted hand with glycerine and tears; Beth felt that even her beloved kittens would fail as a balm for grief like this; Jo wrathfully proposed that Mr Davis be arrested without delay; and Hannah shook her fist at the 'villain', and pounded potatoes for dinner as if she had him under her pestle.

No notice was taken of Amy's flight, except by her mates; but the sharp-eyed demoiselles discovered that Mr Davis was quite benignant in the afternoon, also unusually nervous. Just before school closed, Jo appeared, wearing a grim expression as she stalked up to the desk, and delivered a letter from her mother; then collected Amy's property, and departed, carefully scraping the mud from her boots on the door-mat, as if she shook the dust of the place off her feet.

"Yes, you can have a vacation from school, but I want you to study a little every day with Beth," said Mrs March that evening. "I don't approve of corporal punishment, especially for girls. I dislike Mr Davis's manner of teaching, and don't think the girls you associate with are doing you any good, so I shall ask your father's advice before I send you anywhere else."

"That's good! I wish all the girls would leave, and spoil his old school. It's perfectly maddening to think of those lovely limes," sighed Amy, with the air of a martyr.

"I am not sorry you lost them, for you broke the rules, and deserved some punishment for disobedience," was the severe reply, which rather disappointed the young lady, who expected nothing but sympathy.

"Do you mean you are glad I was disgraced before the whole school?" cried Amy.

"I should not have chosen that way of mending a fault," replied her mother; "but I'm not sure that it won't do you more good than a milder method. You are getting to be rather conceited, my dear, and it is quite time you set about correcting it. You have a good many little gifts and virtues, but there is no need of parading them, for conceit spoils the finest genius. There is not much danger that real talent or goodness will be overlooked long; even if it is, the consciousness of possessing and using it well should satisfy one, and the great charm of all power is modesty."

"So it is!" cried Laurie, who was playing chess in a corner with Jo. "I knew a girl, once, who had a really remarkable talent for music, and she didn't know it; never guessed what sweet little things she composed when she was alone, and wouldn't have believed it if any one had told her."

"I wish I'd known that nice girl, maybe she would have helped me, I'm so stupid," said Beth, who stood beside him, listening eagerly.

"You do know her, and she helps you better than any one else could," answered Laurie, looking at her with such mischievous meaning in his merry black eyes, that Beth suddenly turned very red, and hid her face in the sofa-cushion, quite overcome by such an unexpected discovery.

Jo let Laurie win the game, to pay for that praise of her Beth, who could not be prevailed upon to play for them after her compliment. So Laurie did his best, and sung delightfully, being in a particularly lively humour, for to the Marches he seldom showed the moody side of his character. When he was gone, Amy, who had been pensive all the evening, said suddenly, as if busy over some new idea:

"Is Laurie an accomplished boy?"

"Yes; he has had an excellent education, and has much talent; he will make a fine man, if not spoilt by petting," replied her mother.

"And he isn't conceited, is he?" asked Amy.

"Not in the least; that is why he is so charming, and we all like him so much."

"I see; it's nice to have accomplishments, and be elegant; but not to show off or get perked up," said Amy thoughtfully.

"These things are always seen and felt in a person's manner and conversation if modestly used; but it is not necessary to display them," said Mrs March.

"Any more than it's proper to wear all your bonnets and gowns and ribbons at once, that folks may know you've got them," added Jo; and the lecture ended in a laugh.

THE CONVENT OF
THE BLESSED LIMIT

ANDREW DAVIES

IF YOU have read any other books about Marmalade Atkins, you will know that one of the schools she went to was called the Convent of the Blessed Limit, which was run by a couple of very tough nuns called Sister Purificaton and Sister Conception. Sister Purification was over six feet tall and had a long straggly moustache, and Sister Conception was over three feet thick and carried a baseball bat wherever she went. Sister Purification and Sister Conception struck terror into the hearts of all the little girls at the Convent of the Blessed Limit. Except Marmalade Atkins.

You may think you have heard about all the dreadful deeds done by Marmalade at the Convent, but you haven't. You haven't heard the story of the Bad Girls' Cupboard.

One day, Marmalade had been particularly bad. She had let off a banger during Silent Reading, she had locked Cherith Ponsonby (the Head Girl) in the lavatory, and during Sister Purification's after-dinner nap, she had dyed her moustache green. Sister Purification and Sister Conception knew that something drastic had to be done. They called Marmalade out to the front. They looked at Marmalade. They looked at each other. And they nodded three times.

"Marmalade Atkins," they boomed in unison. "The Bad Girls' Cupboard!"

"What's that, then, cock?" said Marmalade.

"You will find out," said Sister Purification and Sister Conception. And seizing her firmly in their great hairy hands, they led her up a winding stone staircase to a room she had never seen before. In the middle of the room was a huge black cupboard, with iron bolts and bars on the outside.

"The Bad Girls' Cupboard is dark and terrible," said Sister Purification.

"They say there is a ghost in there," said Sister Conception.

"Girls who go in the Bad Girls' Cupboard are never, never naughty again," said Sister Purification.

"Come on then, cock," said Marmalade. "Open the box."

"Ooh, you naughty little girl!" said Sister Conception, brandishing her baseball bat. And they drew back the huge rusty bolts, opened the great creaking doors, and before Marmalade knew what was happening she was inside and the bolts and bars were firmly shut.

"And you can stay there until you have decided to be good," said Sister Purification and Sister Conception, and they went off for a nice game of darts, feeling very pleased with themselves.

It *was* very dark in the Bad Girls' Cupboard. Dark and musty and full of creaks and cobwebs and little icy draughts like the breath of ghosts. But Marmalade was always prepared for emergencies. She got out her Bad Girl's Torch from the special pocket in her Bad Girl's Knickers, and switched it on. She found that she was staring right into the face of a skeleton!

"Hello, cock," said Marmalade. "You must have been in here a good long time. Are you in for moustache dyeing too?"

The skeleton did not reply.

"Cheer up," said Marmalade, getting a pack of cards out. "Let's have a nice game of snap."

Two hours later, the Convent of the Blessed Limit was dark and silent. All the good little girls had gone home hours ago, and not a sound had been heard from the Bad Girls' Cupboard. Sister Purification and Sister Conception decided that it was time to investigate. They clomped up the winding stone staircase and stood in front of the huge black cupboard.

"Marmalade Atkins," said Sister Purification. "You have been in the Bad Girls' Cupboard for two hours. Are you ready to come out and be good?"

Not a sound came from the Bad Girls' Cupboard.

"Marmalade, we're waiting," said Sister Purification.

Silence.

"Speak up, you cheeky little monkey!" roared Sister Conception, banging on the door with her baseball bat. Not a sound. Her voice echoed in the eerie silence. The two toughest nuns in the world began to feel a little bit uneasy.

"She's very quiet, Sister," said Sister Conception.

"She might have fainted," said Sister Purification.

"She might have suffocated!" said Sister Conception.

"She might have died of terror!" said Sister Purification.

Trembling with apprehension, they drew back the great rusty bolts and threw open the great creaking doors. Nothing to be seen except the skeleton.

"It's very dark in there," said Sister Purification. "She might be lying suffocated in the darkest corner!"

"We'd better go in and see!" said Sister Conception.

Trembling and holding hands, they tiptoed in. As they did so, Marmalade crawled out between them, slammed the doors, and shot home the rusty bolts.

"Help!" shouted the nuns. "Let us out!"

Marmalade let them shout for a while, then summoned up her best Cherith Ponsonby impression.

"Ooh! It's ghosts!" she squealed.

"Who's there?" shouted Sister Purification.

"Chewith Ponthonby, the Head Girl!" said Marmalade.

"Let us out, Cherith!" roared Sister Conception.

"No, I won't, I'm afwaid of ghosts," said Marmalade.

Sister Conception lost her temper.

"Let us out, you silly little faggot!" she thundered, banging about with her baseball bat. "We're Sister Purification and Sister Conception!"

"Now I know you're a ghost," said Marmalade. "Because the nice kind nuns wouldn't call the Head Girl a thilly little faggot. I won't let you out, tho there!" And Marmalade went home for her tea.

Far into the night a strange booming sound, like a foghorn with a frog in its throat, could be heard coming from the lonely towers of the Convent of the Blessed Limit. If you listened carefully you could make out what it was saying:

MARMALADE ATKINS! YOU ARE EXPELLED!

After they had recovered from their nervous breakdowns, Sister Purification and Sister Conception went on a course in Modern Methods of Teaching. It lasted for a whole term, during which Marmalade Atkins did not go to school at all, and Mr and Mrs Atkins were pretty close to having nervous breakdowns themselves. Then to their amazement and joy Mrs Allgood came round with the news that the nuns were ready to have Marmalade back, to test out the success of their new approach to education.

"Now, girls," said Sister Purification on the first day of term. "An important announcement. Sister Conception and I have been on a course about *modern education*. It appears that we have been a little bit behind the times. Locking girls in cupboards and chasing them with baseball bats is all a bit old-fashioned, it would appear."

"Huh," said Sister Conception, who had not enjoyed the course very much.

"Now," said Sister Purification, "when girls are naughty, we will have cosy little chats with them and find out what the matter is."

"And *then* we'll whack 'em with baseball bats and lock 'em in cupboards," said Sister Conception.

"*No*, Sister. Just Sister's little joke!" said Sister Purification, who could see her colleague eyeing the baseball bat in the corner. "And today, we are going to start *Child-Centred Projects*."

"Huh," said Sister Conception.

"We want you all to think of something you're very, very interested in, and then you can do a lovely project on it."

"Oooooh!" trilled all the little good girls.

"I can't believe this," said Marmalade Atkins.

"Now tell me what your projects are," said Sister Purification. "Mary O'Malley, Mary McNally, and Mary McSharry?"

40

"Flowers, Sister," said Mary O'Malley.

"Bunnies, Sister," said Mary McNally.

"Penguins, Sister," said Mary McSharry.

"Fine, fine," said Sister Purification. "Eileen Rogan, Eileen Hogan and Eileen Gogan?"

"Doggies, Sister," said Eileen Rogan.

"Pussies, Sister," said Eileen Hogan.

"Penguins, Sister," said Eileen Gogan.

"Yes. All right, I suppose," said Sister Purification, giving Eileen Gogan a rather suspicious look. "Cherith Ponsonby, Head Girl?"

"Please, Sister Purification, Great Nuns in History."

"Creep," said Marmalade Atkins.

"Please, Sister, can I put you in it?" said Cherith.

"If you wish, Cherith," said Sister Purification, twirling her moustache modestly. "Now. Marmalade Atkins?"

"Great Murders in History, cock?" suggested Marmalade.

"Certainly not. Little girls are not interested in murder."

"Torture, then," said Marmalade reasonably.

"No!"

"Oh, I dunno," said Sister Conception. "I think Torture's very interesting. We could get out the old thumbscrews . . ."

"*No*, Sister. Now, Marmalade. Think again."

"Pets," said Marmalade.

"What sort of pets?" said Sister Purification suspiciously.

"All sorts of pets," said Marmalade craftily. "All Creatures Great and Small."

"Well," said Sister Purification. "All right."

"Can I make a model, Sister?"

"Yes, you can, Marmalade," said Sister Purification, thinking how well these Modern Methods worked even with the most revolting . . . the most *difficult* children.

"Huh," said Sister Conception. "Look, can't I give her just a couple of whacks for old times' sake?"

"*No*, Sister. Have faith in Modern Methods."

By the end of the day the projects were going well. The flowers and the bunnies were a joy to behold, the doggies and the pussies would have brought tears to your eyes, and it was an awful pity that someone had painted moustaches on some of the penguins and put baseball bats under their flippers. Still, it had been a good day for Modern Methods. Even Marmalade had been hard at work all day on her model snake.

"What d'you reckon then, cock?" said Marmalade.

"Rubbish," said Sister Conception.

"Now, now," said Sister Purification. "Remember our course. Encourage their little creative spirits."

"Bash their little bottoms," said Sister Conception, who was getting really fed up with Modern Methods.

"Somehow I hoped it would look more sort of real," said Marmalade, looking at her model. "Can I take it home and work on it?"

"Yes, Marmalade," said Sister Purification. "You see, Sister? It's like magic! With Modern Methods, even bad girls want to do homework!"

"Huh," said Sister Conception.

When Marmalade got home, her father was practising his golf shots in the hall, trying to hit the ball into the mouths of a set of very valuable vases belonging to Marmalade's mother. He was not a very good golfer, and tended to hit the ball too hard. After watching him break three of the vases, Marmalade was bored, and went into the living room. Her mother was on the telephone to Harrods as usual and Marmalade sat down to listen.

"Hello. Bracelet Department?" said Mrs Atkins. "I want a good strong pair of handcuffs, and a ball and chain. Suitable for a quite *small* but extremely *strong* girl. What? Absolute balderdash! You tell me that you can supply anything in the world, and now you hum and ha over a perfectly simple . . . yes, I should think so. Express delivery too!"

There was an extra loud crash from the hall.

"Excuse me a moment," said Marmalade's mother. "I must just go and abuse my husband. Hold the line, please."

When her mother had stormed out into the hall, Marmalade picked up the telephone.

"Hello? Harrods?" she said, in her best imitation of her mother's voice. "It's rich Mrs Atkins again. Now can you or can you not supply anything in the world? Good. Pet Department, please!"

By the end of the week, all the Child-Centred Projects were complete. The walls of the convent were festooned with flowers, bunnies, doggies, pussies and penguins, and Sister Purification and Sister Conception were beaming with pride and pleasure.

"Girls," said Sister Purification. "You have all done very well. Hurrah for Modern Methods!"

"Hurrah for Sister Purification!" chorused the Good Girls.

"Huh," said Sister Conception.

"And the prize for the best project of all goes to Cherith Ponsonby, Head Girl, for her lovely project on Great Nuns in History!" announced Sister Purification.

Cherith Ponsonby smiled a smug smile.

"Here, cock," said Marmalade Atkins. "That's not fair. You haven't seen mine yet."

43

All eyes turned to the back of the class. There beside Marmalade's desk was a very long wooden box with holes in it.

"Oh, all right," said Sister Purification. "What is it?"

"My model snake, cock," said Marmalade. "Have a look. Gather round, folks, girls at the front, penguins at the back!"

And she opened the box. The nuns peered inside.

"It *is* very realistic," said Sister Purification grudgingly.

"It works, too," said Marmalade. She put her head in the box. "Wake up, mate!"

The snake, a giant python called Percy, lifted his sleepy head and looked around. The first thing he saw was Sister Purification. She reminded him of a giant fruit-bat, and he decided that there was nothing he would like more than to wind himself round her and give her a cuddle. So that was what he did.

"Er . . . very good Marmalade," said Sister Purification. "Make it stop now."

"Don't know how to, cock," said Marmalade. "Sorry!"

"Help!" screamed Sister Conception. Percy found that he had enough spare coils to give Sister Conception a cuddle as well. And Cherith Ponsonby. And the rest of the Good Girls. He rolled himself round and round them, and then went off to sleep. He was really a very peaceable python, but the nuns did not see it in this light.

"Marmalade Atkins!" they said, in rather muffled tones. "You are expelled again!"

"Fair enough," said Marmalade Atkins. "You can keep Percy to remember me by."

44

A NICE OLD-FASHIONED
ROMANCE WITH LOVE LYRICS
AND EVERYTHING

WILLIAM SAROYAN

MY COUSIN ARAK was a year and a half younger than me, round-faced, dark, and exceptionally elegant in manners. It was no pretence with him. His manners were just naturally that way, just as my manners were bad from the beginning. Where Arak would get around any sort of complication at school with a bland smile that showed his front upper teeth, separated, and melted the heart of stone of our teacher, Miss Daffney, I would go to the core of the complication and with noise and vigour prove that Miss Daffney or somebody else was the culprit, not me, and if need be, I would carry the case to the Supreme Court and prove my innocence.

I usually got sent to the office. In some cases I would get a strapping for debating the case in the office against Mr Derringer, our principal, who was no earthly good at debates. The minute I got him cornered he got out his strap.

45

Arak was different; he didn't care to fight for justice. He wasn't anywhere near as bright as me, but even though he was a year and a half younger than me, he was in the same grade. That wouldn't be so bad if the grade wasn't the fifth. I usually won all my arguments with my teachers, but instead of being glad to get rid of me they refused to promote me, in the hope, I believe, of winning the following semester's arguments and getting even. That's how it happened that I came to be the oldest pupil in the fifth grade.

One day Miss Daffney tried to tell the world I was the author of the poem on the blackboard that said she was in love with Mr Derringer, and ugly. The author of the poem was my cousin Arak, not me. Any poem I wrote wouldn't be about Miss Daffney, it would be about something worthwhile. Nevertheless, without mentioning any names, but with a ruler in her hand, Miss Daffney stood beside my desk and said, I am going to find out who is responsible for this horrible outrage on the blackboard and see that he is properly punished.

He? I said. How do you know it's a boy and not a girl?

Miss Daffney whacked me on the knuckles of my right hand. I jumped out of my seat and said, You can't go around whacking me on the knuckles. I'll report this.

Sit down, Miss Daffney said.

I did. She had me by the right ear, which was getting out of shape from being grabbed hold of by Miss Daffney and other teachers.

I sat down and quietly, almost inaudibly, said, You'll hear about this.

Hold your tongue, Miss Daffney said, and although I was sore as the devil, I stuck out my tongue and held it, while the little Mexican, Japanese, Armenian, Greek, Italian, Portuguese, and plain American boys and girls in the class, who looked to me for comedy, roared with laughter. Miss Daffney came down on my hand with the ruler, but this time the ruler grazed my nose. This to me was particularly

46

insulting, inasmuch as my nose then, as now, was large. A small nose would not have been grazed, and I took Miss Daffney's whack as a subtle comment on the size of my nose.

I put my bruised hand over my hurt nose and again rose to my feet.

You told me to hold my tongue, I said, insisting that I had done no evil, had merely carried out her instructions, and was therefore innocent, utterly undeserving of the whacked hand and the grazed nose.

You be good now, Miss Daffney said. I won't stand any more of your nonsense. You be good.

I took my hand away from my nose and began to be good, I smiled like a boy bringing her a red apple. My audience roared with laughter and Miss Daffney dropped the ruler, reached for me, fell over the desk, got up and began to chase me around the room.

There I go again, I kept saying to myself while Miss Daffney chased me around the room. There I go again getting in a mess like this that's sure to end in murder, while my cousin Arak, who is the guilty one, sits there and smiles. There's no justice anywhere.

When Miss Daffney finally caught me, as I knew she would unless I wanted even more severe punishment from Mr Derringer, there was a sort of free-for-all during which she tried to gouge my eyes out, pull off my ears, fingers, and arms, and I, by argument, tried to keep her sweet and ladylike.

When she was exhausted, I went back to my seat, and the original crime of the day was taken up again: Who was the author of the love lyric on the blackboard?

Miss Daffney straightened her hair and her clothes, got her breath, demanded and got silence, and after several moments of peace during which the ticking of the clock was heard, she began to speak.

I am going to ask each of you by name if you wrote this awful – poem – on the blackboard and I shall expect you to tell the truth. If you lie, I shall find out anyway and your punishment will be all the worse.

She began to ask each of the boys and girls if they'd written the poem and of course they hadn't. Then she asked my cousin Arak and he also said he hadn't. Then she asked me and I said I hadn't, which was the truth.

You go to the office, she said. You liar.

I didn't write any poem on any blackboard, I said. And I'm not a liar.

Mr Derringer received me with no delight. Two minutes later Susie Kokomoto arrived from our class with a message describing my crime. In fact, quoting it. Mr Derringer read the message, made six or seven faces, smiled, snapped his suspenders, coughed and said, What made you write this little poem?

I didn't, I said.

Naturally, he said, you'd say you didn't, but why did you?

I *didn't* write it, I said.

Now don't be headstrong, Mr Derringer said. That's a rather alarming rumour to be spreading. How do you *know* Miss Daffney's in love with me?

Is she? I said.

Well, Mr Derringer said, that's what it says here. What gave you that impression? Have you noticed her looking at me with admiration or something?

I haven't noticed her looking at you with anything, I said. Are *you* in love with *her* or something?

That remains to be seen, Mr Derringer said. It isn't a bad poem, up to a point. Do you really regard Miss Daffney as ugly?

I didn't write the poem, I said. I can prove it. I don't write that way.

You mean your handwriting isn't like the handwriting on the blackboard? Mr Derringer said.

Yes, I said, and I don't write that kind of poetry either.

You *admit* writing poetry? Mr Derringer said.

I write poetry, I said, but not *that* kind of poetry.

A rumour like that, Mr Derringer said. I hope you know what you're about.

Well, I said, all I know is I didn't write it.

Personally, Mr Derringer said, I think Miss Daffney is not only not ugly, but on the contrary attractive.

Well, that's all right, I said. The only thing I want is not to get into a lot of trouble over something I didn't do.

You *could* have written that poem, Mr Derringer said.

Not *that* one, I said. I could have written a good one.

What do you mean, *good*? Mr Derringer said. Beautiful? Or insulting?

I mean beautiful, I said, only it wouldn't be about Miss Daffney.

Up to this point, Mr Derringer said, I was willing to entertain doubts as to your being the author of the poem, but no longer. I am convinced you wrote it. Therefore I must punish you.

I got up and started to debate.

You give me a strapping for something I didn't do, I said, and you'll hear about it.

So he gave me a strapping and *the whole school* heard about it. I went back to class limping. The poem had been erased. All was well again. The culprit had been duly punished, the poem effaced, and order re-established in the fifth grade. My cousin Arak sat quietly admiring Alice Bovard's brown curls.

First thing during recess I knocked him down and sat on him.

I got a strapping for that, I said, so don't write any more of them.

The next morning, however, there was another love lyric on the blackboard in my cousin Arak's unmistakable hand, and in his unmistakable style, and once again Miss Daffney wanted to weed out the culprit and have him punished. When I came into the room and saw the poem and the lay of the land I immediately began to object. My cousin Arak was going too far. In Armenian I began to swear at him. He, however, had become stone deaf, and Miss Daffney believed my talk was for her. Here, here, she said. Speak in a language everybody can understand if you've got something to say.

All I've got to say is I didn't write that poem, I said. And I didn't write yesterday's either. If I get into any more trouble on account of these poems, somebody's going to hear about it.

Sit down, Miss Daffney said.

After the roll call, Miss Daffney filled a whole sheet of paper with writing, including the new poem, and ordered me to take the message to the office.

Why *me*? I said. I didn't write the poem.

Do as you're told, Miss Daffney said.

I went to her desk, put out my hand to take the note, Miss Daffney gave it a whack, I jumped back three feet and shouted, I'm not going to be carrying love-letters for you.

This just naturally was the limit. There was a limit to everything. Miss Daffney leaped at me. I in turn was so sore at my cousin Arak that I turned around and jumped on him. He pretended to be very innocent, and offered no resistance. He was very deft, though, and instead of getting the worst of it, he got the least, while I fell all over the floor until Miss Daffney caught up with me. After that it was all her fight. When I got to the office with the message, I had scratches and bruises all over my face and hands, and the love-letter from Miss Daffney to Mr Derringer was crumbling and in places torn.

What's been keeping you? Mr Derringer said. Here, let me see that message. What mischief have you been up to now?

He took the message, unfolded it, smoothed it out on his desk, and read it very slowly. He read it three or four times. He was delighted, and, as far as I could tell, in love. He turned with a huge smile on his face and was about to reprimand me again for saying that Miss Daffney was ugly.

I didn't write the poem, I said. I didn't write yesterday's either. All I want is a chance to get myself a little education and live and let live.

Now, now, Mr Derringer said.

He was quite pleased.

If you're in love with her, I said, that's your affair, but leave me out of it.

All I say is you could be a little more gracious about Miss Daffney's appearance, Mr Derringer said. If she seems plain to you, perhaps she doesn't seem plain to someone·else.

I was disgusted. It was just no use.

All right, I said. Tomorrow I'll be gracious.

Now that's better, Mr Derringer said. Of course I must punish you.

He reached for the lower drawer of his desk where the strap was.

Oh, no, I said. If you punish me, then I won't be gracious.

Well, what about today's poem? Mr Derringer said. I've

got to punish you for that. Tomorrow's will be another story.

No, I said. Nothing doing.

Oh, all right, Mr Derringer said, but see that you're gracious.

I will, I said. Can I go back now?

Yes, he said. Yes. Let me think this over.

I began to leave the office.

Wait a minute, he said. Everybody'll know something fishy's going on somewhere unless they hear you howl. Better come back here and howl ten times, and then go back.

Howl? I said. I can't howl unless I'm hurt.

Oh, sure you can, Mr Derringer said. Just give out a big painful howl. You can do it.

I don't think I can, I said.

I'll hit this chair ten times with the strap, Mr Derringer said, and you howl.

Do you think it'll work? I said.

Of course it'll work, he said. Come on.

Mr Derringer hit the chair with the strap and I tried to howl the way I had howled yesterday, but it didn't sound real. It sounded fishy, somewhere.

We were going along that way when Miss Daffney herself came into the office, only we didn't know she'd come in, on account of the noise.

On the tenth one I turned to Mr Derringer and said, That's ten.

Then I saw Miss Daffney. She was aghast and mouth-agape.

Just a few more, son, Mr Derringer said, for good measure.

Before I could tell him Miss Daffney was in the office, he was whacking the chair again and I was howling.

It was disgusting.

Miss Daffney coughed and Mr Derringer turned and saw her – his beloved.

52

Miss Daffney didn't speak. She *couldn't*. Mr Derringer smiled. He was very embarrassed and began swinging the strap around.

I'm punishing the boy, he said.

I understand, Miss Daffney said.

She didn't either. Not altogether anyway.

I'll not have any pupil of this school being impertinent, Mr Derringer said.

He was madly in love with her and was swinging the strap around and trying to put over a little personality. Miss Daffney, however, just didn't think very much of his punishing the boy by hitting a chair, while the boy howled, the man and the boy together making a mockery of justice and true love. She gave him a very dirty look.

Oh! Mr Derringer said. You mean about my hitting the chair? We were just rehearsing, weren't we, son?

No, we weren't, I said.

Miss Daffney, infuriated, turned and fled, and Mr Derringer sat down.

Now look what you've done, he said.

Well, I said, if you're going to have a romance with her, have it, but don't mess me up in it.

Well, Mr Derringer said, I guess that's that.

He was a very sad man.

All right, he said, go back to your class.

I want you to know I didn't write them poems, I said.

That's got nothing to do with it, Mr Derringer said.

I thought you might want to know, I said.

It's too late now, he said. She'll never admire me any more.

Why don't you write a poem to her yourself? I said.

I can't write poems, Mr Derringer said.

Well, I said, figure it out some way.

When I went back to class Miss Daffney was very polite. So was I. She knew I knew and she knew if she got funny I'd either ruin the romance or make her marry him, so she was very friendly. In two weeks school closed and when school opened again Miss Daffney didn't show up. Either Mr Derringer didn't write her a poem, or did and it was no good; or he didn't tell her he loved her, or did and she didn't care; or else he proposed to her and she turned him down, *because I knew*, and got herself transferred to another school so she could get over her broken heart.

Something like that.

COUSINS

NOEL STREATFEILD

from **Curtain Up**

Many of the children in Noel Streatfeild's books are destined for a career in the theatre, and several of them attend the Children's Academy of Dancing and Stage Training run by Madame Fidolia. This extract is about the three Forbes children who were sent there during the Second World War.

THE CHILDREN had all noticed one point about the Academy: the right thing for a proper pupil to carry was a little brown attaché case. In it you carried all your belongings to hang up in your locker; in it you carried things like your towel, shoes and spare socks for your classes, and in it you took home any of your belongings which needed to be washed. They did not want or expect the full Academy wardrobe. They were so used to coupons, or rather lack of them, that they knew they could not have clothes just because they needed them; but an attaché case was different. It was not on coupons and it was the sign of being a real pupil rather than a child who just came in for holiday classes.

They decided not to explain about the attaché cases to Hannah. Hannah could not be made to see that anything to do with the Academy really mattered. She looked upon the whole business of their going to the Academy as something that would pass, like having measles. Instead, they told Alice. Alice was the sort of person who understood how having just one of the right things could make all the difference.

Alice lived up to their expectations.

"That's quite right, that is. That's just what you do need. I'll have a word with Hannah about bees and honey, and then you can go shopping Saturday morning."

Saturday morning was wet. Hannah had a great deal to do and only terrific cajoling could get her to go out at all. Alice advised trying the King's Road, Chelsea. They could walk to it, which meant no escalators to put Hannah off. The morning was a dismal failure. They splashed along in the wet, Hannah absolutely refusing to hurry, and they went into every single shop in the King's Road, including Woolworths, that could possibly sell attaché cases. The King's Road is long, and they did not leave one suitable shop unvisited on either side, but it was not until they got to the far end where the shops finished that they faced the awful truth. Cheap attaché cases were one of the things you could no longer buy. In a few places were grand little cases of leather costing pounds and pounds, but the cheap kind could not be bought anywhere.

On Monday morning they went to the Academy each carrying a brown-paper parcel. Inside Sorrel and Holly's parcels were their black tunics, which had been given them second-hand at the Academy, and brought home to be shortened, their black knickers, their black belts, their pink satin knickers and tunics, two pairs of white socks, their dancing sandals and a rough hand towel. In Mark's parcel was a bathing suit, a pair of cotton shorts, some dancing sandals and a rough towel. The nearer the children got to the Academy the worse they felt about the parcels.

56

"If only it was boxes!" said Sorrel. "A little box, now, would be neat and you could carry things about in it."

Mark angrily kicked a stone off the pavement.

"Even that awful Shirley that did Mistress Mary and was only a holiday pupil had an attaché case."

Sorrel and Mark were walking fast and Holly had to run and skip to catch up.

"And so has even that smallest child who is almost a baby – she's so small that she doesn't even carry her case herself, her mother does – and here's us, old enough to go to the Academy alone, and not an attaché case between us."

Sorrel slowed up because the Academy was in sight.

"I wouldn't mind if it wasn't for us being grandmother's grandchildren. People expect us to be good at everything because of her and because of our mother and the uncles and aunts and all the rest of it, and because of our having scholarships, and it's bad enough that we aren't good, but when as well we haven't got anything but brown-paper parcels we really look most peculiar."

The Academy was quite a different place now that the term had started. Winifred was standing at the Students' entrance with some lists in her hand, and she told the girls to hurry up and put on their black tunics with their white socks and dancing sandals, which they would wear for lessons. Sorrel and Holly had lockers side by side in one changing room, Mark's was in the boys' room down the passage. Sorrel opened her locker quickly and pushed her parcel inside and tried to unpack it in there. There did not seem to be many of the girls about that she knew, but all the same she thought she would like to get her parcel undone and everything hung up before anyone noticed. All round the room there was a flow of chatter.

"Hullo! Had a good holiday?"

"Hullo, Doris! Have you come back to live in London?"

"Have you heard Freda will not be back until half term, she's still with that concert party in Blackpool, lucky beast."

Then it happened. Somebody hurrying by tripped over

Sorrel's feet and the back half of her that was sticking out of her locker and a voice said:

"Oh, bother! I nearly fell," and then added, "One of the new girls grubbing about with a paper parcel."

Holly was sitting on the floor changing her socks. She did not so much care what anybody said to her, but she would not have anyone being rude to Sorrel. She raised her voice to what Ferntree School, who had not approved of such behaviour, would have called a shout.

"We would have attaché cases if we could, but we can't because there is a war on. Perhaps you didn't know that."

There was a lot of laughter, and then somebody said, "That's put you in your place, Miranda."

Miranda! Sorrel turned, her cheeks crimson. What an awful start she had made with her cousin. What an even worse start Holly had made, shouting like that. Miranda was walking up the line of lockers, she ran after her and caught hold of her arm.

"Are you Miranda? I – I mean we – are your cousins. We're Sorrel, Holly and Mark Forbes. Mark isn't here just now, he's in the boys' room changing."

Miranda turned and Sorrel gave a little gasp of surprise, Miranda was so very like what grandmother must have been like when she was a child. The same brown hair – it hung down at the back, of course, but the top part was piled up into curls – the same dark eyes, the same effect of being a patch of colour in a dull room. Only grandmother was like a sparkling bit of colour and Miranda was more like the last smouldering red cinder lying amongst grey ash. Miranda was evidently not a person who minded if she had been rude to her cousins or not, or rather she seemed to have forgotten it, for she put on a very grown-up gracious air.

"How do you do? I heard you were coming. We shall be quite a family gathering this term, for Uncle Mose is sending Miriam, did you know? You're a beginner, aren't you? I'm afraid that means we shan't see much of each other."

Sorrel wished most heartily that this were going to be the

case, but she remembered what Winifred had said about their both being in the same class. Quite time enough, however, for Miranda to find that out if it happened. So she just smiled politely and admitted to being a beginner and went back to her changing.

Sorrel and Holly had just got into their overalls and were fastening their belts when the changing-room door was thrown open and a little girl dashed in. She had on a frock of bright orange linen, against which her thin little face looked pale and yellowish, in fact there seemed hardly any face at all, it was so surrounded by a fuzz of black hair. In one hand she carried a grand leather attaché case of the sort which cost pounds and pounds. She glanced imperiously round the room.

"Which is my cousin Holly?"

Holly was shy of being called out in front of all the big girls and she spoke in a very small voice.

"Me."

The child dashed over to her, put her attaché case on the floor and gave her a kiss.

"We're cousins. I'm Miriam Cohen. You're just a tiny bit older than me, I won't be eight until the end of this month."

This was so insulting that Holly forgot to be shy.

"If you don't mind my saying so, I'm a great deal older than you. I shall be nine just after Christmas."

Miriam seemed to be a person who did everything quickly. She snapped her attaché case undone and threw everything in it out on to the floor.

"Never mind, let's be friends. Mum says if we're friends I can ask you to tea. I can't come to you because we're not on speaking terms with grandmother just now. We hardly ever are, you know, except at Christmas. Of course, we always go to grandmother's then."

Sorrel and Holly rather liked the look of Miriam, who was, at any rate, friendly. Sorrel knelt down beside her and began collecting the things that Miriam had upset.

"I'm a cousin, too. I'm Sorrel. Do you know which your locker is?" She picked up a white satin tunic and knickers and gave them a shake. "These will get awfully dirty on the floor."

Miriam got up and began tearing her orange linen frock over her head.

"Mum's made me two tunics and two knickers. She cut up one of her best nightdresses. I think that was pretty decent of her, don't you? She said I'd have to have two, she knew I wouldn't be clean a minute if I only had one. I've got the locker next to Holly, they told me so at the door."

Sorrel hung up Miriam's tunic and knickers and her linen frock and helped her into her black knickers and tunic. Holly passed Miriam her dancing sandals.

"Are you absolutely new, like me, or have you learnt it before?"

Miriam sat on the floor to put on her sandals.

"Learnt what?"

Holly crouched down beside her.

"All these routines and things the big girls do, and that tap and that work at the bar."

Miriam tied the tapes of one of her sandals.

"I began tap when I was three, then I started acrobatic

work, you know, flip flaps and all that. I learnt to sing when I was four. I did some shows with Dad for charity when I was five. I don't really ever remember a time when I wasn't learning, but mostly I went to special classes or learnt at home. That's why they've sent me here. It's to see which way I'm heading – at least, that's what Dad says. He thinks it's time I specialized. He says I'm too plain for the glamour type and I ought to do a lot of acrobatic work and become a comedienne. But I shan't, I'm going to dance. He knows that really." She tied her second sandal tapes. "There's no doubt about it, I'm a bitter disappointment."

A bell clanged in the passage. At once there was a crash of locker doors and everybody hurried out. Winifred was standing at the foot of the stairs with a list in her hand.

"Get in line, please, children, and come past me slowly."

Sorrel leaned a little way out of the line and looked up the passage for Mark. Boys were easy to pick out amongst that mass of black tunics and white socks. Mark had changed into his sandals, otherwise he was dressed exactly as he had started out in the morning. He saw Sorrel and gave her a grin. It was a cheerful grin, but she knew that inside he was feeling very much as she was, sort of sinking and wishing they were not so new.

Winifred had stopped Miranda and told her to wait. She was standing at the foot of the stairs when Sorrel arrived at the head of the queue. Winifred laid a hand on Sorrel's arm.

"I expect you've met Miranda in the changing room." She looked at Miranda. "I want you to look after Sorrel. You two are in the same form."

Miranda gaped at Winifred.

"But she's younger than I am and she's never done a thing."

Winifred spoke nicely, but you could not help feeling she was not sorry to be able to say what she did.

"She may be younger, but from the paper I set her she's well up to the standard of work in the upper middle, and, as well, Madame has granted her the scholarship Pauline

Fossil has given for dramatic work."

This last remark seemed to stun Miranda into silence. She caught Sorrel by the hand and pulled her up the stairs after her. It was only when they were outside the door of the practice room in which the upper middle worked that she suddenly stopped.

"I didn't know you could act, nobody told me."

"I don't know that I can."

"What did Madame see you do?"

Sorrel was just going to tell her and then she thought better of it. Perhaps Madame had been over-generous in granting her the scholarship. Perhaps she had not really seen very much talent, but if that was so she was certainly not going to let Miranda know about it. Like a distant light at the end of a long tunnel a thought shaped in Sorrel's head. She had not ever thought of being an actress, but she was the daughter of one and the grandchild of an actor and an actress, and the great-grandchild of a very great actor indeed, if all they said about that old Sir Joshua was right. Anyway, there was every bit as much reason why she should be an actress as why Miranda should. Why should not she see if she could be good? If she could really be worth Pauline Fossil's scholarship? She answered Miranda casually:

"Oh, just a bit of a play that she asked us to do. Is this the classroom?"

In the next few weeks the children were so busy that they had no time to think if they liked London or the Academy, or living with grandmother or anything else. Every morning they left the house at a quarter past eight to be ready and dressed for their first class at nine. They worked at lessons until twelve. From twelve till one Mark and Holly played games with the smaller children in the garden near the Academy, but Sorrel had special ballet classes with Winifred. At one o'clock they went down to the dining-room, which was in the basement, and had lunch, which was brought in vast containers from the British Restaurant. They were then sent out when it was fine, or, if it was wet, did what they liked indoors until two-thirty, they then did lessons until four-thirty. Sometimes they had singing or dancing or an acting class in the afternoon, and then they did extra lessons after tea. Normally, tea was at four-thirty, and from five till six-thirty they had special classes; ballet one night, tap dancing the next and on each night acting in either French or English, or a mime class.

All day long, unless there was a special class, the girls worked in their black overalls, white socks and sandals; but if there was a special class, such as Sorrel's extra ballet lesson before lunch, or Holly had an extra ballet lesson in the afternoon, then down they had to rush to the changing room, get into their tunics and knickers, snatch up their towels and go up to their class. At the end of that, after a quick rub down, back they had to dash into their overalls. "It's not so bad as it used to be," the other children told them. "Now, until you get to wearing block shoes, the same sandals do for everything except tap, and the world doesn't come to an end if you just wear your tunic knickers and a shirt for tap; but when we could get the stuff there was all that changing into rompers, and we'd special satin sandals for ballet. It was change, change, all the time."

As far as the lessons were concerned the children found things easy. The Academy standard was reasonably high, but nothing like as high as it had been at their previous schools, and some subjects were dropped altogether, such as Latin, but, of course, other things took their place. There was a tremendous lot of history of dancing and of the theatre, and any amount of time given to music. They had not only to learn the theory of music, but there were special classes on rhythm and special classes on appreciation, when music was played to them on gramophone records, and they were taught how to listen to it and to understand it. Music was an afternoon class. A Doctor Felix Lente came every afternoon and taught the whole school.

The children could have kept pace with all the ordinary school things, even the music, for, as a whole, the pupils were not exceptionally musical, but it was the dancing they found so difficult. In spite of extra coaching and the fact that all three were quite intelligent, they were taking a long time to catch up. Sorrel, in fact, was obviously never going to catch up with her age, and when she was finally put to bar work with a class, it was with girls of Holly's age. Holly and Mark worked with a special little class of beginners.

As well as all the dancing they had to memorize, each of the children had two or three acting parts. In those first weeks they frequently found themselves trying to do three things at once. Have a bath, say a part out loud, and stick out one foot, murmuring with half their minds, plié and rise, plié and rise.

Everything was much more difficult for Sorrel than for Holly and Mark. Mark took his dancing lessons very lightly. He tried to remember all he could but he felt it was a shocking waste of time for somebody who was going into the Navy. Holly had only to compete with the new girls, who knew no more than she did, and very soon she began to like dancing and became one of the best in her small class. It was not saying much, but it was something to show for the person who held the Posy Fossil scholarship. But, for Sorrel, life was pretty tough. Every girl of her age had been learning dancing for at least two years, most of them had been working on their points for quite a while. Of course the majority had been evacuated for about a year during the heavy bombing, but they had kept up fairly well by working under a local ballet teacher. Sorrel could see that however hard she worked and however many extra classes she had she was never really going to be a dancer. It was not even as though she had any especial talent. She was light on her feet and quick at remembering, but it took more than that to make a dancer. Sometimes, in the night, she thought desperately of going to Madame and asking if she could not drop all this dancing, but even before she had framed the thought she knew it would be hopeless. Madame's Academy was primarily for dancing, and to get inside those doors you had to dance.

What Sorrel did find as the weeks went by was that she looked forward to all the acting classes. Mime, where you acted scenes with no words spoken at all, she loved. Then there were her speaking parts. She had the part of the queen in a French version of *The Sleeping Beauty*. She had a scene or two of Rosalind's in *As You Like It* and she had Friar Tuck in *Robin Hood*. Every acting class, she liked acting more. She found things happened to her. One day, quite suddenly, she knew what her hands should be doing. Another, she discovered how she should get from one place to another across the stage. She found that she knew what it meant when Miss Jay said, "You were well in the scene, Sorrel dear." She began to know how to be acting, and yet to sound natural. Quite a lot of these things she could not possibly have explained, but they were each becoming clear thoughts, so that she knew that presently each one would be sorted out and she would be able to say, "I did that because . . ."

All the time in front of her at the acting classes there was Miranda to watch. Miranda in the school, or Miranda at a dancing class, or Miranda listening to an appreciation of music lesson was just an ordinary schoolgirl. But Miranda acting was something so special that you forgot she was Miranda. It did not matter to Miranda that she was dressed in a black overall and white socks and black sandals, and looked just like all the other girls, for when she was acting she became the person she was meant to be. As the princess as a child in *The Sleeping Beauty* you knew that she was very young and wearing stiff satin, and that she had never heard there were such things as needles in the world, and when the needle pricked her, though there was no needle there, you could see that it had gone in and had hurt her, and you could watch her going to sleep and know it was not just an ordinary sleep but would last for a hundred years. In her Rosalind scene she took the words and they sang out of her mouth in a golden stream, and yet, somehow, she made them ordinary words and Rosalind a real girl. And so it was when she played Maid Marian. Miranda always played the best parts; she never thought that she would not play them, and it seemed to be the rule that she picked what she liked and the rest of the class shared out what was over. Both Miss Jay and Madame Moulin treated Miranda as something special when she was acting. When she was not acting they treated her as the rather conceited schoolgirl that she was. It was all very muddling. In what little time Sorrel had to think about anything except her work, she thought about Miranda. Miranda was full of talent, she had inherited all the family gifts, everybody said so. To Madame Moulin and Miss Jay it was something wonderful to be descended from the Warrens. Sorrel respected Madame Moulin and Miss Jay, and so what they thought mattered to her. She still thought of herself as Forbes, but just now and again, when she was watching Miranda act, something stirred in her, and she felt excited and then part of her mind said, "You're a Warren too. You're a Warren too."

M.13 IN FORM
ONCE MORE

GENE KEMP

Told by X who never dares to give his/her name. The Cat's revenges are terrible and timeless.

"**B**OOKS IS COMIN'," yelled Mandy the Boot, blundering into the classroom in her father's size 12 army boots and knocking Slasher Ormeroyd flying, which caused him to leap up with a mad roar and lurch to attack her, except that the Cat (Felix Delaney) paused in the middle of a poker game with Lia Tansy, Chinky Fred and Tom Lightfinger to call out, "Cool it, Slasher," so that he hauled back his huge maulers, for he always does what the Cat tells him. As we all do.

"What books?" enquired the Cat gently, for he was a great reader: crime and horror.

"A crateful. Old Perkins is turning 'em over an' oinkin' like a ma pig with piglets. There's at least a hundred."

"Mr Perkins has comed back to us, doody, doody,"

crooned Daisy Chain, blue eyes beaming, bright hair bobbing. She loved Mr Perkins, and he was fond of her, not that he had much choice, M.13 not being noted for its lovable characters. Mind you, we were all pleased to see him. He'd been absent on a course and the teacher they sent instead left in tears on Wednesday morning, making the rest of the week very tedious. The Headmaster took us. His name is Mr Bliss and it's a lie.

"That's great," said Bat Pearson, resident genius. "And about the books. We need new ones. Not that I read much fiction, haven't the time" – she was wading through *A Study of Bog Burial in Scandinavia and Europe* (funny place to bury people, said Mandy) – "but I like to keep Killer going and he can't stand *Little Women*."

Killer, six feet two and growing, nodded, for Bat does all his work. In return he's her Minder. Most of us need one. M.13 isn't popular in the school, not that it's popular out of it either.

"I like Enid Blyton," cried Hot Chocolate, the class prefect. "I've read them all. Sir once said they'd made me what I am."

"Yeah," growled Mandy the Boot, "fascist, sexist and racist, which in your case especially is disgusting."

"Speak for yourself," shrieked Lia Tansy, the Cat's woman, she of the golden skin and golden eyes.

"Belt up," bellowed Hag Stevens from the doorway, "Mr Perkins is on his way." We were all so pleased to see him that we arranged ourselves nicely, looking keen and eager. And instead of sighing as he usually does at the sight of us, he smiled, which smoothed out all his wrinkles like an American with a face-lift.

"It's so nice to see you all again," he said warmly, and as if that wasn't enough he was dressed in cords and check shirt. Where was his old chalky? What was up?

"As you know, I've been on a course, a language course, which I really enjoyed, and now I feel we can go forward with a new outlook."

"A wha ...?" asked Brain Drain, dim even by M.13's standards.

"A new outlook on the rest of our year together. Speaking to you honestly, as your friend as well as teacher, that course came just in the nick of time, for I'd begun to despair at the thought of us struggling and drowning together ..."

"I wunt let yer drown, Sir," interrupted Brain Drain, breathing hard, for more than two words was difficult, "I kin swim."

"Quite," Sir agreed. "Now let's see if my old friends are all here ... Abdullah, Asra, Brian ..."

Killer and Slasher were despatched to carry in the heavy crate, Bat, Lia and Mandy to organize the class resource centre. The rest of the school has a central area, but it was decided that M.13 should just keep theirs in the classroom, after Tom Lightfinger flogged all the cassette players and musical instruments to some teenage pals to start a group.

"Any 'orror comics or girlie mags?" Slasher asked Killer hopefully.

"No, shurrup. The Cat looks after that side, and y'know he don't think it right for old Perkins to learn about such things. Not at his age."

Eventually all the splendid new books were arranged and the classroom transformed. Mr Perkins had done well, something for everyone: Dr Seuss for Brain Drain and Daisy and The Heap, *War and Peace* for Bat, *An Anthology of Horror* for the Cat. He beamed at us all.

"Yes, you shall soon get at them, but first something new for a new day. Has anyone a poem for me? A suitable poem, mind, Ormeroyd."

A mind-boggling hush fell for we always turned to the Cat or Bat or Mandy to represent us on these occasions and they all three despised poetry (wet, useless, boring). And then Brain Drain lumbered to his feet.

"I know one about an ickle worm." And he recited it while Sir grinned like a maniac.

"Jolly good," he cried. "They told me it would work. Good old M.13. Don't let me down. Surely you must know a poem, Beatrice."

Bat stood up, grimacing horribly, embarrassed. "The only one I know is a dead boring one from Horace, about a smelly, skinny youth. Dates back to my classical hang-up last year. Sorry. Will that do?"

Sir nodded, and the Latin phrases hung in the classroom already quite well known for its language. Killer smiled approvingly. His Bat was doing well even if no one could understand a word of it. And Tom Lightfinger got up, brick red. "Know one about a dicky bird," he said, head down. "Learnt it in the Infants." One by one M.13 made their offerings, the Cat last, with the lyrics of an obscure cult rock group.

A week later anyone walking into M.13's classroom, and most people preferred not to, would have had to weave their way through poems everywhere – on the walls, on the windows, standing in displays, hanging on string, swinging in mobiles, for M.13 had taken to poetry, writing poems, reading poems, reciting poems, illustrating poems. Mr Perkins had seen a miracle in his lifetime and walked on air. The school grapevine had it that the class had either gone barmy or had reformed at last. Actually it was, as usual, the Cat.

Shoulders hunched, black glasses, white face, he said,

"I want old Perkins happy. De poetry makes him happy. So we get with de poetry. See?" We saw.

When it wasn't poetry, it was stories. M.13 went book mad, reading all of the time all over the place, even walking round the playground reading with Killer and Slasher ready to settle anyone foolish enough to find it funny. Those who understood what those squiggles on a page meant helped those who didn't.

So occupied were we, we didn't notice that the school's big issue was now Conservation. A famous celebrity had addressed the school on the subject and projects mushroomed everywhere. But it wasn't until a very pretty lady came to tell the school of the plight of a butterfly that was about to die out unless money could be raised to provide a Nature Reserve where it could breed that M.13 realized it was needed.

"Dat poor ickle 'utterfly," muttered Brain Drain, moved.

Now despite everything – lies, thefts, vandalism, dishonesty, cheating, bullying, greed, truancy, you name it, M.13's got it – despite all these or as well as, M.13 has Heart. Disasters, they weep over disasters. Earthquakes bring contributions from them faster than anyone. Tom Lightfinger has been known to pinch the Save the Children bottle from the corner shop to contribute to the class's gift. So when the very pretty lady said there was to be a prize for the best school contribution – a silver medal – and a framed poem about a butterfly written by the very pretty lady herself for the best class collection, there could be no doubt about it. M.13 intended to get that prize, that poem on their wall.

No one needed to tell M.13 about fund-raising. They have

71

a natural talent for it: begging, gambling, sponsoring, busking, collecting, blackmailing, grovelling, stealing, shop-lifting, extorting, bullying, even selling, they went about it all in the way that suited each of them best. Yet in the final week but one, the grapevine informed the Cat that Hadley Grove School were the favourites, their rich parents being plushier than ours.

Mr Perkins was heard to remark with pleasure on the industry of his class, most pleased, most pleased. Reading, writing and money-raising thrived. An experienced teacher, though, every Friday he collected in the books that had worked the miracle (he thought) and checked them. That Friday only Bat's was missing and she promised faithfully etc. Mr Perkins went home. Happy.

On Monday morning all the shelves were empty. All the books had disappeared. So had every leaflet, magazine, poster and map in the resources area. His face sagged back into all those wrinkles as he took the register, all present, except for Brain Drain.

"Right, what have you lot done with them?" He didn't look at all like that nice Mr Perkins. He looked more like Hanging Judge Jeffreys.

"Delaney, what have you organized?"

"Nothing, Sir," the Cat at a loss, for once, "honest."

"You don't know what honesty is, Delaney."

But the Cat stood firm; it was nothing to do with him nor anyone else that he knew about.

"Then Lightfinger, it just has to be you."

"No, no, no. I liked the books. They just took what I was half-way in the middle of and I haven't finished. And I dint read the ending first, for once."

"Hard luck," snapped Mr Perkins, cruelly.

And the door crashed open as the vast, shaggy head of Brain Drain appeared, then the rest of him, waving a fistful of money.

"For de 'utterfly pome, Mr Perkins. For de pome. We win it now, won't we? Look at all de lolly. And I did it for you,

Mr Perkins, becos you give me all dem pomes and I love pomes now."

"Brian, look at me and stop gabbling. Where did you get that money? And do you know what's happened to all our books?"

"I've conserved our books. Dey'll go on f'ever an' ever. An' dey gived me lolly for 'em. Look."

"But how?" groaned Mr Perkins.

Brain Drain was panting like an old train at full steam ahead. "Me Auntie Mave. Cleanin' after school, an' she give me this dustbin bag an' I put 'em all in an' took 'em to our church for rebikin' . . ."

"For what?" Mr Perkins looked as if he was going demented.

"Recycling," translated Bat.

"An' they said what a good cause, and gived me money an' we'll win the pome now, wun't we?" he beamed. He sat down and bobbed up again in the heavy silence. "Mr Perkins, Sir?"

"Yes, Brian?" came a low moan.

"I conserved them books and the 'utterfly, dint I?"

"Oh, Brian, you did, you did."

After a long time the Cat spoke, and for possibly the first time in his life, his voice was full of pity.

"M.13. Listen. De kindness, get it? From now on we are going to be kind to Mr Perkins."

How M.13 later visited the recycling plant, rescued all the books (not very suitable anyway, they said), was spotted by the Mayor, also visiting, got its picture in all the papers (such keen children), won the school medal and the butterfly poem (more pictures in the papers – what fine, hardworking children, an example to others) so that at last Brain Drain could hang the pome on the wall – except they'd gone on to computer games by then – and as usual were hated bitterly by the rest of the school (good, hardworking, boring children) is another story.

THE DAY POSY BATES
MADE HISTORY

HELEN CRESSWELL

THIS IS the story of the Great Paxton School Jubilee and Anniversary Procession, and about mistakes. The first mistake was in the village schoolmistress, Miss Perlethorpe, thinking she had a good idea. (Miss Perlethorpe, who always dressed in autumnal shades of brown, and did jig-saws in the evenings, had never had a good idea in her life.)

It all happened the summer of the village school's anniversary.

"We shall be one hundred years old next month, children," Miss Perlethorpe told her pupils.

"You don't look it, miss," observed William, who was nine, and the eldest of the Bates children.

"It's *terribly* exciting," she told the school. There were twenty-six children in it altogether and they all had their lessons in one large room. "I always think that once something becomes more than one hundred years old, it becomes historical. Imagine – we shall be historical!"

Nobody was much excited by this prospect.

"We shall have celebrations," announced Miss Perlethorpe.

The children did brighten somewhat at this.

"Food?" they asked. "Eats? Sausages on sticks and jelly? Smashing!"

"I was not thinking of food," said Miss Perlethorpe rather quellingly, "and am disappointed that it should be the first thing that sprang to your minds. No, I have thought of a perfectly lovely idea – something quite, quite different."

It was then that Miss Perlethorpe told the children what was – or so she mistakenly believed – the first good idea she had ever had.

"This year is, of course, the Silver Jubilee of our Queen. We shall celebrate our passing into history by all becoming kings and queens!" she cried.

The school looked stonily back at her.

"We shall have a splendid procession! We shall have a procession of all the kings and queens of England! We shall all have the most enormous fun making our own crowns and costumes, and then we shall parade through the village on July the Sixth!"

"Bags I Harold," said Peter Potter instantly. "I shall have a whacking big arrow in my eye."

"You may have an arrow, Peter," Miss Perlethorpe told him, "but certainly not in your eye. Your mother would never allow it."

"I shall be Charles the First," announced William.

"Lovely, William!" Miss Perlethorpe was delighted about this because she had only last week been telling the children about King Charles being beheaded. What she did not know was that William intended to walk in the procession with his head covered in blood and tucked underneath his arm.

"I still think there ought to be food," Kate said. (She was the middle one of the Bates.) "There ought to be a feast, or something. Kings and queens were always having feasts and banquets. If we had a big banquet with crisps and bangers and cream buns and jellies that would be really historical. I'm going to be the Queen of Hearts. Then there'll have to be some tarts."

"The Queen of Hearts was not really a Queen of England, Kate," Miss Perlethorpe told her.

"Where *was* she queen of, then?" Kate asked.

Miss Perlethorpe was floored by this.

"Very well, Kate," she told her, "you may be the Queen of Hearts."

"Which queen can I be?" piped up Posy Bates. Miss Perlethorpe was again stumped. Posy was the youngest member of the school and only four and not altogether reliable. She had played the part of one of the Three Kings in the school Nativity Play, and when it came to her turn to present the Infant Jesus with her gift, had refused to part with it.

"He's not having it!" she had shrieked, as the other two kings tried vainly to wrest it from her grasp.

"He's got lots of presents already. And I haven't got nothing yet. He's not having it, he's *not*!"

The gift Posy was supposed to present was in fact Miss Perlethorpe's own string of imitation pearls, and she herself had the greatest difficulty in retrieving her property. Posy, sobbing and struggling, had to be pulled off into the wings by Miss Perlethorpe, who had to abandon her post at the piano to do this. She had then had a violent tug-of-war with Posy, who had run back on to the stage, and the string had finally snapped, sending pearls everywhere. The Nativity Play had then broken up in disorder with angels, kings, shepherds and even the Virgin Mary herself all scrambling about after the scattered beads, and the audience laughing until they cried, which audiences are not meant to do at Nativity Plays.

The memory of this terrible event was still painfully clear, and Miss Perlethorpe wished no repetition.

"I do not think you had better be a queen, Posy dear," she told her firmly. "I think you are too young to be either a king or a queen."

"What can I be then?" persisted Posy.

Miss Perlethorpe cast swiftly round for something relatively safe.

"You may be a lady-in-waiting," she told Posy. "You can carry the train of one of the queens, which is, of course, a tremendous honour. I shall myself – ahem – appear at the head of the procession as the present queen at her coronation. People have told me there is a likeness."

"So shall I carry your train, miss?" Posy asked.

"Yes, Posy, you shall," Miss Perlethorpe told her.

"Posy is, after all, only four," she thought, "and cannot do much harm."

She had made her second mistake. Posy Bates, without even trying, could do more harm than everyone else in Paxton put together.

From then on the school was busy preparing for the Jubilee and Anniversary Procession. The whole village was, for that matter. Miss Perlethorpe had relented and decided that there should, after all, be a banquet, to be organized by the mothers and laid out on trestle tables on the village green.

"If it rains," Miss Perlethorpe told the school, "we shall have it in the schoolroom. But we must all pray earnestly that it will not rain."

Ordinary lessons had to go on as usual, of course, and this is how another mistake came to be made. It is not easy to teach twenty-six children aged between four and eleven in a single large room, though Miss Perlethorpe strove valiantly to do so. It means that sometimes as many as four different lessons were going on at once, and inevitably Miss Perlethorpe now and again became flustered and got mixed up. This very thing happened the day following the announcement of the Procession.

The older children were busy writing and drawing about Charles I and Miss Perlethorpe had to keep going and peering over their shoulders to make sure that they were not being silly and putting too much blood into the pictures of

77

the execution. At the same time she was trying to tell the younger ones about Noah and his Ark. They liked this story very much, especially Posy, who lived on a farm and wondered if that would ever be flooded so that her father could build an ark. She hoped so.

"And now I want to see some really lovely pictures, children," Miss Perlethorpe told them. "And remember that the animals went in pairs, and remember that a pair means *two*."

She then went to take a look at the King Charles children, and Posy, carefully drawing a giraffe, had an idea.

"Was Noah a king, miss?" she asked.

Miss Perlethorpe was not really listening, and her mind was on kings anyway, and she murmured absently, "Yes. Yes, dear, of course."

"Good," thought Posy. She thought that she had now had the best idea she had ever had in *her* whole life. But something told her that Miss Perlethorpe would probably *not* think it a good idea, so she kept it to herself.

She did not really think it fair that everyone in the school should be a king or queen except herself. She decided, therefore, that she would be King Noah. She knew that most people in the Bible wore long flowing robes, so decided that she would secretly make her costume from one of her mother's sheets and a striped bath towel, as the shepherds had in the Nativity Play. But Posy was not only going to be King Noah. She intended to have a retinue.

"I only need two of everything," she thought, "and we've got a lot more than two of pigs and cows and cats and dogs and sheep and hens and goats and things. No elephants and no giraffes, though."

Posy regretted the elephants and giraffes.

From then on two quite separate Processions were being planned. Miss Perlethorpe, in her mind's eye, could see a stately line of Kings and Queens moving with slow dignity along the flag lined village street. Posy could see a

Procession of farm animals, two by two and good as gold, with herself at their head.

Every day, while the children were busy making golden crowns and cardboard shields and coats of armour, Miss Perlethorpe would tell them exactly what they were to do.

"I am what is called a Producer," she told them. "Every procession must have a Producer, just as a play must. Now I want you all to stop for a moment, and march round the room just as you will on the day. Lovely. Shoulders back, William! *That's* it. Lift your head just a teeny shade higher, Denise. You are a queen, remember. Splendid! You *won't* wear those striped socks on the day, will you, Caroline dear?"

Posy realized that she must be the Producer of her own procession, and every day after school she conscientiously trotted off to rehearse her own team. She went to the pigs first, mostly. She had to stand on a bucket to see over the wall.

"Now listen, pigs," she told them, "I'm your Producer for the procession. Only two of you can be in it, so I'll pick the best. I hope you are listening."

The pigs did not look as if they were listening, but Posy was not deterred.

"You've got to walk side by side," she told them. "You mustn't run, and you must keep your heads up."

She tried to produce the hens as well, even though they never did stand still while she was talking. On the whole, the cows seemed to listen best. They stood perfectly still as Posy stood on the five-barred gate and shouted her instructions.

"I'm King Noah!" she shouted. "I am your leader!"

They stood and stared and chewed, and it really did seem to Posy as if they were listening.

"It's going to be lovely," she told herself. "I think I'm good as a Producer, and Miss Perlethorpe will be really surprised and pleased."

She broke the news to Miss Perlethorpe that she would rather not, after all, carry her train.

"I think I'd rather walk at the back of everybody," she told her. "I think I'm rather little to carry a long train."

"How *sensible*, Posy!" cried Miss Perlethorpe. She was secretly relieved. She had decided, after some misgiving, to use one of her best velvet floor-length curtains as a train. The velvet had been very expensive, but she had determined to risk it.

"I am not, after all," she told herself, "a queen *every* day."

The day of the Great Paxton School Jubilee and Anniversary Procession dawned warm and sunny. Miss Perlethorpe spent the morning hurrying about the village supervising last-minute details, and Posy went and gave her team their last run through.

"It's today!" she told the pigs, hens, cats, dogs, sheep, cows and goats. "I want you to remember everything I told you. The main thing is to be clean and tidy and hold your heads up."

It was only at two o'clock when the Procession began to assemble in the High Street that Posy realized that her job as Producer was much more complicated than Miss Perlethorpe's. The dogs and cats presented no problem. It was when Posy began the attempt to sort the other animals into pairs that she saw that she might, possibly, have bitten off more than she could chew.

Luckily her family had already gone down to the village and thought that she had, too. It took her a long time to get the door of the sty open and prod two of the pigs out with a stick. Wearing a large sheet and bath towel did not help.

"Wait here," she told the pigs and hens, "while I fetch the rest."

It was easy enough to untether the goats, but the cows just seemed to want to lie and chew daisies, and sheep, of course, are notoriously difficult to organize. Posy battled valiantly on. She was King Noah, and a Producer, and had a job to do.

Meanwhile Miss Perlethorpe ran up and down making a last-minute inspection of her own Procession, with her velvet curtain clutched up with one hand and hanging on to her tiara with the other.

"Oh Caroline – *not* football socks! You are Mary Queen of Scots, remember. Graham, do pull your garters up, and put that lollipop away. Don't chew gum, Felicity dear, there's a good girl."

She did not notice that William Bates did not appear to have a head and was hiding something under his cloak. The clock struck the half-hour, the band broke into *Land of Hope and Glory*, and Miss Perlethorpe felt tears of pride and pleasure spring to her eyes.

"Heads up, everybody!" she cried. "Forward – march!"

The Procession set off. Everyone marched very straight and tall to begin with, except William, who could not see very well through the slits he had made for his eyes.

The first inkling that anything was going wrong was when the crowd, instead of clapping and singing, began to point and stare at something higher up the street. Nigel Walker, who was holding Miss Perlethorpe's train, dropped it while he turned round to see what was happening. She did not notice this, and went marching on, quite unaware that her Procession was no longer with her. Everyone in it had halted, turned, and was now staring at the amazing cavalcade now fast approaching in clouds of dust.

Posy had not managed to shut the door of the sty properly, so that there were fourteen pigs, all grunting and squealing and trying to get from under the hooves of six cows in hot pursuit. (It was not that Posy could not count, just that she had not been able to control the cows.) Hens and ducks flapped everywhere and two thoroughly bewildered sheepdogs were vainly nipping among the muddled cows and sheep trying to sort them out. Somewhere in the middle of this throng was a small figure draped in a striped towel and being towed along fast by a charging goat on the end of a rope. It was King Noah, in tears.

"I meanted it to be lovely!" sobbed Posy Bates as the pigs charged the trestle tables. After that the pigs were very little trouble, because they were busy eating. They made very short work indeed of the sausage rolls and bangers and egg sandwiches and trifle. The cows did quite a lot of damage, though, and Miss Perlethorpe was tripped by one of the goats and had her velvet curtain irremediably ruined. Hens squawked, ducks quacked, and there seemed to be sheep everywhere, and the Kings and Queens in the Procession certainly had no intention of marching forward with their heads held up with all this going on. William Bates had his head butted from underneath his arm by a billy goat, who then careered into the crowd with the blood-covered head on his horns and a lot of women and children screamed and tried to get away. King Noah turned tail and ran sobbing off up the street but fell over his sheet and was caught, though nobody had the heart to spank him.

The Great Paxton School Jubilee and Anniversary

Procession received a lot of publicity, and later both King Noah and Miss Perlethorpe appeared on local television.

"I meanted it as a lovely surprise," Posy kept saying. "But it all turned out horrid. I don't want to be King Noah any more."

"I have never been so mortified in my whole life," Miss Perlethorpe told the interviewer, "and shall remember this occasion in all its awful detail till the day I die."

And on that point, everyone was agreed. The Great Paxton School Jubilee and Anniversary Procession might not have turned out as planned but it had, most certainly, been a day to remember.

History, one might almost say.

THE WOOLLEN BANK
FORGERIES

KEITH WATERHOUSE

WHEN I WAS nine years old I developed an insane passion for a cricket set on Woolworth's toy counter. This was in the days when everything at Woollie's cost either threepence or sixpence. Sixpence for the bat, ball sixpence, stumps sixpence, bails threepence, pads sixpence apiece, analysis book threepence, total three shillings. I made up my mind that I was going to have the cricket set. Long before I worked out how I was going to steal the money I was rehearsing what I would say to my mother when I took the gear home for the first time.

"No, only they've started a cricket team in our class. And do you know who's got to look after all the stuff, mam? Me."

Immediate suspicion. "How do you mean, you've got to look after it? Why can't they look after their own stuff?"

"Ah well, it's not really a school team, it's just our teacher. Old Webby. Mr Webb. He sees us all playing cricket in the street with an old tennis ball, so he says we could start our own team up in that field, and all look after the stuff in turns. He said we shouldn't be playing in the street."

"Yes, and I've told you not to play in the street as well."

My mother, with her flat damp voice, was so predictable

that I could make up whole conversations with her before I got into the house, examining and re-examining each statement for flaws, leading myself up my own garden path and reconnoitring for trip-wires.

"Who paid out for it, then?"

"Mr Webb. He paid out for it himself."

"What's *he* want to buy you cricket things for?" And so on.

First I had to get the money. I had several sources of income, but none large enough to get three shillings together at one go. The blue cup on the panshelf where she kept the pennies for the gas, that was worth twopence at one swoop, or perhaps threepence, depending on how full it was, but never more. Or the fish and chips: by buying twopennyworth instead of threepennyworth I could save a penny, but it was a risk. She always knew.

I thought for a long time that she had someone down there in the fish shop who ran back and told her what I'd bought.

"How many chips did you get?"

"Threepennorth."

"How many chips did you get?"

"Threepennorth."

"How – many – chips – did – you – get?"

"Told you, threepennorth."

"You didn't get threepennorth at all. You got twopennorth. Didn't you?"

"No."

"Didn't you?"

"No."

"*Did*n't you?"

"Yes."

"Where's that penny?"

"What penny?"

"I'll give you what penny, my lad! What have you done with it?"

"Lost it!"

"You didn't lose it at all. You've spent it! Have you spent it? You can't keep your hands off nothing, can you?"

I got sixpence a month from the church for singing in the choir, and threepence to take to the Wolf Cubs on Friday night towards the excursion to the Zoo. And sixpence on Monday morning to take to school and put in the bank. And twopence milk money, which I spent on myself as a matter of course.

Bank day was the big ceremony of the week. Each one of us at school had a little, green, linen-backed bank book, and on Monday mornings we paid in our sixpences or, in some rare cases, shillings and even half-crowns, to the Woollen Bank. The teacher acted as agent or collector for the bank. We started first thing, after the attendance register had been called. Webby would call out the names again, in a different order for some obscure reason, and this time we would march up in turn and pay out our money and have it entered in our little green books.

"Littlewood?"

"Here, sir."

"Yes, we can see you're here, Littlewood. Where's your bank money?"

"Forgot it, sir."

"You'd forget your head if it was loose, wouldn't you, Littlewood? All right. Patterson?"

"Sir."

It cut very nicely into the geography class.

Some boys drew their money out regularly every four or five weeks, in florins and half-crowns, whenever their fathers were on short time; and some never had anything in the bank at all except an erratic sixpence on the wrong side of Christmas.

My own account usually went up to ten or twelve shillings before my mother made me draw it out to buy a pair of boots or something, and then we would start again at sixpence a week.

"Parker?"

"Sir."

"Richards?"

"Drawing out, sir."

"You're always drawing out, Richards."

I had nothing in the bank. A neat red double line marked the last withdrawal and the new boots were squeaky on my feet. A sixpence screwed up in newspaper was ready to start the account again.

"Newbould."

"Sir."

"Well, move yourself, Newbould."

"Haven't anything to put in, sir."

"Why not?"

"My mother says we can't afford it this week, sir."

"All right, Newbould. – Baker?"

"Sir."

"Jordan?"

"Sir."

I had sixpence in my pocket, wrapped up in a piece torn from the margin of the *Argus*. The first shiver ran down my back as I imagined dropping it in the playground and Webby recognizing it as bank money.

"It's what my mother gave me to get a cut loaf, sir."

Five more like this would make three shillings. Twopence milk money would pay the tram fare to and from Woollie's.

"Here, why hasn't Mr Webb filled your bank book up?"

"Eh? Oh, he doesn't, sometimes. He sometimes leaves it till the end of the month."

"Well, that's a funny way of doing it. How does he know how much you've paid in?"

"Ah, well, he's got a big book with it all written down."

I never got the cricket set. On the way home from school, going the long way round while I worked out full and detailed dialogues with my mother about the bank book, I passed the Chocolate Cabin, the sweetshop belonging to the Regal cinema. In the little side window there was always a card advertising this or that assortment, and today there

was a new card all about Ascot Royal, the new quarter-
pound selection box. I went in and bought it, a box slightly
smaller than the dummy in the window, and told them it
was for my mother's birthday.

I ate the chocolates in quick bites all the way home. I
never knew there were so many in a quarter of a pound.
Even accounting for the bits of chocolate-coloured straw in
three corners, I couldn't eat them all. I had five left when I
approached our street. I put two in a privet hedge, gave one
away to a little girl who was playing in her vest at the side of

88

the road, and carried two home. I told my mother Mr Webb
had given them to me.

"What's he want to give you chocolates for?"

"I don't know. He gave us all two each out of a big box."

"He must have more money than sense."

The sixpences slid slowly by. The second one I spent on
my way to school on sugared almonds, which I had always
fancied. The third one I kept until night and then went to
the Regal and saw a film about a train in which the carriage
door opens and someone throws a severed hand into the
compartment.

I have dreamt about it since but I did not dream about it
then, although I would lie awake wondering what was
going to happen about the bank money. The fourth one I
spent on an enormous wood-fibre scribbling block and told
my mother that the rag and bone man was giving them
away outside our school. The fifth sixpence was rolled away
in pennies at a small and shoddy fair that halted for the day
on some waste ground.

When I had got through two and sixpence my mother
looked in the bank book. It was bound to happen sooner or
later, and each Monday morning when she gave the book
to me and each Monday dinnertime when I handed it
back, another sixpence spent, I would jump small hurdles
of apprehension, my eyes scouring her face for traces of
suspicion and my ears strained to catch faint lilts of
accusation.

It was, as a matter of fact, on a Wednesday. She had been
going on about my wearing down the heels of my new boots
and as usual she went on to drag up some other topic. My
mother was too tired for spontaneous wrath. The graver
sins were always hoarded until she could launch her rage
with the touch-paper of some pettier misdemeanour.

"And another thing, why hasn't Mr Webb filled in your
bank book?"

It suddenly seemed ridiculous that she had only now got
round to asking about it.

"Eh? Oh, he doesn't, sometimes. He sometimes leaves it till the end of the month."

"How do you mean, he leaves it to the end of the month? Of course he doesn't leave it to the end of the month."

"Ah no, but he's started doing, because he's got 2B's books to do as well. So he like collects them and fills them in at the end of the month."

"Have you been paying that money in?"

"Eh? Course I've been paying it in, what do you think I've been doing with it? He just marks it up every month, that's all."

"Well, there's five weeks here not marked up. If I find out you've taken that money yourself . . ."

"Course I haven't taken it, what do I want with it?" I had rehearsed this too. I had rehearsed it, under the sweating blankets, every inch of the way to the reformatory. "He just hasn't marked it up. He's got a big book and he puts it in that."

"Well, he can just take it out again. Because I'm drawing it out. You can just get that money drawn out on Monday. Because I need it. And you can just tell him to mark that book in future."

"I've told him. He doesn't take any notice."

"He will take notice if I go down to that school."

I prayed. Please God, get me out of this one and don't let her count the gas money on the panshelf, then I'll be all right.

It was a question of two and six. Better than letting it drag on until there was ten shillings to find, or twelve shillings. At the back of my mind I had already planned where the money was coming from. The Cub excursion to the Zoo was about eight weeks off. The full cost of the outing was five shillings, and there was three shillings so far in the kitty.

On Friday, while a game of British Bulldog was going on, I straightened my jersey and sought out Baloo at the back of the hall and told her I would not be going on the excursion.

"Why not?"

"My mother says we can't afford it."

"But it's only threepence a week. Surely she can spare threepence a week?"

"No, it's not that, miss. She wants to draw out what we've put in already. To get a shirt."

Baloo gave me her keen social worker's glance but I was not afraid of that.

"'Cos I've only got one shirt and it's all torn."

"Well, it's a shame. It's only two shillings and you'd have enough to go on the trip."

"I know. She says I can go another year."

At the end of the evening, after Taps, Baloo put the three shillings in a clean envelope and handed it over. I kept it in my pocket and worried all night in case my mother went through my trousers and found it.

"What's this money?"

"Eh? Oh, it's what I drew out of the bank for you. Forgot to tell you, they always pay out on Fridays now."

"Well you only had two and six in. What's this extra?"

"Interest."

On Saturday morning I spent my last sixpence on toffee, reducing the sum to half a crown. On Saturday afternoon, when my mother was over at the cemetery, I got out the blue ink and the red ink and got to work on the bank book.

It wasn't a bad forgery. First of all I added five sixpences together, copying five consecutive Mondays' dates from the doggy calendar by the mantelpiece. And then, carefully tracing an imitation of Webby's scrawl, I put 'Withdrn. – 2s. 6d.' Drew a double red line under it, as he did. Blotted it. Panicked, at the sudden realization that my mother might look at the bank book again before Monday. Prayed. Burned the blotting paper and disturbed the ash with the poker so that she could not fish it out and decipher what I had written.

At Monday dinnertime she got her half-crown and her bank book back. She glanced at the green book perfunctorily and put it away for ever. I had already decided to lose it down the fever drain if she ever opened that account again. I went out into the yard and stood on my hands against the lavatory door, for pleasure, and it was Friday, Club night, before the gnawing fears began again and I began to wonder what would happen if she ever ran into Baloo.

I spent the threepence she gave me for the Zoo excursion. I was having some very rich weeks. I had a feeling that when it came to it they might take me on the excursion for nothing, out of charity, and my only worry as the weeks passed was whether Baloo would call at the house and put this proposition to my mother.

"Just come in here. Now then. What have you done with all that money I gave you to give to Miss Dickinson?"

But when the last Friday came there was no question of it. They made their elaborate arrangements, to meet for the long trip at the Corn Exchange at seven in the morning with a packed dinner and a packed tea, and to go to the lavatory before they got on the coach.

I was up at six on Saturday morning and in my uniform, neckerchief straight, green garter tabs in position, by half-past. My last fear was that my mother would insist on taking me to the Corn Exchange. But she gave me my meals in a large brown paper bag, twopence for the tram fare and twopence for myself, and kissed me, I should think for the first time since I was in my pram. I went slowly up the empty street with sevenpence in my pocket – fourpence from my mother and threepence the last instalment on the Zoo money – planning the long day and marvelling at the cold brightness of the workman's morning.

I went to the park where the gates were still locked, climbed the railings and had the lake to myself to walk round twenty times before the ranger appeared in the distance and I ran into the woods nearby where the ferns were still wet. I sat for a long time on a green bench and ate the first sandwich, cheese and onion, from my paper bag. I went from tree to tree, counting a hundred by each one before moving on. I nearly slept in the long grass. I took a

piece of stone and tried to scrape my initials in the old men's shelter and then took fright and ran away again. The sandwiches were finished and I was down to the bun and apple.

At the top of the hill on the edge of the woods, at the far side of the park, I stopped at the ramshackle wooden shop and bought some liquorice bootlaces and a twopenny chocolate whirl. I sat on the long low wall by the side of the road and eventually a man came by and stopped and turned round and gave me the Wolf Cub salute. Shyly, without getting up, I put up my own two fingers and saluted him back.

"I'm the Akela of the 23rd South-east Pack. What's your Pack?"

"Twenty-second North-east, sir."

"And where are they?"

"They've gone off to Manchester for the day, sir, to the Zoo. Only my mother wouldn't let me go."

He moved off and full of guilt I went back into the woods and walked around the trees while the day wore on.

When the sky was getting dark and I was tired, I set off home slowly, the longest way, sometimes walking backwards to waste the last half hour, and rehearsing what I would say to my mother. The street was empty again. My mother was in the kitchen, washing clothes and straining her eyes in the gloom to save the light. I flopped down on the buffet by the empty fire and waited for her to speak so that I could discover what she knew.

"Just look at you! Where've you been?"

"Zoo, where do you think I've been?"

"I'd have thought you'd been down the pit to look at you. You're black bright! Just look at your jersey."

For the first time I examined my clothes, stained with grass and tree-bark, my boots streaked with white where the dew had dried on them, my hands and knees lined with rust where I had stood so long gripping the railings round the woods, remembering what I had read or seen at the Regal about zoos.

"Well, it's mucky, is the Zoo. We sat down on some grass for a picnic."

"You look as though you've been sat down in a coal cellar."

"Hey, mam, did you know elephants squirt water at each other when they have a bath?"

"You look as though *you* need a bath, never mind the elephants."

"Well they do, they squirt each other. And we saw all these monkeys having a party."

"Anyone'd think you were a monkey to look at you. And what's that tear in your trousers?"

I kept her talking, giving her opportunities to accuse me if she wanted to, but there was no more than routine disapproval in her voice. I told her about the zebras, the camel, the seals catching fish and the chimpanzee that stole a schoolboy's cap and ran away with it. She rubbed at my face and knees with a cold flannel caked in soap and listened to all I had to say. At the end she said:

"And who said you could give that tip-up lorry away to Jackie Hardcastle?"

"I didn't give it to him. I only lent it to him."

"Well you can just stop lending things. And you get it back tomorrow morning. And don't you lend out things again."

I went to bed and undressed in the dark. I slept and in the morning it was Sunday and I went to church. I still had three pennies left out of my sevenpence. I put them on the collection plate, for my criminal career was over. I was glad she had found out about the tip-up lorry, and for the first time in many months I had no fears at all. I was going to stop stealing the gas-money.

In the robing room, one of the other choirboys spoke to me.

"Hey, Newbouldy, where had you been yesterday afternoon in your Cub clothes?"

"When?"

"Yesterday, when do you think? You hadn't been on that Zoo excursion, I know that much, because they didn't come back till ten o'clock last night."

"Where did you see me, then? On the golf-links?"

"No, in your street. You were just going home."

I felt the low, watery thud at the bottom of my stomach. Struggling out of my surplice I said, "What time was it?"

"Don't ask me, kid. 'Bout half past twelve. One o'clock.

When it got right dark. Just before it started pelting down with rain."

I ran all the way home, almost crying, and too seized with fear to rehearse any explanations about being sent home early from the Zoo by special coach. I had time to wonder why I hadn't thought to come down this way, past the church, and see the time by the old clock. Half-remembered snatches of the previous night's talking darted through my head, and it seemed now that her words had been larded with suspicion and disbelief, and that she was just waiting for some little incident to spark her off into the grand recrimination.

"Why did you tell me you'd been on that excursion?"

"What excursion?"

"I'll give you what excursion before I've finished, my lad."

But in the house everything was quiet. She was making Yorkshire puddings and she asked me if I would like to stir the batter, a great favour.

I tested her, deliberately talking about the Zoo and giving her a chance to contradict me.

"Hey, the Scouts are going to that Zoo next month as well. Where we went to."

"Never mind the Scouts, just watch what you're doing."

"I bet their coach doesn't go as fast as ours. It didn't half go fast. We were there in no time."

"Just watch what you're doing."

I created the little incident, giving her an opening to get on to the bigger issues; I splashed batter over the clean newspapers that lined the kitchen table. But she only said: "You're going to have that on the floor if you don't stop your chattering and watch what you're doing."

I tested her and tested her for a week before I let the subject drop. And she never said anything. A fortnight later she met Baloo while she was out shopping and had a long talk with her. I tested her again about the Zoo. But she never said anything.

GREEN GRAVEL

JILL PATON WALSH

"**WHAT ABOUT THAT?**" the woman said, pointing at the card in the estate agent's window.

"You want to go back to school?" the man said, smiling.

"Nothing else here looks even possible," she said. "Do look, Mark."

"Development opportunity," he read. "The Old School House, Ravensway, with planning permission for conversion to a four-bedroomed luxury detached home . . ."

"It's pretty," she said. "Nice new thatch. I like the belfry on the roof. It's got a little land; not too much. And I think I remember us driving through Ravensway last year, and liking the look of it."

"Hmm," he said. "I suppose the Education Committee will have kept the basic fabric in good repair. Lots of room. Could be good. OK, let's go and look."

"You go in and fix it while I hop across the road and buy us a picnic," she said. "We'll be starving otherwise."

"I'm starving now," he said.

Returning to the car with a bulging plastic bag she said, "I

97

got French bread, and paté, and tomatoes. Will that keep the wolves at bay?"

"Lovely. It's unoccupied. A Miss Flewin right next door has the keys. She's expecting us."

"Off we go then."

But they didn't go straight there. They drove round Ravensway, sussing it out, finding the village shop, the Post Office, the little railway station. They ate their lunch on a sagging bench under a chestnut tree, on the village green, eyeing in the distance the School House under its cosy brown thatch, taking their time, getting the feel of the place A deeply quiet feel. A good contrast with the frenetic life they led in town.

Mark spread out the plans the estate agent had given him. They frowned over them, trying to make sense of the faint blue lines.

"I don't think so," he said. "It would be nicer to leave the space open to the roof, don't you think? Come on, eat up. I'm getting interested in this."

"First find Miss Flewin," she said, standing up, brushing crumbs from her skirt.

Miss Flewin's house was easily found. The School House itself overlooked the green, standing well back, and a few yards further up the lane, a tiny gabled house in similar bricks, with similar distinctive pointed windows stood guard over the escapes from the erstwhile playground to a patch of enticing, promising woodland.

"Miss Flewin has what was once the schoolmistress's house," said Mark, assessing it. They knocked on the sun-cracked, green-painted door.

Nobody came. They stood waiting, mildly disconcerted. A bird sang rapturously in the wood behind the gables. Mark tried again.

"Perhaps she was expecting us sooner. Perhaps we shouldn't have taken time for lunch. Really, we've been very leisurely about it."

"Bother!" said Mark. "I shall be very disappointed if . . ."

He banged the door again, and as he did so they could hear a faint sound within the house, a door opening, footfalls, someone coming after all.

You could see why she was slow the moment you caught sight of her. A very old, very frail lady, thin and tall in spite of her stoop, seeming to be made of bones and cardigan, with a lovely ancient tortoiseshell comb in her upswept white hair. A diaphanous halo of fine strands escaped the comb, and surrounded her deeply wrinkled face. A pair of disconcertingly sharp lilac-blue eyes stared at an uptilted angle – for really she was very stooped – at her visitors.

The woman felt at once ashamed, ashamed they had banged three times, vulgarly, bossily, in the presence of such self-possession.

"Mr Chittenden? You'll be Mr Chittenden," said Miss Flewin, "and Mrs Chittenden . . ."

"And thank God I am," the woman thought, a sudden

perception making her shudder at what she would have been, otherwise, in the cold lilac eyes of Miss Flewin.

"You have the keys of the Schoolhouse, I believe," Mark was saying.

"I'll get them," the old lady said, "and I'll just get my shoes on."

"Oh, but surely . . ." said Mark. But he was addressing the bent back of Miss Flewin as she shuffled slowly away down her hall, sliding her worn slippers on the lino.

He pulled a face at his wife. He was fidgeting, longing to get the keys in his hands and get into the school. He was quick at everything: quick moving, quick thinking, quick to act. It was agony for him to wait for people; long ago she had learnt to say, "Go without me," or, "I'll catch up."

And now they were caught, suspended. They could hardly walk into the open door of the house, and demand the keys. They could equally hardly abandon the quest and walk away . . . The bird sang frantically, as though busking a waiting crowd. "It's a lovely situation," she said in a while, filling time.

"Oh, I've got high hopes," he said. "If the inside is promising this could be it; don't you think so, Jean?"

"I saw it first," she said, smugly. "I liked it first."

"This is maddening!" he cried, in a while longer. "Wherever has that crazy old biddy got to?"

"Hush, hush, she might hear you! She's putting on her shoes."

"But we don't want her trailing along . . ."

Mark was always constrained, formal, with strangers. Only alone with her had she ever seen him real. Of course he wanted to see over the building, discuss what to do with it, without the tedious Miss Flewin. Just the same she shushed him.

"Oh, she's bound to be deaf!" he said. But, Jean thought, just in case she's not . . . I'm a bit afraid of her.

"She has that in her face I would fain serve . . ." she murmured.

100

"What's that?" said Mark, treading on the spot, like one treading water.

"Authority . . ." she said. But it was no good playing quotations with Mark.

"Oh, do come on!" he said to the absent Miss Flewin.

And she still took so much longer that he couldn't bear it. "I'll take a closer look at the outside, I think," he said, and strode away, almost running down the lane, and disappearing towards the school gate.

Miss Flewin came back wearing black button boots, half way up her shin, the sort of thing that needed a buttonhook, Jean remembered, from the time she had played Eliza in a school production of *My Fair Lady*. No wonder it had taken a while to get them on. She had a lilac woollen knitted hat askew on her erratic hair. She reached for a pair of huge iron keys hanging on the hatstand, which had been within reach all the time, and Jean said, trying for Mark's sake to walk free with them, "Please don't trouble yourself. You needn't bother to come. The School is unoccupied, isn't it?"

"In a way," Miss Flewin said.

"Well, then . . . We'll bring them back as soon as we're through with them. And you can stay indoors."

"I am entrusted with them," the old woman said. "I would rather come."

They found Mark prancing round the building. He had fetched a notebook and his camera from the car, and was writing things down, and taking snapshots. Miss Flewin walked so slowly that Jean could watch this going on while they approached like snails. And, she thought, we must be careful of this old woman, we must be patient, we must be kind, she may be our neighbour until she dies . . .

"When you get to be ninety," her companion said, as though answering the unspoken thought, "there's a lot of time for things. There has to be."

The Schoolhouse door, framed by a little porch, was double. Once, long since, there had been two ways in, one marked 'Boys' the other marked 'Girls'. At some more rational period the door had been widened, made into a single, somewhat shapeless, wide archway, with the stone-cut labels left where they had always been, above it. The door creaked enthusiastically, as they went in. The Schoolhouse was a single, large room. Tall windows that didn't reach down enough to allow for looking out stood on its sunny side; it was open to the pitch of the roof, and wooden beams braced by iron rods painted green crossed the roofspace. At one end a pair of doors led through to a little lobby, with coathooks and lockers, and an old enamel sink. The one tap above it was lagged with strips of sacking. Lines of green mould ran down the walls, and a musty smell proclaimed the damp of ages.

But Mark was seized with delight. The cloakroom, he said, would be the kitchen, large, exquisitely fitted, opening into the main living space. That should certainly not be divided into boxes to make the usual number of rooms, all the wrong shape; instead they should build a gallery round three sides, leaving the main area open to the roof, and put in a lovely Coalbrookdale iron stove on a tiled hearth.

"Where do we sleep?" Jean asked, trying to follow his flights of fancy.

"In the gallery."

"Open to the living room?"

He smiled at her with a ghost of uncertainty in the smile. *Don't take this wrong*, his smile said. *Don't trip me up . . .* "Dearest, if we ever do manage to get you in the family way, we can just put up some partition for the baby's room." If they had been alone he would have put his arms round her, but any strangers made him stiff and remote . . .

"Of course," she said. "OK . . ."

"Hold the tape measure against that wall, will you?" he said. She stood, holding it, watching Miss Flewin, who had stepped into the cloakroom with them, reappear. Miss Flewin walked across an invisible grid in the floor. She was walking, Jean thought, round the desks that had once been there. She came slowly and stood quietly, hands folded, in

102

front of the worn blackboard on the end wall. She was holding herself very straight, and gazing sternly and steadily at the vacant room.

She let the tape end drop and he wound it back, saying, "Acres of space for everything!"

But Jean was staring at Miss Flewin. She could have sworn that the silent building was suddenly hushed, that Miss Flewin's glance had brought order, silence, a sense of expectation . . . she almost expected her next to rap the non-existent desk with a ruler, and announce morning prayers. And, she saw, completely certain, without the smallest scrap of a reason, that Miss Flewin did not just live in what had once been the schoolmistress's cottage, she had been the schoolmistress. Mark was holding out the end of the tape to her again, to take the measurement the other way.

"Mark, look! What's that?" she said, pointing upwards. A rope descended through a hole in the ceiling, looped sideways, and was hitched round a hook on the wall.

"The school bell!" Mark said, delighted. "Don't you remember the pretty little lantern in the roof? The actual bell will have been taken down and sold, I expect."

Miss Flewin smiled faintly. She made her way across the floor to the rope, taking again a curious right-angled route, as though her path were obstructed by things in rows. She unhooked the rope, and held the flocked end out to Jean, smiling faintly, interrogatively. Jean walked over to her, took the rope, and tugged it. For a moment she was back in the polished marble front hall of her own school, wearing her prefect's badge, feeling the resistance of her serge gymslip to her upward stretching arms. It was just the same now: for the first count, nothing . . . then a delayed loud bronze note. Recalling the way of it she tugged the rope with surprising energy, spacing the tugs. The notes rang late and regular, a fast imperious song.

Mark beamed. "Oh, wonderful!" he said. "We won't touch that. We'll find a way of ringing that from the new gallery level . . . how fantastic! Why, Jean, are you all right?

103

Whatever is the matter?"

For Jean was drained of colour, and staring fixedly ahead. She was hearing things. As the last note of the bell died down, a tide of children's voices; children shouting, calling . . . a crowd of them, all over the vanished playground, their yelling and singing melded into a roar of sound, heard through each window, each wall : . . She thought at first it was a private madness, that her secret longing had finally tripped her reason; then she saw that Mark was frozen too, standing with the tape measure in his hands as though he were playing statues, and on Miss Flewin's face there was an expression of satisfaction. Head cocked, she was listening, smiling. The others were hearing it too. That joyful outburst, going on and on . . .

"You wouldn't think they would want to close a school with so many children round it," Miss Flewin said, suddenly. "They say there aren't enough children any more . . . I keep telling them, but they pay no heed. No heed of me at all."

"But . . . where did they spring from?" said Mark, bewildered. "Oughtn't they to be . . . ?"

"At school?" said Miss Flewin. "But of course they ought. They know that. But they don't know not to come here."

Drifting through the window came a snatch of skipping song. Little girls' chirpy voices, singing:

> *Green gravel, green gravel, the grass is so green,*
> *The fairest young lady that ever was seen!*
> *Oh Liza, oh, Liza, your lover is dead!*
> *And here comes a letter to turn round your head!*

"They can tell the actual parents, of course," Miss Flewin said. "They can put letters in the post, telling them the school is closed, telling them to go to the one in Hampden, telling them about the school bus; but of course they can't tell these."

"Ghosts?" said Mark, trying to laugh.

104

"Bless you, no, Mr Chittenden! Ghosts are the dead walking, aren't they? And these are not dead, oh, no."

"But who are they?" asked Jean, a tremor running up and down her spine.

"I can tell if I listen," the old lady said. "That's John Thoroughgood shouting like that; and Tom Parsons answering him back. There's Grace and Netty Ramsey singing, and Ann Newbolt, and Bertie Hapgood counting skipping – always plays with the girls, that one – and . . . but there. Names don't mean a thing to you. How could they?"

"And you remember them all?" said Mark, quietly.

"How could I ever forget them," she said, "when two of them are mine? Will they trouble you, do you think, Mrs Chittenden? I mean, if you take the school?"

"Children's voices?" Jean said. "No. I like them."

"Well then," the old lady said. "And you won't hear them often. I'll keep away. I'll keep my own side of that new fence. And you'll not often ring the bell for play."

A unison chant sounded loud and clearly, above the other noise: "The *wolf* has gone to *Devon*shire, and *won't* be back for *seven* year!"

"Good God!" said Mark. "I haven't heard that since I was eight . . ."

Miss Flewin reached for the rope. She pulled three notes on the bell, and the voices ceased. They died down rapidly to whispers, shuffling of boots, complete silence . . . Straining her ears Jean heard once more the bird on the bush outside, and a car going along the road on the far side of the green . . .

"I knew the right people wouldn't mind," Miss Flewin said, as she turned the iron key behind them in the door. "There's been a lot of wrong people looking over it."

They saw her to her gate, and took their leave of her, and walked away together across the green.

"Yes," Jean said. "Yes, this is it, love. Let's go and buy it."

"You don't mind the neighbour being as mad as a bat?" he said. "But, oh, just you wait, love! Just wait till you see what

105

a house we can make of that! Such fun. We'll find an architect, but we'll keep him under control . . . I wonder where the old biddy keeps that tape-recorder; it had me shaken rigid for a bit."

"They won't trouble us much, Mark," she said. "The voices, I mean. But they will be there sometimes. You'd better say now if you're going to mind them. They will be there sometimes, because I shall have Miss Flewin to tea now and then, and now and then I shall ring that bell."

Their path back to the car led them across the green, past the war memorial, rather a florid one, with a bronze soldier, bayonet drawn, head bowed.

Mark stopped. "My God, Jean," he said. "You can see why they put a stop to neighbourhood recruiting after the First World War. They seem to have lost half a regiment, all from this tiny place . . ."

But Jean was fixed in a silent stare again, staring at the long list of names and dates, the dates of young men who died just into adulthood, before anything had begun for them; and the names: Oliver Parsons, Ernest Thoroughgood, John Ramsey, Michael Newbolt, Percy Hapgood . . . What had Miss Flewin said? "How could I forget them when two of them are mine . . ."

Suddenly Jean was crying, weeping again helplessly, her too frequent tears flowing now for the long forgotten defeat of natural hopes; not for the childless young men so much, quenched in the mud and chaos, nor even for the long solitudes they left to their girls behind them, but for the laughing and quarrelling and singing children who were not dead, having never been born.

THE PRIZE POEM

P. G. WODEHOUSE

SOME QUARTER of a century before the period with which this story deals, a certain rich and misanthropic man was seized with a bright idea for perpetuating his memory after death, and at the same time harassing a certain section of mankind. So in his will he set aside a portion of his income to be spent on an annual prize for the best poem submitted by a member of the Sixth Form of St Austin's College, on a subject to be selected by the Headmaster. And, he added – one seems to hear him chuckling to himself – every member of the Form must compete. Then he died. But the evil that men do lives after them, and each year saw a fresh band of unwilling bards goaded to despair by his bequest. True, there were always one or two who hailed this ready market for their sonnets and odes with joy. But the majority, being barely able to rhyme 'dove' with 'love', regarded the annual announcement of the subject chosen with feelings of the deepest disgust.

The chains were thrown off after a period of twenty-seven years in this fashion.

Reynolds of the Remove was indirectly the cause of the change. He was in the infirmary, convalescing after an attack of German measles, when he received a visit from Smith, an ornament of the Sixth.

"By Jove," remarked that gentleman, gazing enviously round the sick-room, "they seem to do you pretty well here."

"Yes, not bad, is it? Take a seat. Anything been happening lately?"

"Nothing much. I suppose you know we beat the M.C.C. by a wicket?"

"Yes, so I heard. Anything else?"

"Prize poem," said Smith, without enthusiasm. He was not a poet.

Reynolds became interested at once. If there was one role in which he fancied himself (and, indeed, there was a good many), it was that of a versifier. His great ambition was to see some of his lines in print, and he had contracted the habit of sending them up to various periodicals, with no result, so far, except the arrival of rejected MSS. at mealtimes in embarrassingly long envelopes. Which he blushingly concealed with all possible speed.

"What's the subject this year?" he asked.

"The College – of all idiotic things."

"Couldn't have a better subject for an ode. By Jove, I wish I was in the Sixth."

"Wish I was in the infirmary," said Smith.

Reynolds was struck with an idea.

"Look here, Smith," he said, "if you like I'll do you a poem, and you can send it up. If it gets the prize –"

"Oh, it won't get the prize," Smith put in eagerly. "Rogers is a cert. for that."

"If it gets the prize," repeated Reynolds, with asperity, "you'll have to tell the Old Man all about it. He'll probably curse a bit, but that can't be helped. How's this for a beginning?

"Imposing pile, reared up 'midst pleasant grounds,
The scene of many a battle, lost or won,

    At cricket or at football; whose red walls
    Full many a sun has kissed 'ere day is done."

"Grand. Couldn't you get in something about the M.C.C. match? You could make cricket rhyme with wicket." Smith sat entranced with his ingenuity, but the other treated so material a suggestion with scorn.

"Well," said Smith, "I must be off now. We've got a housematch on. Thanks awfully about the poem."

Left to himself, Reynolds set himself seriously to the composing of an ode that should do him justice. That is to say, he drew up a chair and table to the open window, wrote down the lines he had already composed, and began chewing a pen. After a few minutes he wrote another four lines, crossed them out, and selected a fresh piece of paper. He then copied out his first four lines again. After eating his pen to a stump, he jotted down the two words 'boys' and 'joys' at the end of separate lines. This led him to select a third piece of paper, on which he produced a sort of *édition de luxe* in his best handwriting, with the title 'Ode to the College' in printed letters at the top. He was admiring the neat effect of this when the door opened suddenly and

violently, and Mrs Lee, a lady of advanced years and energetic habits, whose duty it was to minister to the needs of the sick and wounded in the infirmary, entered with his tea. Mrs Lee's method of entering a room was in accordance with the advice of the Psalmist, where he says, 'Fling wide the gates'. She flung wide the gate of the sick-room, and the result was that what is commonly called 'a thorough draught' was established. The air was thick with flying papers, and when calm at length succeeded storm, two editions of 'An Ode to the College' were lying on the grass outside.

Reynolds attacked the tea without attempting to retrieve his vanished work. Poetry is good, but tea is better. Besides, he argued within himself, he remembered all he had written, and could easily write it out again. So, as far as he was concerned, those three sheets of paper were a closed book.

Later on in the afternoon, Montgomery of the Sixth happened to be passing by the infirmary, when Fate, aided by a sudden gust of wind, blew a piece of paper at him. "Great Scott," he observed, as his eye fell on the words 'Ode to the College'. Montgomery, like Smith, was no expert in poetry. He had spent a wretched afternoon trying to hammer out something that would pass muster in the poem competition, but without the least success. There were four lines on the paper. Two more, and it would be a poem, and capable of being entered for the prize as such. The words 'imposing pile', with which the fragment in his hand began, took his fancy immensely. A poetic afflatus seized him, and in less than three hours he had added the necessary couplet,

> How truly sweet it is for such as me
> To gaze on thee.

"And dashed neat, too," he said, with satisfaction, as he threw the manuscript into his drawer. "I don't know whether 'me' shouldn't be 'I', but they'll have to lump it. It's a poem, anyhow, within the meaning of the act." And he strolled off to a neighbour's study to borrow a book.

Two nights afterwards, Morrison, also of the Sixth, was enjoying his usual during prep siesta in his study. A tap at the door roused him. Hastily seizing a lexicon, he assumed the attitude of the seeker after knowledge, and said, 'Come in.' It was not the Housemaster, but Evans, Morrison's fag, who entered with pride on his face and a piece of paper in his hand.

"I say," he began, "you remember you told me to hunt up some tags for the poem. Will this do?"

Morrison took the paper with a judicial air. On it were the words:

> Imposing pile, reared up 'midst pleasant grounds,
> The scene of many a battle, lost or won,
> At cricket or at football; whose red walls
> Full many a sun has kissed 'ere day was done.

"That's ripping, as far as it goes," said Morrison. "Couldn't be better. You'll find some apples in that box. Better take a few. But look here," with sudden suspicion, "I don't believe you made all this up yourself. Did you?"

Evans finished selecting his apples before venturing on a reply. Then he blushed, as much as a member of the junior school is capable of blushing.

"Well," he said, "I didn't exactly. You see, you only told me to get the tags. You didn't say how."

"But how did you get hold of this? Whose is it?"

"Dunno. I found it in the field between the pavilion and the infirmary."

"Oh! well, it doesn't matter much. They're just what I wanted, which is the great thing. Thanks. Shut the door, will you?" Whereupon Evans retired, the richer by many apples, and Morrison resumed his siesta at the point where he had left off.

111

"Got that poem done yet?" said Smith to Reynolds, pouring out a cup of tea for the invalid on the following Sunday.

"Two lumps, please. No, not quite."

"Great Caesar, man, when'll it be ready, do you think? It's got to go in tomorrow."

"Well, I'm really frightfully sorry, but I got hold of a grand book. Ever read –"

"Isn't any of it done?" asked Smith.

"Only the first verse, I'm afraid. But, look here, you aren't keen on getting the prize. Why not send in only the one verse? It makes a fairly decent poem."

"Hum! Think the old 'un'll pass it?"

"He'll have to. There's nothing in the rules about length. Here it is if you want it."

"Thanks. I suppose it'll be all right? So long! I must be off."

The Headmaster, known to the world as the Rev. Arthur James Perceval, M.A., and to the school as the old 'un, was sitting at breakfast, stirring his coffee, with a look of marked perplexity upon his dignified face. This was not caused by the coffee, which was excellent, but by a letter which he held in his left hand.

"Hum!" he said. Then "Umph!" in a protesting tone, as if someone had pinched him. Finally, he gave vent to a long-drawn "Um-m-m," in a deep bass. "Most extraordinary. Really, most extraordinary. Exceedingly. Yes. Um. Very." He took a sip of coffee.

"My dear," said he, suddenly. Mrs Perceval started violently. She had been sketching out in her mind a little dinner, and wondering whether the cook would be equal to it.

"Yes," she said.

"My dear, this is a very extraordinary communication. Exceedingly so. Yes, very."

"Who is it from?"

Mr Perceval shuddered. He was a purist in speech. "*From

112

whom, you should say. It is from Mr Wells, a great College friend of mine. I – ah – submitted to him for examination the poems sent in for the Sixth Form Prize. He writes in a very flippant style. I must say, very flippant. This is his letter: – 'Dear Jimmy (really, really, he should remember that we are not so young as we were); dear – ahem – Jimmy. The poems to hand. I have read them, and am writing this from my sick-bed. The doctor tells me I may pull through even yet. There was only one any good at all, that was Rogers', which, though – er – squiffy (tut!) in parts, was a long way better than any of the others. But the most taking part of the whole programme was afforded by the three comedians, whose efforts I enclose. You will notice that each begins with exactly the same four lines. Of course, I deprecate cribbing, but you really can't help admiring this sort of thing. There is a reckless daring about it which is simply fascinating. A horrible thought – have they been pulling your dignified leg? By the way, do you remember' – the rest of the letter is – er – on different matters."

"James! How extraordinary!"

"Um, yes. I am reluctant to suspect – er – collusion, but really here there can be no doubt. No doubt at all. No."

"Unless," began Mrs Perceval, tentatively. "No doubt at all, my dear," snapped Reverend Jimmy. He did not wish to recall the other possibility, that his dignified leg was being pulled.

"Now, for what purpose did I summon you three boys?" asked Mr Perceval, of Smith, Montgomery, and Morrison, in his room after morning school that day. He generally began a painful interview with this question. The method had distinct advantages. If the criminal were of a nervous disposition, he would give himself away upon the instant. In any case, it was likely to startle him. "For what purpose?" repeated the Headmaster, fixing Smith with a glittering eye.

"I will tell you," continued Mr Perceval. "It was because I desired information, which none but you can supply. How comes it that each of your compositions for the Poetry Prize

113

commences with the same four lines?" The three poets looked at one another in speechless astonishment.

"Here," he resumed, "are the three papers. Compare them. Now," – after the inspection was over – "what explanation have you to offer? Smith, are these your lines?"

"I-er-ah-*wrote* them, sir."

"Don't prevaricate, Smith. Are you the author of those lines?"

"No, sir."

"Ah! Very good. Are you, Montgomery?"

"No, sir."

"Very good. Then you, Morrison, are exonerated from all blame. You have been exceedingly badly treated. The first-fruit of your brain has been – ah – plucked by others, who toiled not, neither did they spin. You can go, Morrison."

"But, sir –"

"Well, Morrison?"

"I didn't write them, sir."

"I – ah – don't quite understand you, Morrison. You say that you are indebted to another for these lines?"

"Yes, sir."

"To Smith?"

"No, sir."

"To Montgomery?"

"No, sir."

114

"Then, Morrison, may I ask to whom you are indebted?"

"I found them in the field on a piece of paper, sir." He claimed the discovery himself, because he thought that Evans might possibly prefer to remain outside this tangle.

"So did I, sir." This from Montgomery. Mr Perceval looked bewildered, as indeed he was.

"And did you, Smith, also find this poem on a piece of paper in the field?" There was a metallic ring of sarcasm in his voice.

"No, sir."

"Ah! Then to what circumstance were you indebted for the lines?"

"I got Reynolds to do them for me, sir."

Montgomery spoke. "It was near the infirmary that I found the paper, and Reynolds is in there."

"So did I, sir," said Morrison, incoherently.

"Then am I to understand, Smith, that to gain the prize you resorted to such underhand means as this?"

"No, sir, we agreed that there was no danger of my getting the prize. If I had got it, I should have told you everything. Reynolds will tell you that, sir."

"Then what object had you in pursuing this deception?"

"Well, sir, the rules say everyone must send in something, and I can't write poetry at all, and Reynolds likes it, so I asked him to do it."

And Smith waited for the storm to burst. But it did not burst. Far down in Mr Perceval's system lurked a quiet sense of humour. The situation penetrated to it. Then he remembered the examiner's letter, and it dawned upon him that there are few crueller things than to make a prosaic person write poetry.

"You may go," he said, and the three went.

And at the next Board Meeting it was decided, mainly owing to the influence of an exceedingly eloquent speech from the Headmaster, to alter the rules for the Sixth Form Poetry Prize, so that from thence onward no one need compete unless he felt himself filled with the immortal fire.

Marv
Hammerman

THE EIGHTEENTH EMERGENCY

BETSY BYARS

"HEY, MOUSE!" It was Ezzie.

He got up from the sofa quickly and went to the window. "What?" he called back.

"Come on down."

His mother said in the kitchen, "You've got to eat."

"I've got to eat, Ezzie."

"Well, hurry up. I'll wait."

He stood at the window and watched Ezzie sit down on the steps. The dog had finished with his Cracker Jacks and was now sitting in front of Ezzie, looking at him hopefully. The smell of chicken and noodles was coming from one of the windows, and the dog thought it was coming from Ezzie. The dog wanted some chicken and noodles so badly that his nose had started to run.

Ezzie patted the dog once. "I haven't got anything," he told him. "And quit looking at me." Once the dog had looked at Ezzie so long that Ezzie had gone in the house and fixed him a devilled egg sandwich. "I haven't got anything," Ezzie said again and turned his head away. Ezzie had named the dog Garbage Dog because of his eating habits. "Go *on*." Slowly Garbage Dog got up. He circled once like a

116

radar finder and then began slowly to move in the direction of the chicken and noodles.

"Come to supper," Mouse's mother called. He went into the kitchen where his mother was putting the food on the table. She sat down, spread a paper napkin on her lap and said, "Why doesn't Ezzie help you with those boys?"

"What?"

"Why doesn't Ezzie help you fight those boys?" she repeated, nodding her head towards the window.

"Oh, Mom."

"I mean it. If there were *two* of you, then those boys would think twice before –"

"Oh, Mom!" He bent over his plate and began to smash his lima beans with his fork. He thought about it for a moment, of stepping in front of Marv Hammerman and Tony Lionni and the boy in the black sweat shirt and saying in a cool voice, "I think I'd better warn you that I've got my friend with me."

"Who's your friend?"

"*This* is my friend." At that Ezzie would step out from the shadows and stand with him.

Marv Hammerman would look at them, sizing them up, the two of them, this duo his mother had created for strength. Then with a faint smile Hammerman would reach out, grab them up like cymbals and clang them together. When Hammerman set them down they would twang for forty-five minutes before they could stumble off.

"Well, I know what I'm talking about, that's all," his mother said. "If you could get Ezzie to help you –"

"All right, Mom, I'll ask him."

He ate four lima beans and looked at his mother. "Is that enough? I'm not hungry."

"Eat."

He thought he was going to choke. Emergency Five – Being Choked by a Boa Constrictor. When you were being strangled by a boa constrictor, Ezzie had said, what you had to do was taunt the boa constrictor and get him to *bite* you

117

instead of *strangle* you. His bite, Ezzie admitted, was a little painful but the strangulation was worse.

This had seemed a first rate survival measure at the time. Now he had trouble imagining him and Ezzie in the jungle being squeezed by the boa constrictor. He tried to imagine Ezzie's face, pink and earnest, above the boa constrictor's loop. He tried to hear Ezzie's voice taunting, "Sure you can strangle, but can you bite? Let's see you try to bite us!"

"Hey, Mouse, you coming?" Ezzie had opened the door to the hall now, and his voice came up the stairs as if through a megaphone.

"I'll eat the rest later," Mouse said. He was already out of his chair, moving towards the door.

"Oh, all right," his mother said, "go on."

He ran quickly out of the apartment and down the stairs. Ezzie was waiting for him outside, sitting down. As soon as he saw Mouse, Ezzie got up and said, "Hey, what happened? Where'd you go after school?"

Mouse said, "Hammerman's after me."

Ezzie's pink mouth formed a perfect O. He didn't say anything, but his breath came out in a long sympathetic wheeze. Finally he said, "*Marv* Hammerman?" even though he knew there was only one Hammerman in the world, just as there had been only one Hitler.

"Yes."

"Is after *you*?"

Mouse nodded, sunk in misery. He could see Marv Hammerman. He came up in Mouse's mind the way monsters do in horror movies, big and powerful, with the same cold, unreal eyes. It was the eyes Mouse really feared. One look from those eyes, he thought, just one look of a certain length – about three seconds – and you knew you were his next victim.

"What did you do?" Ezzie asked. "Or did you do anything?"

At least, Mouse thought, Ezzie understood that. If you were Marv Hammerman, you didn't need a reason. He sat down on the steps and squinted up at Ezzie. "I did something," he said.

"What?" Ezzie asked. His tongue flicked out and in so quickly it didn't even moisten his lips. "What'd you do? You bump into him or something?"

Mouse shook his head.

"Well, what?"

Mouse said, "You know that big chart in the upstairs hall at school?"

"What'd you say? I can't even hear you, Mouse. You're muttering." Ezzie bent closer. "Look at me. Now what did you say?"

Mouse looked up, still squinting. He said, "You know that big chart outside the history room? In the hall?"

"Chart?" Ezzie said blankly. "What chart, Mouse?"

"This chart takes up the whole wall, Ez, how could you miss it? It's a chart about early man, and it shows man's progress up from the apes, the side view of all those different kinds of prehistoric men, like Cro-Magnon man and Homo erectus. *That* chart."

"Oh, yeah, I saw it, so go on."

Mouse could see that Ezzie was eager for him to get on to the good part, the violence. He slumped. He wet his lips. He said, "Well, when I was passing this chart on my way out of history – and I don't know why I did this – I really don't. When I was passing this chart, Ez, on my way to math –" He swallowed, almost choking on his spit. "When I was passing this chart, Ez, I took my pencil and I wrote Marv Hammerman's name on the bottom of the chart and then I drew an arrow to the picture of Neanderthal man."

"What?" Ezzie cried. *"What?"* He could not seem to take it in. Mouse knew that Ezzie had been prepared to sympathize with an accident. He had almost been the victim of one of those himself. One day at school Ezzie had reached for the handle on the water fountain a second ahead of Marv Hammerman. If Ezzie hadn't glanced up just in time, seen Hammerman and said quickly, "Go ahead, I'm not thirsty," then this sagging figure on the steps might be him. "What did you do it for, Mouse?"

"I don't know."

"You crazy or something?"

"I don't know."

"Marv Hammerman!" Ezzie sighed. It was a mournful sound that seemed to have come from a culture used to sorrow. "Anybody else in the school would have been better. I would rather have the principal after me than Marv Hammerman."

"I know."

"Hammerman's big, Mouse. He's flunked a lot."

"I know," Mouse said again. There was an unwritten law that it was all right to fight anyone in your own grade. The fact that Hammerman was older and stronger made no difference. They were both in the sixth grade.

"Then what'd you do it for?" Ezzie said.

"I don't know."

"You must want trouble," Ezzie said. "Like my grandfather. He's always provoking people. The bus driver won't even pick him up any more."

"No, I don't want trouble."

"Then, why did you –"

"I don't *know*" Then he sagged again and said, "I didn't even know I had done it really until I'd finished. I just looked at the picture of Neanderthal man and thought of Hammerman. It does look like him, Ezzie, the sloping face and the shoulders."

"Maybe Hammerman doesn't know you did it though," Ezzie said. "Did you ever think of that? I mean, who's going to go up to Hammerman and tell him his name is on the prehistoric man chart?" Ezzie leaned forward. "Hey, Hammerman," he said, imitating the imaginary fool, "I saw a funny thing about you on the prehistoric man chart! Now, who in their right mind is going to –"

"He was right behind me when I did it," Mouse said.

"What?"

"He was right behind me," Mouse said stiffly. He could remember turning and looking into Hammerman's eyes. It was such a strange, troubling moment that Mouse was unable to think about it.

Ezzie's mouth formed the O, made the sympathetic sigh. Then he said, "And you don't even know what you did it for?"

"No."

Ezzie sank down on the steps beside Mouse. He leaned over his knees and said, "You ought to get out of that habit, that writing names and drawing arrows, you know that? I see those arrows everywhere. I'll be walking down the street and I'll look on a building and I'll see the word DOOR written in little letters and there'll be an arrow pointing to the door and I know you did it. It's crazy, labelling stuff like that."

"I never did that, Ez, not to a door."

"Better to a door, if you ask me," Ezzie said, shaking his

head. He paused for a moment, then asked in a lower voice, "You ever been hit before, Mouse? I mean, hard?"

Mouse sighed. The conversation had now passed beyond the question of whether Hammerman would attack. It was now a matter of whether he, Mouse Fawley, could survive the attack. He said thickly, remembering, "Four times."

"Four times in one fight? I mean, you stood up for four hits, Mouse?" There was grudging admiration in his voice.

Mouse shook his head. "Four hits – four fights."

"You went right down each time? I mean POW and you went down, POW and you went down, POW and you went –"

"Yes!"

"Where did you take these hits?" Ezzie asked, straightening suddenly. Ezzie had never taken a single direct blow in his life because he was a good dodger. Sometimes his mother chased him through the apartment, striking at him while he dodged and ducked, crying, "Look out, Mom, look out now! You're going to hit me!"

He asked again, "Where were you hit?"

Mouse said, "In the stomach."

"All four times?"

"Yeah." Mouse suddenly thought of his stomach as having a big red circular target on it with HIT HERE printed in the centre.

"Who hit you?"

"Two boys in Cincinnati when I was on vacation, and a boy named Mickey Swearinger, and somebody else I don't remember." He lowered his head because he remembered the fourth person all right, but he didn't want to tell Ezzie about it. If he had added the name of Viola Angotti to the list of those who had hit him in the stomach, Ezzie's face would have screwed up with laughter. "Viola Angotti hit you? No fooling, Viola Angotti?" It was the sort of thing Ezzie could carry on about for hours. "Viola Angotti. *The* Viola Angotti?"

And Mouse would have had to keep sitting there saying over and over, "Yes, Viola Angotti hit me in the stomach.

Yes, *the* Viola Angotti." And then he would have to tell Ezzie all about it, every detail, how one recess long ago the boys had decided to put some girls in the school trash cans. It had been one of those suggestions that stuns everyone with its rightness. Someone had said, "Hey, let's put those girls over there in the trash cans!" and the plan won immediate acceptance. Nothing could have been more appropriate. The trash cans were big and had just been emptied, and in an instant the boys were off chasing the girls and yelling at the tops of their lungs.

It had been wonderful at first, Mouse remembered. Primitive blood had raced through his body. The desire to capture had driven him like a wild man through the school yard, up the sidewalk, everywhere. He understood what had driven the cave man and the barbarian, because this same passion was driving him. Putting the girls in the trash cans was the most important challenge of his life. His long screaming charge ended with him red-faced, gasping for breath – and with Viola Angotti pinned against the garbage cans.

His moment of triumph was short. It lasted about two seconds. Then it began to dim as he realized, first, that it *was* Viola Angotti, and, second, that he was not going to be able to get her into the garbage can without a great deal of help.

He cried, "Hey, you guys, come on, I've got one," but behind him the school yard was silent. Where was everybody? he had wondered uneasily. As it turned out, the principal had caught the other boys, and they were all being marched back in the front door of the school, but Mouse didn't know this.

He called again, "Come on, you guys, get the lid off this garbage can, will you?"

And then, when he said that, Viola Angotti had taken two steps forward. She said, "Nobody's putting *me* in no garbage can." He could still remember how she had looked standing there. She had recently taken the part of the Statue of Liberty in a class play, and somehow she seemed taller and stronger at this moment than when she had been in costume.

He cried, "Hey, you guys!" It was a plea. "Where are you?"

And then Viola Angotti had taken one more step, and with a faint sigh she had socked him in the stomach so hard that he had doubled over and lost his lunch. He hadn't known it was possible to be hit like that outside a boxing ring. It was the hardest blow he had ever taken. Viola Angotti could be heavyweight champion of the world.

As she walked past his crumpled body she had said again, "Nobody's putting me in no garbage can." It had sounded like one of the world's basic truths. The sun will rise. The tides will flow. Nobody's putting Viola Angotti in no garbage can.

Later, when he thought about it, he realized that he had been lucky. If she had wanted to, Viola Angotti could have capped her victory by tossing his rag-doll body into the garbage can and slamming down the lid. Then, when the principal came out on to the playground calling, "Benjamin Fawley! Has anybody seen Benjamin Fawley?" he would have had to moan, "I'm in here." He would have had to climb out of the garbage can in front of the whole school. His shame would have followed him for life. When he was a grown man, people would still be pointing him out to their children. "*That*'s the man that Viola Angotti stuffed into the garbage can."

Now he thought that Marv Hammerman could make Viola Angotti's blow seem like a baby's pat. He wanted to double over on the steps.

Ezzie said, "You ought to watch out for your stomach like a fighter, protect your body. There's a lot of valuable stuff in there."

"I know."

"The trick of it," Ezzie said, "is moving quickly, ducking, getting out of the way." Ezzie did a few quick steps, his feet flashing on the sidewalk. "You dance, Mouse, like this." Mouse suddenly remembered that Ezzie had once told him that if you were ever bitten by a tarantula (Emergency Six) you had to start dancing immediately. Ezzie said you were supposed to do this special Italian folk dance, but any quick lively steps would probably do.

Mouse had a picture of himself doing this lively dance in front of Hammerman. Hammerman would watch for a moment. There would be no expression on his face. The dance would reach a peak. Mouse's arms and legs would be a blur of motion. And then Hammerman would reach down, a sort of slow graceful movement like he was bowling, and come up effortlessly right into Mouse's stomach.

Mouse leaned forward, shielding his body with his arms. He cleared his throat. "Did anybody ever hit you, Ezzie?"

Ezzie stopped dancing. "Sure."

"Who?"

"Well, relatives mostly. You can't hardly walk through my living-room without somebody trying to hit you – for any little thing. I accidentally step on my sister's feet – she's got long feet, Mouse, she can't hardly buy ordinary shoes, and she takes it as an insult if you step on one of them. She's fast too, Mouse. That's how I learned about getting out of the way."

"But nobody like Hammerman ever hit you?"

"No." He sounded apologetic.

Mouse sighed. Above him his mother called, "Benjie, come up now, I want you to do something for me."

"I got to go." Mouse still sat there. He hated to leave the warmth of Ezzie's understanding. Ezzie didn't want to leave either. Mouse had taken on a fine tragic dimension in his eyes, and there was something about being with a person like that that made him feel good.

Ezzie had felt the same way about their teacher last fall when he had told them he had to go to the hospital. For the first time, Mr Stein in his baggy suit had seemed a fine tragic figure, bigger than life. Ezzie would have done anything for Mr Stein that day. But then, when Mr Stein came limping back the next week – it turned out he had had some bone spurs removed from his heels – he had been his normal size.

"Benjie, come up now," his mother called again.

"I'm coming."

"Did you tell your mom about Hammerman being after you?" Ezzie asked.

"Yeah."

"What'd she say?"

He tried to think of the most impossible statement his mother had made. "She said I'll laugh about it in a week or two."

"Laugh about it?"

"Yeah, through my bandages."

Ezzie's face twisted into a little smile. "Hey, remember Al Armsby when he had those broken ribs? Remember how he would beg us not to make him laugh? And I had this one

126

joke about a monkey and I would keep telling it and keep telling it and he was practically on his knees begging for mercy and –"

Mouse got slowly to his feet. "Well, I better go," he said.

Ezzie stopped smiling. "Hey, wait a minute. Listen, I just remembered something. I know a boy that Hammerman beat up, and he said it wasn't so bad."

"Who?"

"A friend of my brother's. I'll find out about it and let you know."

"All right," Mouse said. He did not allow himself to believe it was true. Sometimes Ezzie lied like this out of sympathy. If you said, "My stomach hurts and I think I'm going to die," and if Ezzie really liked you, he would say, "I know a boy whose stomach hurt worse than that and *he* didn't die!" And if you said, "Who?" Ezzie would say, "A friend of my brother's." Ezzie's brother had only one friend that Mouse knew about, and this friend would have had to have daily brushes with death to fulfil all of Ezzie's statements.

Still, it made Mouse want to cry for a moment that Ezzie would lie to spare him. Or maybe he wanted to cry because Hammerman was going to kill him. He didn't know. He said, "Thanks, Ez," in a choked voice. He turned and walked quickly into the apartment building.

BILLY THE KID

WILLIAM GOLDING

William Golding is one of our finest and most famous novelists and in 1983 he won the Nobel Prize for Literature. All great writers, however, have to begin somewhere. In this story he remembers his first term at school.

ON THE FIRST DAY, Lily, my nurse, took me to school. We went hand-in-hand through the churchyard, down the Town Hall steps, and along the south side of the High Street. The school was at the bottom of an alley; two rooms, one downstairs and one upstairs, a staircase, a place for hanging coats, and a lavatory. 'Miss' kept the school – handsome, good-tempered Miss, whom I liked so much. Miss used the lower room for prayers and singing and drill and meetings, and the upper one for all the rest. Lily hung my coat up, took me upstairs and deposited me among a score or so of children who ranged in age from five to eleven. The boys were neatly dressed, and the girls over-dressed if anything. Miss taught in the old-fashioned way, catering for all ages at once.

I was difficult.

No one had suggested, before this time, that anything mattered outside myself. I was used to being adored, for I was an attractive child in an Anglo-Saxon sort of way. Indeed, my mother, in her rare moments of lyricism, would declare that I had 'eyes like cornflowers and hair like a field of ripe corn'. I had known no one outside my own family – nothing but walks with Lily or my parents, and long holidays by a Cornish sea. I had read much for my age but saw no point in figures. I had a passion for words in themselves, and collected them like stamps or birds' eggs. I had also a clear picture of what school was to bring me. It was to bring me fights. I lacked opposition, and yearned to be victorious. Achilles, Lancelot and Aeneas should have given me a sense of human nobility but they gave me instead a desire to be a successful bruiser.

It did not occur to me that school might have discipline or that numbers might be necessary. While, therefore, I was supposed to be writing out my tables, or even dividing four oranges between two poor boys, I was more likely to be scrawling a list of words, butt (barrel), butter, butt (see goat). While I was supposed to be learning my Collect, I was likely to be chanting inside my head a list of delightful words which I had picked up God knows where – deebriss and Skirmishar, creskant and sweeside. On this first day, when Miss taxed me with my apparent inactivity, I smiled and said nothing, but nothing, until she went away.

At the end of the week she came to see my mother. I stuck my field of ripe corn round the dining-room door and listened to them as they came out of the drawing-room.

My mother was laughing gaily and talking in her front-door voice.

"He's just a little butterfly, you know – just a butterfly!"

Miss replied judiciously.

"We had better let that go for a while."

So let go it was. I looked at books or pictures, and made up words, dongbulla for a carthorse; drew ships and aeroplanes with all their strings, and waited for the bell.

I had quickly narrowed my interest in school to the quarter of an hour between eleven and fifteen minutes past.

This was Break, when our society at last lived up to my expectations. While Miss sat at her desk and drank tea, we spent the Break playing and fighting in the space between the desks and the door. The noise rose slowly in shrillness and intensity, so that I could soon assess the exact note at which Miss would ring a handbell and send us back to our books. If we were dull and listless, Break might be extended by as much as ten minutes; so there was a constant conflict in my mind – a desire to be rowdy, and a leader in rowdiness, together with the knowledge that success would send us back to our desks. The games were numerous and varied with our sex. The girls played with dolls or at weddings. Most of the time they played Postman's Knock among themselves – played it seriously, like a kind of innocent apprenticeship.

> Tap! Tap!
> "Who's there?"
> "A letter for Mary."

We boys ignored them with a contempt of inexpressible depth. We did not kiss each other, not we. We played tag or fought in knots and clusters, while Miss drank tea and smiled indulgently and watched our innocent apprenticeship.

Fighting proved to be just as delightful as I had thought. I was chunky and zestful and enjoyed hurting people. I exulted in victory, in the complete subjugation of my adversary, and thought that they should enjoy it too – or at least be glad to suffer for my sake. For this reason, I was puzzled when the supply of opponents diminished. Soon, I had to corner victims before I could get a fight at all.

Imperceptibly the gay picture altered. Once back in our desks, where the boys were safe from me, they laughed at me, and sniggered. I became the tinder to a catch word. Amazed, behind my eager fists, I watched them and saw they were – but what were they? Appearances must lie; for of course they could not drive themselves from behind those

130

aimed eyes, could not persuade themselves that I, ego Billy, whom everyone loved and cherished, as by nature, could not persuade themselves that I was not uniquely woven of precious fabric –

Could it be?

Nonsense! Sky, fly, pie, soup, hoop, croup – geourgeous.

But there were whisperings in corners and on the stairs. There were cabals and meetings. There were conversations which ceased when I came near. Suddenly in Break, when I tried to fight, the opposition fled with screams of hysterical laughter, then combined in democratic strength and hurled itself on my back. As for the little girls, they no longer played Postman's Knock, but danced on the skirts of the scrum, and screamed encouragement to the just majority.

That Break ended early. When we were back at our desks, I found my rubber was gone, and no one would lend me another. But I needed a rubber, so I chewed up a piece of paper and used that. Miss detected my fault and cried out in mixed horror and amusement. Now the stigma of dirt was added to the others.

At the end of the morning I was left disconsolate in my desk. The other boys and girls clamoured out purposefully. I wandered after them, puzzled at a changing world. But they had not gone far. They were grouped on the cobbles of the alley, outside the door. The boys stood warily in a semi-circle, their satchels swinging loose like inconvenient shillelaghs. The girls were ranged behind them, ready to send their men into the firing line. The girls were excited and giggling, but the boys were pale and grim.

"Go on!" shouted the girls, "go on!"

The boys took cautious steps forward.

Now I saw what was to happen – felt shame, and the bitterest of all my seven beings. Humiliation gave me strength. A rolled-up exercise book became an epic sword. I went mad. With what felt like a roar, but must really have been a pig-squeal, I leapt at the nearest boy and hit him squarely on the nose. Then I was round the semi-circle,

131

hewing and thumping like Achilles in the river bed. The screams of the little girls went needle sharp. A second or two later, they and the boys were broken and running up the alley, piling through the narrow entry, erupting into the street.

I stood alone on the cobbles and a wave of passionate sorrow engulfed me. Indignation and affront, shame and frustration took command of my muscles and my lungs. My voice rose in a sustained howl, for all the world as though I had been the loser, and they had chased Achilles back to his tent. I began to zigzag up the alley, head back, my voice serenading a vast sorrow in the sky. My feet found their way along the High Street, and my sorrow went before me like a brass band. Past the Antique Shoppe, the International Stores, Barclay's Bank; past the tobacconist's and the Green Dragon, with head back, and grief as shrill and steady as a siren –

How can one record and not invent? Is there any point in understanding the nature of a small boy crying? Yet if I am to tell the small, the unimportant truth, it is a fact that my sorrows diminished unexpectedly and woefully up the street. What had been universal, became an army with banners, became soon so small that I could carry it before me, as it were, in two hands. Still indignant, still humiliated, still moving zigzag, with little running impulses and moments of pause, I had my grief where I could hold it out and see it – look! Some complexity of nature added three persons to my seven devils – or perhaps brought three of the seven to my notice. There was Billy grieving, smitten to the heart; there was Billy who felt the unfairness of having to get this grief all the way home where his mother could inspect it; and there was scientific Billy, who was rapidly acquiring know-how.

I suspected that my reservoirs were not sufficient for the waters of lamentation, suspected that my voice would disappear, and that I was incapable of a half-mile's sustained emotion. I began to run, therefore, so that my sorrow would last. When suspicion turned to certainty, I cut my crying to a whimper and settled to the business of getting it home. Past the Aylesbury Arms, across the London Road, through Oxford Street by the Wesleyan Chapel, turn left for the last climb in the Green – and there my feelings inflated like a balloon, so that I did the last twenty yards as tragically as I could have wished, swimming through an ocean of sorrow, all, paradoxically enough, quite, quite genuine – swung on the front door knob, stumbled in, staggered to my mother –

"Why, Billy! Whatever's the matter?"

– balloon burst, floods, tempests, hurricanes, rage and anguish – a monstrous yell –

"THEY DON'T LIKE ME!"

My mother administered consolation and the hesitant suggestion that perhaps some of the transaction had been my fault. But I was beyond the reach of such footling ideas. She comforted, my father and Lily hovered, until at last I was quiet enough to eat. My mother put on her enormous hat and went out with an expression of grim purpose. When she came back, she said she thought everything would be all right. I continued to eat and sniff and hiccup. I brooded righteously on what was going to happen to my school-fellows now that my mother had taken a hand. They were, I thought, probably being sent to bed without anything to eat, and it would serve them right and teach them to like me and not be cruel. After lunch, I enjoyed myself darkly (scaffole, birk, rake), inventing possible punishments for them – lovely punishments.

Miss called later and had a long talk with my mother in the drawing-room. As she left, I stuck my field of ripe corn round the dining-room door again and saw them.

"Bring him along a quarter of an hour late," said Miss. "That's all I shall need."

My mother inclined her stately head.

"I know the children don't really mean any harm – but Billy is so sensitive."

We were back to normal again, then. That night, I suffered my usual terrors; but the morning came and I forgot them again in the infinite promise of day. Lily took me to school a quarter of an hour later than usual. We went right in, right upstairs. Everyone was seated and you could have stuck a fork into the air of noiseless excitement. I sat in my desk, Lily went, and school began. Wherever I looked there were faces that smiled shyly at me. I inspected them for signs of damage but no one seemed to have suffered any crippling torment. I reached for a rubber, and a girl in pink and plaits leaned over.

"Borrow mine."

A boy offered me a handkerchief. Another passed me a note with 'wil you jine my ggang' written on it. I was in. We began to say our tables and I only had to pause for breath before giving an answer to six sevens for a gale of whispers to suggest sums varying from thirty-nine to forty-five. Dear Miss had done her work well, and today I should enjoy hearing her fifteen minutes' homily on brotherly love. Indeed, school seemed likely to come to a full stop from sheer excess of charity; so Miss, smiling remotely, said we would have an extra long break. My heart leapt, because I thought that now we could get on with some really fierce, friendly fighting, with even a bloody nose. But Miss

134

produced a train set. When the other boys got down to fixing rails, the girls, inexpressibly moved by the homily, seized me in posse. I never stood a chance against those excited arms, those tough, silken chests, those bird-whistling mouths, that mass of satin and serge and wool and pigtails and ribbons. Before I knew where I was, I found myself, my cornflowers popping out of my head, playing Postman's Knock.

The first girl to go outside set the pattern.

"A parcel for Billy Golding."

In and out I went like a weaver's shuttle, pecked, pushed, hugged, mouthed and mauled, in and out from fair to dark to red, from Eunice who had had fever and a crop, to big Martha who could sit on her hair.

I kissed the lot.

This was, I suppose, my first lesson; and I cannot think it was successful. For I did not know about the homily, I merely felt that the boys and girls who tried to do democratic justice on me had been shown to be wrong. I was, and now they knew it, a thoroughly likeable character. I was unique and precious after all; and I still wondered what punishments their parents had found for them which had forced them to realize the truth.

I still refused to do my lessons, confronting Miss with an impenetrable placidity. I still enjoyed fighting if I was given the chance. I still had no suspicion that Billy was anything but perfect. At the end of term, when I went down to Cornwall, I sat in a crowded carriage with my prize book open on my knees for six hours (keroube, serrap, konfeederul), so that passengers could read the inscription. I am reading it now:

BILLY GOLDING

1919

PRIZE FOR

GENERAL IMPROVEMENT

MAM'ZELLE'S 'TREEK'

ENID BLYTON

from In The Fifth At Malory Towers

*The girls mentioned in this extract appear elsewhere in the novel, but
the heroine here is Mam'zelle Dupont, butt of many harmless practical
jokes by the girls, who has confiscated their mail order catalogues and
secretly ordered a joke of her own . . .*

CERTAINLY EVERYTHING was much better now. Alicia
went to see June and addressed a good many sound
and sensible words to that much chastened and
subdued first-former. It would be a long time before June
forgot them, if she ever did. She didn't think she ever
would.

Moira was basking in a new-found admiration and liking,
that made her much more amenable to the others'
suggestions, and rehearsals became a pleasure. Even the
sulky Bridget came smiling into the fifth-form common-
room to say she was glad Moira had saved June. "It makes
me feel you might do the same for *me*, Moira!" she said.

"Well – I would," said Moira, shortly, and Bridget went
out, pleased.

Mam'zelle had been very shocked and upset about

everything. "But it is terrible! How could June do such a thing? And Moira – *Moira*, that hard Moira to go and save her like that! Miss Potts, never would I have thought that girl had a generous action in her! Miss Potts – it shocks me that I know so little of my girls!"

"Oh, you'll get over the shock," said Miss Potts, cheerfully. "And you'll have plenty more. Well, well – the girls have cheered up a lot – the fifth-formers I mean. They really were a worried, miserable, quarrelsome crew last week! I was seriously thinking of playing a trick on them to cheer them up!"

Mam'zelle looked at Miss Potts. In her desk were the trick teeth which had arrived that morning. Miss Potts must not play a trick – if a trick was to be played, she, Mam'zelle, would play it. Ah yes – to cheer up the poor girls! That would be a kind act to do.

There was a house-match that afternoon – North Tower girls against West Tower. Mam'zelle decided she would appear as a spectator at the match – with her teeth!

Ah, those teeth! Mam'zelle had tried them on. They might have been made for her! They fitted over her own teeth, but were longer, and projected slightly forward. They were not noticeable at all, of course, when she had her mouth shut – but when she smiled – ah, how sinister she looked, how strange, how fierce!

Mam'zelle had shocked even herself when she had put in the extraordinary teeth and smiled at herself in the glass. "*Tiens!*" she said, and clutched her dressing-table. "I am a monster! I am truly terrible with these teeth . . ."

That afternoon she put them in carefully over her others and went downstairs to the playing-fields, wrapping herself up warmly in coat, scarf and turban. Darrell saw her first, and made room for her on the form she was on.

"Thank you," said Mam'zelle, and smiled at Darrell. Darrell got a tremendous shock. Mam'zelle had suddenly looked altogether different – quite terrifying. Darrell stared at her – but Mam'zelle had quickly shut her mouth.

The next one to get the Smile was little Felicity who came up with Susan. Mam'zelle smiled at her.

"Oh!" said Felicity in sudden horror, and Susan stared. Mam'zelle shut her mouth. A desire to laugh was gradually working up inside her. No, no – she must not laugh. Laughing spoilt tricks.

She did not smile for some time, trying to conquer her urge to laugh. Miss Linnie, the sewing-mistress, passed by and nodded at Mam'zelle. Mam'zelle could not resist showing her the teeth. She smiled.

Miss Linnie looked amazed and horrified. She walked on quickly. "Was that *really* Mam'zelle?" she wondered. "No, it must have been someone else. What awful teeth!"

Mam'zelle felt that she must get up and walk about. It was too cold to sit – and besides she so badly wanted to laugh again. Ah, now she understood why the girls laughed so much and so helplessly when they played their mischievous tricks on her.

She walked along the field, and met Bill and Clarissa. They smiled at her and she smiled back. Bill stood still, thunderstruck. Clarissa hadn't really noticed.

"Clarissa!" said Bill, when Mam'zelle had gone. "What's tha matter with Mam'zelle this afternoon? She looks *horrible*!"

"Horrible? How?" asked Clarissa in great surprise.

"Well, her *teeth*! Didn't you see her teeth?" asked Bill. "They seem to have changed or something. Simply awful teeth she had – long and sticking-out."

Clarissa was astonished. "Let's walk back and smile at her again," she said. So back they went. But Mam'zelle saw their inquisitive looks, and was struggling against a fit of laughter. She would not open her mouth to smile.

Matron came up. "Oh, Mam'zelle – do you know where Gwen is? She's darned her navy gym pants with grey wool again. I want her indoors this afternoon!"

Mam'zelle could not resist smiling at Matron. Matron stared as if she couldn't believe her eyes. Mam'zelle shut her mouth. Matron backed away a little, looking rather alarmed.

"Gwen's over there," said Mam'zelle, her extra teeth making her words sound rather thick. Matron looked even more alarmed at the thick voice and disappeared in a hurry. Mam'zelle saw her address a few words to Miss Potts. Miss Potts looked round for Mam'zelle.

"Aha!" thought Mam'zelle. "Matron has told her I look terrible! Soon Miss Potts will come to look at my Smile. I shall laugh. I know I shall. I shall laugh without stopping soon."

Miss Potts came up, eyeing Mam'zelle carefully. She got a quick glimpse of the famous teeth. Then Mam'zelle clamped her mouth shut. She would explode if she didn't keep her mouth shut! She pulled her scarf across her face, trying to hide her desire to laugh.

"Do you feel the cold today, Mam'zelle?" asked Miss Potts anxiously. "You – er – you haven't got toothache, have you?"

A peculiar wild sound came from Mam'zelle. It startled Miss Potts considerably. But actually it was only Mam'zelle trying to stifle a squeal of laughter. She rushed away hurriedly. Miss Potts stared after her uncomfortably. What *was* up with Mam'zelle?

Mam'zelle strolled down the field by herself, trying to recover. She gave a few loud gulps that made two second-formers wonder if she was going to be ill.

Poor Mam'zelle felt she couldn't flash her teeth at anyone for a long time, for if she did she would explode like Irene. She decided to go in. She turned her steps towards the school – and then, to her utter horror, she saw Miss Grayling, the head mistress, bearing down on her with two parents! Mam'zelle gave an anguished look and hurried on as fast as she could.

"Oh – there's Mam'zelle," said Miss Grayling's pleasant voice. "Mam'zelle, will you meet Mrs Jennings and Mrs Petton?"

Mam'zelle was forced to go to them. She lost all desire for

laughter at once. The trick teeth then suddenly stopped being funny, and became monstrosities to be got rid of at once. But how? She couldn't spit them into her handkerchief with people just about to shake hands with her.

Mrs Jennings held out her hand. "I've heard so much about you, Mam'zelle Dupont," she said, "and what tricks the naughty girls play on you, too!"

Mam'zelle tried to smile without opening her mouth at all, and the effect was rather peculiar – a sort of suppressed snarl. Mrs Jennings looked surprised. Mam'zelle tried to make up for her lack of smile by shaking Mrs Jennings' hand very vigorously indeed.

She did the same with Mrs Petton, who turned out to be a talkative mother who wanted to know *exactly* how her daughter Teresa was getting on in French. She smiled gaily at Mam'zelle while she talked, and Mam'zelle found it agony not to smile back. She had to produce the suppressed snarl again, smiling with her mouth shut and her lips firmly over her teeth.

Miss Grayling was startled by this peculiar smile. She examined Mam'zelle closely. Mam'zelle's voice was not quite as usual either – it sounded thick. "As if her mouth is too full of teeth," thought Miss Grayling, little knowing that she had hit on the exact truth.

At last the mothers went. Mam'zelle shook hands with them most vigorously once more, and was so relieved at parting from them that she forget herself and gave them a broad smile.

They got a full view of the terrible teeth. Miss Grayling, too. The head stared in the utmost horror – *what* had happened to Mam'zelle's teeth? Had she had her old ones out – were these a new, false set? But how TERRIBLE they were! They made her look like the wolf in the tale of Red Riding Hood.

The two mothers turned their heads away quickly at the sight of the teeth. They hurried off with Miss Grayling who hardly heard what they said, she was so concerned about

Mam'zelle's teeth. She determined to send for Mam'zelle that evening and ask her about them. Really – she couldn't allow any of her staff to go about with teeth like that! They were monstrous, hideous!

Mam'zelle was so thankful to see the last of the mothers that she hurried straight into a little company of fifth-formers going back to the school, some to do their piano practice and some to have a lesson in elocution.

"Hallo, Mam'zelle!" said Mavis. "Are you coming back to school?"

Mam'zelle smiled. The fifth-formers got a dreadful shock. They stared in silent horror. The teeth had slipped a little, and now looked rather like fangs. They gave Mam'zelle a most sinister, big-bad-wolf look. Mam'zelle saw their alarm and astonishment. Laughter surged back into her. She felt it swelling up and up. She gasped. She gulped. She roared.

She sank on to a bench and cried with helpless laughter. She remembered Matron's face – and Miss Grayling's – and the faces of the two mothers. The more she thought of them the more helplessly she laughed. The girls stood round, more alarmed than ever. What *was* the matter with Mam'zelle? What was this enormous joke?

Mam'zelle's teeth slipped out altogether, fell on to her lap, and then to the ground. The girls stared at them in the utmost amazement, and then looked at Mam'zelle. She now looked completely normal, with just her own small teeth

showing in her laughing face. She laughed on and on when she saw her trick teeth lying there before her.

"It is a treek," she squeaked at last, wiping her eyes with her handkerchief. "Did you not give me a dare? Did you not tell me to do a treek on you? I have done one with the teeth. They are treek teeth. Oh, *là là* – I must laugh again. Oh my sides, oh my back!"

She swayed to and fro, laughing. The girls began to laugh, too. Mam'zelle Rougier came up, astonished to see the other French mistress laughing so much.

"What is the matter?" she asked, without a smile on her face.

Irene did one of her explosions. She pointed to the teeth on the ground. "Mam'zelle wore them – for a trick – and they've fallen out and given the game away!"

She went off into squeals of laughter again, and the other girls joined in. Mam'zelle Rougier looked cold and disapproving.

"I see no joke," she said. "It is not funny, teeth on the grass. It is time to see the dentist when that happens."

She walked off, and her speech and disapproving face sent everyone into fits of laughter again. It was altogether a most successful afternoon for Mam'zelle, and the 'treek' story flew all through the school immediately.

Mam'zelle suddenly found herself extremely popular, except with the staff. "A little *undignified*, don't you think?" said Miss Williams.

"Not a thing to do *too* often, Mam'zelle," said Miss Potts, making up her mind to remove the trick booklets from Mam'zelle's desk at the first opportunity.

"Glad you've lost those frightful teeth," said Matron, bluntly. "Don't do that again without warning me, Mam'zelle. I got the shock of my life."

But the girls loved Mam'zelle for her 'treek', and every class in the school, from top to bottom, worked twice as hard (or so Mam'zelle declared) after she had played her truly astonishing 'treek'!

MIDGE PROVOKES HYSTERIA

WINIFRED HOLTBY

from South Riding

Playing jokes on the staff is not always harmless fun. Midge Carne wins friends and followers at Kiplington High School by tormenting Miss Sigglesthwaite, the biology mistress, without understanding the harm she is causing.

T HE BICYCLE SHED stood behind the High School buildings, a long dim jungle of steel and wire beneath a sloping roof. Showers dancing on corrugated iron almost deafened the members of the Anti-Sig Society huddled together in one corner with winter coats bunched round their ears and cheeks bulging with liquorice allsorts.

Above them hung a notice-board on which was pinned a sheet torn out of an exercise book bearing the peculiar inscription, "A.S.S."

Judy	6
Nancy	4+
Gwynneth⎫	
Midge ⎭	3
Enid	2

Maud ⎫
Phyllis ⎭   0

From time to time day-girls entered, abstracted bicycles and pedalled off into the rain, paying small attention to the conspiratorial group in the dark corner. The bicycle shed was a recognized committee-room for unofficial school societies.

"Judy's got top marks. Judy presides," said Nancy.

A plump child with limp straw-coloured hair wriggled on to the lamp shelf.

"Midge Carne has an idea," she announced.

"We ought to re-read the rules of the society."

"Why?"

"That's the right thing. Before every meeting."

"No – not the rules, the minutes."

"Well, we haven't any minutes."

"I founded the society," said Midge. "I say it's the rules. Judy can read them."

Judy lit a bicycle lamp and bent forward to bring a battered exercise book into range of its narrow delta of light. She read:

"This society shall be called the Anti-Sig Society or A.S.S.

"Its object is the abolition of the Sigglesthwaite monster from Kiplington School.

"Members are elected by a committee consisting of Midge Carne, Gwynneth Rogers, Nancy Grey and Judy Peacock.

"The society meets weekly and gives marks to the members, judged by their behaviour towards the Sig.

"Marks shall be given for the following points:

Ordinary cheek in class	1
Personal insults	2
Picking up dropped hairpins	2
Drawings – (if good)	2
If good and in a public place	3

A really splendid piece of cheek, affecting
   every one   10
Also whoever does it shall be called Queen A.S.S. for
   the term and preside at all meetings.
Top marks otherwise for the week make a president.
"This society was the idea of M.C."

"I have a really splendid idea," announced Midge.
"All right. Get up on to the president's seat."
Judy slid down; Midge climbed.
She sat on the shelf dangling her legs, looking down on to the ring of upturned faces in the lamplight.

These were Them. These were her friends. She had triumphed. In the first term of her second year she sat there, presiding over Judy and Maud and Gwynneth, warm and secure in the confidence of their friendship. She was one of a Group, a Family. She belonged.

Her triumph was all the more sweet because she had nearly lost it. She had returned to Maythorpe after the Measle Term to the worst summer holidays that she had ever known. After the bright precision of Miss Burton's little house, after the discipline and companionship of school, Maythorpe seemed lost in unhappy desolation.

The neglected lawns grew tall as a watered meadow. The unpruned roses straggled across the paths and dripped from the leaning archways. Apples rotted as they fell below the orchard trees. No callers came, but as human life receded from the old house it seemed to take to itself its own non-human populace. Mice scratched and whimpered under the bedroom floors; bats hung in the attic; earwigs and spiders ran up the window curtains. When Midge tossed her tennis ball accidentally against the ivy, sparrows and starlings flew out with such shrill chatter that the whole house seemed to have come alive to scold her.

Her loneliness first bored, then terrified her. Elsie, disgruntled and dour, banged about the kitchen. Her father was out all day. Castle was worse. The harvest had not gone well. Hicks was just awful. Daddy had sold three hunters before harvest. The morning when they went away, Trix, Ladybird and the Adjutant, Midge stood on the step that led from the little tiled back-yard to the great gravelled stable-yard, and watched Hicks lead out of the stable first the big bay, then the grey flea-bitten spotted mare, the Ladybird, then her father's bright golden heavyweight, the Adjutant. Carne took the bridle reins, looked at their mouths, bent down and felt their knees. Ladybird was saddled; the other two wore their stable cloths. Hicks mounted the grey, and Carne handed him the bridle reins of the others.

"Be back about four?" asked Carne.

Hicks did not speak. Midge saw his ugly, rather comical face distorted by an odd convulsion. He nodded; he chirruped to the horses; he was off down the drive, riding one, leading two. Carne watched them go.

Midge ran down to him, torn by forebodings, urgent to ask, "Daddy, where's he gone? What's happening?"

But Carne did not seem to hear her. He strode off past the stables towards the hind's house beyond the western stackyard without a word, his face set hard as stone.

So Midge was glad when the holidays were over.

She returned to school eager yet suspicious, sniffing its atmosphere, shying back from innovation like a suspicious and timid little animal. Her habit of suspecting the worst made her inclined to see every change as frightful. There were over fifty new girls and they were awful, slummy, common, with appalling accents. There was another boarding-house along Cliff Terrace. There was a new form, the Remove, and Midge was in it. "It's for us duds," said the irrepressible Judy. "Not at all," Midge replied. "It's for delicate girls who need special attention and don't take matric. That's why I'm in it. I had measles *very* badly, and Dr Campbell says I must be careful of my heart."

But, heart or no, Midge missed the special privileges of illness. Miss Burton had withdrawn from her brief intimacy. She was preoccupied with new buildings, new girls and reorganization. People said that the school was being a success, but what mattered to Midge was whether she could be a success inside the school. She was uncertain again, and insecure.

So something had to be done, or life would be too wretched. "The sensitive girl, aristocratic and delicate, looked with dismay upon the vulgar 'rabble surrounding her," she told herself. It was bad enough that Miss Carne of Maythorpe should be herded with all these tradesmen's just too frightful daughters, but if, on top of that, she was to find herself, Lord Sedgmire's granddaughter, despised by her

147

inferiors, she could not bear it.

Then, with a sudden ecstasy of creation, she invented the Anti-Sig Society.

Ragging the Sig was fun and it was easy. It was part of a popular and legitimate Kiplington fashion. It was Sporting.

There was no intention of malice in it. Mistresses, with their huge statutory powers, were fair game. They were not human beings. They did not possess the common human feelings. Their lives were mysterious. They appeared at the beginning of term and vanished at its close. From the Great Deep to the Great Deep they went, incalculable, inapproachable, unreal.

Therefore for girls to persecute them was heroic. All the risk, all the adventure, lay on the side of youth, which must brave the anger of entrenched authority. Therefore, Midge, swinging her thin brown legs in the light of the bicycle lamp after second school, surveyed her audience with legitimate pride.

"Listen," she said. "You know our nature prep.?"

" 'Write a study of some living creature whose habits you have observed for yourself,' " quoted Maud.

"I've got a marvellous idea. You know how she loves the stickleback. The little stickleback? Why not the Sigglesback? Who'll dare to write an essay on the Sigglesback? We've studied it, haven't we? We've observed it for ourselves?"

She watched her great idea rippling across their faces like light on water.

"The sigglesback – a bony little creature – cold-blooded – lives in the mud."

"Builds nests."

"In its hair."

The idea was catching on.

Here was creation. Here was glory.

"It prefers dirty water."

"It never mates."

Glory, glory, glory. Midge was a leader. She was popular. She was safe. Friendship encircled her. Leadership enthroned her. When had she doubted? When had she been afraid?

"It's marvellous!"

"Midge, you're priceless!"

"Shu-uh!"

The creaking door at the far end of the shed opened. The Sigglesback herself, dank hair in a fringe below her drenched felt hat, mackintosh dripping about her tall bowed figure, botany specimen tin slung from her shoulders, entered pushing her bicycle.

She found difficulty in shoving it into its place. She had been collecting leaves and bark and Mycetozoa for tomorrow's lesson. She was almost blind and half crying with exhaustion after pedalling her cycle against the blustering wind. She was a figure irresistibly comic.

The choking giggles in the corner roused her.

149

She raised her mild short-sighted eyes and saw Midge Carne enthroned, the ring of girls below her, the A.S.S. notice fluttering by her head.

Pushing her bicycle painfully into its place, panting with effort, she withdrew. The suppressed giggles broke into a guffaw as she shut the door.

"My dear, I could have died!"

"Midge, you were *awful*."

"Do you think she'll guess?"

"Whatever *will* she say?"

"She'll never dare do anything. She can't report us unless she shows our essays to Sally and she'll never dare do that! The Sigglesback. Long live the Sigglesback!"

"Bet you she never even sees the point at all."

It did not occur to them that their gloating voices rang clear and unmistakable through the wooden wall, and that Miss Sigglesthwaite, trudging up the path to the science room, heard every word.

She did not stop to listen. She had been educated according to a code which declared eavesdropping to be dishonourable. But though she despised these children, though they bored her inexpressibly, she could not learn complete indifference to them.

When on Thursday evening she packed the pile of nature notebooks into her basket and cycled back with them to her lodgings, she was acutely aware of hatred and contempt surrounding her.

Miss Sigglesthwaite's landlady served her with high tea. It was less trouble. She had tonight provided a smoked kipper. Because Agnes was late it seemed a peculiarly dried and bony kipper, yet its oily effulgence penetrated the air of the bed-sitting-room as though it had been the fattest and juiciest on the east coast. Before she entered the room, Agnes had a headache; she had not been there long before she felt sick as well. Edie's letter was no more cheerful than usual. Her wireless battery had run down and she had decided to economize by selling the whole thing.

150

She dismissed her tea uneaten, closed her window because the fire smoked when she opened it, and shut herself in with the nature notebooks.

There was no reason why she should dread them so much. She scolded her apprehensive mind and cowardly heart. After all – what were these vulgar stupid little adolescents? Why should she care whatever they did or said?

She laid the books on the crimson tablecloth; she brought out her red ink and her marking pen. She sat down stalwartly beside them. She breathed her prayer for grace, "Lord, give me patience."

She opened Gwynneth Rogers' composition upon 'The Life and Habits of the Sigglesback'.

Gwynneth, Maud, Nancy, Enid, Midge. Mechanically underlining words, surrounding blots with red circles, counting spelling faults, Agnes Sigglesthwaite went through the blurred uneven pages. She learned that she was dull, dirty, ugly, boring; that she had silly manners; that her hair was a bird's nest and her dress untidy.

"The sigglesback never mates; it is too bony. Also it has a most peculiar smell. It builds nests in its hair for breeding purposes. It has no voice but a kind of piping squeak when it is angry."

They were not clever children. They had small powers of invention. Their venom outran their wit.

But it was enough for Agnes. It was too much.

Oh, cruel, cruel! They want to drive me away.

Do they think I *like* it? Do they think I want to stay here? Do they think it's fun to put aside the important work I know I could do, and set nature essays to be mangled by their crude nasty little minds?

But they're right. They're right. That is what makes it intolerable. Because I ought not to be here. I'm no use with children. I dislike them. They bore me.

But Mother – Edie? How can I let them down? 'My clever daughter, Agnes.' Oh, God, what shall I do?

Wasn't it enough that I had to hate my work? Must they make me hate myself too?

Unattractive, dreary, tired. . .

Ought I to have gone on wearing that old jumper?

But it doesn't smell. Oh, no, it doesn't smell!

Am I like that? "It has no voice – but a kind of piping squeak when it is angry."

I am Agnes Sigglesthwaite. I won a scholarship to Cambridge. Professor Hemingway said I had a distinguished mind.

She touched her withered cheek with anxious explorative fingers. She moved to the looking-glass and gazed at her thin defenceless face, the mild blue eyes, the soft small unformed chin, the pretty mouth undeveloped as a child's, the long reddened dyspeptic nose. She looked and looked. She could not believe that Agnes Sigglesthwaite, her father's darling daughter, the brilliant scholar, the beloved respected sister, had come to this.

Oh, no! she moaned. Oh, no!

The landlady turned off the lights in the basement and went to bed. The public house at the corner closed, and the men tramped home. The last train whistled, leaving the coast for Kingsport. Face downwards on the floor of her

152

dreary room, beneath the white singing light of the incandescent gas, Agnes lay, calling upon her God who had turned His countenance from her, her father, who was dead, and her own fortitude, which had been exhausted. In her room at Maythorpe, watching the slow march of the moon, Midge lay and shuddered. God, I've been brave. I've proved myself a leader. Let them like me, God, please make me popular.

But Midge slept long before the science mistress. Agnes woke to hear her landlady on the stairs, panting up with the clattering breakfast tray. She crawled to her feet and stood as the door opened.

"Dressed already? Early this morning, aren't you?"

"Yes," murmured Agnes.

The hot tea revived her a little. But she felt so strange that she had to sit, clutching the arms of her chair as the room waltzed round her, up and down, swaying sideways, like the golden swans on a merry-go-round.

It was nine o'clock before she rose from the table. She must go to school. She must not be late for prayers. She gathered her books together.

Half-way down the stairs she remembered that she had not washed her face. That was very dirty. She climbed up again panting, but once in her room could no longer remember why she had returned.

She was late for prayers after all, so went straight through to Form Remove, where she was due to take first period. When the girls filed into the form room, marching demurely, they saw her standing vaguely beside the blackboard, white-faced, red-eyed, her hair in wild disorder.

Members of the A.S.S. glanced at each other. They winked to keep up their spirits.

"Good-morning, Miss Sigglesthwaite."

"Good-morning, girls. Sit down" – the customary formula.

They sat.

153

There was a pause. She looked vacantly at them.

Jennifer Howe, form prefect, who was not a member of the A.S.S., said helpfully:

"Shall I give out the notebooks for you, Miss Sigglesthwaite?"

"The notebooks. The nature notebooks."

Agnes lifted a green-covered book and looked at it. Her voice sounded thick and strange. "Yes. I have read your nature essays. I have also read notices in the cycle shed. We will have a viva-voce examination. Midge Carne!"

Midge sprang to her feet, vibrating with heroic tension.

"What does the A.S.S. stand for?"

"I – I – "

"Nancy!" pause. "Gwynneth!"

No answer.

"Come here, Midge."

Midge marched to the desk, swaggering. If she also trembled none knew it – not even herself.

"Is this your work?"

"Yes, Miss Sigglesback."

It was a slip of the tongue, a trick of nerves. Midge gulped back a snigger.

"You formed the A.S.S.?"

"Yes."

"You are its president?"

"Yes."

"You organized this – this – " a thin dirty finger trembled on the offending books. The snigger broke from control. Midge began to giggle.

"So you think it's funny, do you! To persecute someone who never did you harm? To drive me away when I have my living to make? To organize a cruel malicious attack, a – a – Because your father's a school governor you think you can do what you like. But I tell you, I tell you . . ."

The mumbling furious voice scared Midge out of all sense. Her terrified giggling rose to shrill frightened laughter.

"You laugh now! You dare to laugh at me!"

The science mistress rose from her chair and towered above the child.

"You beast! You little beast!" she hissed, and with the ruler in her hand struck twice at the child's thin sallow face.

Midge gasped.

Never in her life had anyone struck her.

For a moment shock overcame her pain.

Then, as at the second blow, the sharp edge of the ruler caught and cut her delicate skin, she shrank back with a startled cry.

Miss Sigglesthwaite looked down at her handiwork and for the first time she knew what she had done. Her violence had restored her sanity. She became completely calm.

Carefully she laid down the ruler on the blotting-paper, straightening it with meticulous precision.

"Girls," she said, "get out your botany text books. Turn to page 184. Start learning the lists that you will find there. Midge, go back to your seat. Jennifer, you are in charge."

She turned to the door. Jennifer, astonished beyond question, sprang to open it. With a dignity that she had never shown before, Miss Sigglesthwaite left the room and stalked down the passage.

She went straight to Miss Burton's office and entered. She saw the head mistress seated at her desk.

"Yes? Well, Miss Sigglesthwaite, what is it?"

Sarah was none too pleased at the interruption. The time-table over her desk showed her that Miss Sigglesthwaite should be giving a natural history lesson to Form Remove.

"I wish to hand in my resignation."

"Your what?"

"My resignation. I am leaving at once. I have hit Midge Carne. I have cut her cheek open."

"Hit – Midge?"

"I wanted to kill her," observed Agnes calmly. Then, with a vague gesture, "I don't – feel – very well."

She sat down on the chair facing Sarah's desk and, with a mumbled apology, lost consciousness.

155

FRIDAY

SUSAN COOPER

THE AIR-RAID siren went at the beginning of the afternoon, in an English lesson, while Mrs Wilson was reading them *Children of the New Forest*. At first they couldn't hear the siren at all for the school whistles: a chorus of alarm, their own indoor warning, shrilling down all the corridors at once.

"Ma'am, ma'am! A raid, ma'am!"

Mrs Wilson closed the book with a deliberate snap and stood up. "All right now, children, quickly and quietly. Books in your desks, take out your gas masks, all stand up. Anybody not got his gas mask? Very good. Now I want a nice neat line to the shelter, and no running."

A hand was waving wildly at the front of the class. "Ma'am, is it a real raid, ma'am?"

"It's a drill," said a scornful voice.

"It's the wrong time for a drill."

Mrs Wilson scowled, and they knew the scowl and were quiet. "We don't know yet. Door monitor?"

Little Albert Russell was already stiff at attention by the open door, the strap of his gas-mask case neat across his chest. Out they went into the corridor, from one row of desks at a time, their double file jostling the filing classes from the other rooms, out to the air-raid shelters in the playground.

156

Derek and Peter had desks near the classroom window. Geoffrey was behind them.

"Can you see anything?"

"Nah. Hear the siren now, though. Listen."

The head-splitting school whistles had stopped, and Derek listened as he walked, and heard the distant wail of the siren rise and fall until they were down the corridor and going out of the big double door. He and Peter and Geoff were nearly at the end of the line; Mrs Wilson was counting heads just in front of them. He shivered; the sun was shining through broken clouds, but there was a chill wind. Most of the other classes, the younger ones, were made to take their overcoats into the shelters, but his group, the farthest from the cloakrooms, had no time ever to fetch theirs.

He became conscious suddenly of the drone of engines somewhere high up.

"Look!" Peter stopped, excited, pointing.

The three couples behind them fell over their feet as he stopped, and then skirted him and went nervously, disapprovingly on. Only Geoffrey paused. The girl who had been walking with him called over her shoulder, "Come on," but she was Susan Simmons, who was always bossy, and the boys took no notice, but stood where they were and stared up.

Where Peter was pointing, there was a pattern of slow-moving dots in the sky. The deep hum of the engines grew as he watched, and developed a kind of throbbing sound. The clouds were very high, and the planes were flying below them; they seemed light-coloured and were not easy to see unless the sun went behind a cloud. Their noise seemed so loud now that Derek looked all around the rest of the sky for more, but saw nothing except the familiar floating shapes of the seven barrage balloons, three near, four far off, fat silver ovals hanging up there with bulbous fins at their tails, like great friendly bloatēd fish. The balloons were filled with hydrogen, he knew, and tethered by thick cables; they were there to get in the way of any Nazi pilot coming in low to drop his bombs.

"Junkers," Geoffrey said confidently. "Junker eighty-eights."

What with his own excitement and the height of the formation, Derek could not really make out the silhouette of any individual plane; but by the same token he knew that Geoff couldn't either. "No, no," he said. "Dorniers."

And then in the second that they still paused on the black asphalt playground, with the grubby concrete boxes that were the air-raid shelters looming ahead of them, they saw the unbelievable happen. Suddenly the rigid, steadily advancing formation of enemy planes broke its pattern, lost its head as plane after plane broke away and dived; and they heard a new higher noise and glimpsed, diving through a broad gap in the clouds out of the sun, a gaggle of other smaller planes scattering the bombers as a dog scatters sheep. It was a furious sky now, full of coughing gunfire.

They heard other guns open up, deeper, closer, on the ground.

"Gosh!" Derek said. He had forgotten entirely where he was; he hopped in delight. His gas-mask case banged at his back. "*Gosh!*"

"Fighters, our fighters!" Peter waved madly at the sky. "Look!"

And they were lost in breathless looking and in the growing scream of engines and the thumping of gunfire, as an urgent hand came down and Mrs Wilson dragged them off towards the shelter.

"You *stupid* boys, come under cover *at once!*" Her voice was a squeak of anxious rage, and it was only the realization that she was angrier than they had ever seen her that brought them skidding into the entrance to the shelter. But even then Peter was still staring back over his shoulder, and all at once he let out a yell of such joyful surprise that all four of them, even Mrs Wilson, paused, hypnotized, for a last glimpse of the sky.

"He's got him, he's got him, he's got him!"

It was a Hurricane – Derek could see the blunt nose now – and it had dived after one of the weaving bombers, with its guns making bright flashes on its wings. And the bomber had been hit: it was trailing a ragged path of black smoke behind it and lurching erratically across the sky and down. It was still firing its guns; you could hear them and see them among the puffs of smoke in the sky that were the bursts of shells fired from the ground. Nearer and nearer the ground the plane came, a long way away from them but still visible, and as it dived, it veered close to one of the motionless silver barrage balloons, and suddenly there was a sound like a soft 'whoomph' and a great burst of flame.

The plane dropped and vanished, with the victorious

Hurricane above it swooping off to join the battle that they could still hear but no longer see; the sound of the crash was no more than a faraway thump, like the firing of one of the anti-aircraft guns, but enough to galvanize Mrs Wilson into thrusting them ahead of her around the right-angle bend of the entrance into the shelter itself. But still Derek had one moment's last quick sight over his shoulder of the burning barrage balloon, hanging there in the sky as it always had but beginning strangely to droop, with its flat inflated fins no longer sticking firmly out but curving gently, wearily, down.

When they came out of the shelter about half an hour later, the barrage balloon was no longer there. Instead, there was a gap in the sky and only six floating guardian shapes. The raid had not lasted for very long; there had been time for a handful of songs – the other three classes of children in their shelters had been singing 'Waltzing Matilda' when they came in – and the distribution of one boiled sweet each. Then the noise outside, which they heard only in the brief gap between one song and the next, had died away, and the long single note of the 'all clear' had shrilled out. They went back to their classrooms, in as neat a double file as before, and bossy Susan Simmons made a shocked face at Derek and Peter and Geoff and whispered to her friends as they passed.

The three boys stayed after school, hovering at their desks until everyone else had left, to apologize to Mrs Wilson, and curiously she did no more than give them a brief lecture on the perils of being out in the open when a raid was on, and the undeniable extra crime of giving someone else the risk of coming to haul them inside.

"She's nice," Derek said on the way home. "I mean, she could have sent us to the Head, and then they'd have told our parents, and there'd have been an awful row."

"She ought to be grateful, if you ask me," Peter said. "If she hadn't had to come and find us, she'd have missed all the fun."

THE EXERCISE

BERNARD MACLAVERTY

"WE NEVER GOT the chance," his mother would say to him. "It wouldn't have done me much good but your father could have bettered himself. He'd be teaching or something now instead of serving behind a bar. He could stand up with the best of them."

Now that he had started grammar school Kevin's father joined him in his work, helping him when he had the time, sometimes doing the exercises out of the text books on his own before he went to bed. He worked mainly from examples in the Maths and Language books or from previously corrected work of Kevin's. Often his wife took a hand out of him, saying "Do you think you'll pass your Christmas Tests?"

When he concentrated he sat hunched at the kitchen table, his non-writing hand shoved down the back of his trousers and his tongue stuck out.

"Put that thing back in your mouth," Kevin's mother would say, laughing. "You've a tongue on you like a cow."

His father smelt strongly of tobacco for he smoked both a pipe and cigarettes. When he gave Kevin money for sweets he'd say, "You'll get sixpence in my coat pocket on the bannisters."

Kevin would dig into the pocket deep down almost to his elbow and pull out a handful of coins speckled with bits of yellow and black tobacco. His father also smelt of porter, not his breath, for he never drank but from his clothes and Kevin thought it mixed nicely with his grown up smell. He loved to smell his pyjama jacket and the shirts that he left off for washing.

Once in a while Kevin's father would come in at six o'clock, sit in his armchair and say, "Slippers".

"You're not staying in, are you?" The three boys shouted and danced around, the youngest pulling off his big boots, falling back on the floor as they came away from his feet, Kevin, the eldest, standing on the arm of the chair to get the slippers down from the cupboard.

"Some one of you get a good shovel of coal for that fire," and they sat in the warm kitchen doing their homework, their father reading the paper or moving about doing some job that their mother had been at him to do for months. Before their bedtime he would read the younger ones a story or if there were no books in the house at the time he would choose a piece from the paper. Kevin listened with the others although he pretended to be doing something else.

But it was not one of those nights. His father stood shaving with his overcoat on, a very heavy navy overcoat, in a great hurry, his face creamed thick with white lather. Kevin knelt on the cold lino of the bathroom floor, one elbow leaning on the padded seat of the green wicker chair trying to get help with his Latin. It was one of those exercises which asked for the nominative and genitive of: an evil deed, a wise father and so on.

"What's the Latin for 'evil'?"

His father towered above him trying to get at the mirror, pointing his chin upwards scraping underneath.

"Look it up at the back."

Kevin sucked the end of his pencil and fumbled through the vocabularies. His father finished shaving, humped his back and spluttered in the basin. Kevin heard him pull the

plug and the final gasp as the water escaped. He groped for the towel then genuflected beside him drying his face.

"Where is it?" He looked down still drying slower and slower, meditatively until he stopped.

"I'll tell you just this once because I'm in a hurry."

Kevin stopped sucking the pencil and held it poised, ready and wrote the answers with great speed into his jotter as his father called them out.

"Is that them all?" his father asked, draping the towel over the side of the bath. He leaned forward to kiss Kevin but he lowered his head to look at something in the book. As he rushed down the stairs he shouted back over his shoulder.

"Don't ever ask me to do that again. You'll have to work them out for yourself."

He was away leaving Kevin sitting at the chair. The towel edged its way slowly down the side of the bath and fell on the floor. He got up and looked in the wash-hand basin. The bottom was covered in short black hairs, shavings. He drew a white path through them with his finger. Then he turned and went down the stairs to copy the answers in ink.

Of all the teachers in the school Waldo was the one who commanded the most respect. In his presence nobody talked, with the result that he walked the corridors in a moat of silence. Boys seeing him approach would drop their voices to a whisper and only when he was out of earshot would they speak normally again. Between classes there was always five minutes uproar. The boys wrestled over desks, shouted, whistled, flung books while some tried to learn their nouns, eyes closed, feet tapping to the rhythm of declensions. Others put frantic finishing touches to last night's exercise. Some minutes before Waldo's punctual arrival, the class quietened. Three rows of boys, all by now strumming nouns, sat hunched and waiting.

Waldo's entrance was theatrical. He strode in with strides as long as his soutane would permit, his books clenched in his left hand and pressed tightly against his chest. With his right hand he swung the door behind him, closing it with a crash. His eyes raked the class. If, as occasionally happened, it did not close properly he did not turn from the class but backed slowly against the door snapping it shut with his behind. Two strides brought him to the rostrum. He cracked his books down with an explosion and made a swift palm upward gesture.

Waldo was very tall, his height being emphasized by the soutane, narrow and tight-fitting at the shoulders, sweeping down like a bell to the floor. A row of black gleaming buttons bisected him from floor to throat. When he talked his Adam's apple hit against the hard, white Roman collar and created in Kevin the same sensation as a fingernail scraping down the blackboard. His face was sallow and immobile. (There was a rumour that he had a glass eye but no one knew which. Nobody could look at him long enough because to meet his stare was to invite a question.) He abhorred slovenliness. Once when presented with an

164

untidy exercise book, dog-eared with a tea ring on the cover, he picked it up, the corner of one leaf between his finger and thumb, the pages splaying out like a fan, opened the window and dropped it three floors to the ground. His own neatness became exaggerated when he was at the board, writing in copperplate script just large enough for the boy in the back row to read – geometrical columns of declined nouns defined by exact, invisible margins. When he had finished he would set the chalk down and rub the used finger and thumb together with the same action he used after handling the host over the paten.

The palm upward gesture brought the class to its feet and they said the Hail Mary in Latin. While it was being said all eyes looked down because they knew if they looked up Waldo was bound to be staring at them.

"Exercises."

When Waldo was in a hurry he corrected the exercises verbally, asking one boy for the answers and then asking all those who got it right to put up their hands. It was four for anyone who lied about his answer and now and then he would take spot checks to find out the liars.

"Hold it, hold it there," he would say and leap from the rostrum, moving through the forest of hands and look at each boy's book, tracing out the answer with the tip of his cane. Before the end of the round and while his attention was on one book a few hands would be lowered quietly. Today he was in a hurry. The atmosphere was tense as he looked from one boy to another, deciding who would start.

"Sweeny, we'll begin with you." Kevin rose to his feet, his finger trembling under the place in the book. He read the first answer and looked up at Waldo. He remained impassive. He would let someone while translating unseens ramble on and on with great imagination until he faltered, stopped and admitted that he didn't know. Then and only then would he be slapped.

"Two, nominative. *Sapienter Pater*," Kevin went on haltingly through the whole ten and stopped, waiting for a comment from Waldo. It was a long time before he spoke. When he did it was with bored annoyance.

"Every last one of them is wrong."

"But sir, Father, they couldn't be wr . . ." Kevin said it with such conviction, blurted it out so quickly that Waldo looked at him in surprise.

"Why not?"

"Because my . . ." Kevin stopped.

"Well?" Waldo's stone face resting on his knuckles. "Because my what?"

It was too late to turn back now.

"Because my father said so," he mumbled very low, chin on chest.

"Speak up, let us all hear you." Some of the boys had heard and he thought they sniggered.

"Because my father said so." This time the commotion in the class was obvious.

"And where does your father teach Latin?" There was no escape. Waldo had him. He knew now there would be an exhibition for the class. Kevin placed his weight on his arm and felt his tremble communicated to the desk.

"He doesn't, Father."

"And what does he do?"

Kevin hesitated, stammering.

"He's a barman."

"A barman!" Waldo mimicked and the class roared loudly.

"*Quiet*." He wheeled on them. "You, Sweeny. Come out here." He reached inside the breast of his soutane and with a flourish produced a thin yellow cane, whipping it back and forth, testing it.

Kevin walked out to the front of the class, his face fiery red, the blood throbbing in his ears. He held out his hand. Waldo raised it higher, more to his liking, with the tip of the cane touching the underside of the upturned palm. He held it there for some time.

"If your brilliant father continues to do your homework

166

for you, Sweeny, you'll end up a barman yourself." Then he whipped the cane down expertly across the tips of his fingers and again just as the blood began to surge back into them. Each time the cane in its follow-through cracked loudly against the skirts of his soutane.

"You could have made a better job of it yourself. Other hand." The same ritual of raising and lowering the left hand with the tip of the cane to the desired height. "After all, I have taught you some Latin." *Crack*. "It would be hard to do any worse."

Kevin went back to his place resisting a desire to hug his hands under his armpits and stumbled on a schoolbag jutting into the aisle as he pushed into his desk. Again Waldo looked round the class and said, "Now we'll have it *right* from someone."

The class continued and Kevin nursed his fingers, out of the fray.

As the bell rang Waldo gathered up his books and said, "Sweeny, I want a word with you outside. Ave Maria, gratia plena . . ." It was not until the end of the corridor that Waldo turned to face him. He looked at Kevin and maintained his silence for a moment.

"Sweeny, I must apologize to you." Kevin bowed his head. "I meant your father no harm – he's probably a good man, a very good man."

"Yes, sir," said Kevin. The pain in his fingers had gone.

"Look at me when I'm talking, please." Kevin looked at his collar, his Adam's apple, then his face. It relaxed for a fraction and Kevin thought he was almost going to smile, but he became efficient, abrupt again.

"All right, very good, you may go back to your class."

"Yes, Father," Kevin nodded and moved back along the empty corridor.

Some nights when he had finished his homework early he would go down to meet his father coming home from work. It was dark, October, and he stood close against the high wall at the bus-stop trying to shelter from the cutting wind. His thin black blazer with the school emblem on the breast pocket and his short grey trousers, both new for starting grammar school, did little to keep him warm. He stood shivering, his hands in his trouser pockets and looked down at his knees which were blue and marbled, quivering uncontrollably. It was six o'clock when he left the house and he had been standing for fifteen minutes. Traffic began to thin out and the buses became less regular, carrying fewer and fewer passengers. There was a moment of silence when there was no traffic and he heard a piece of paper scraping along on pointed edges. He kicked it as it passed him. He thought of what had happened, of Waldo and his father. On the first day in class Waldo had picked out many boys by their names.

"Yes, I know your father well," or "I taught your elder brother. A fine priest he's made. Next."

"Sweeny, Father."

"Sweeny? Sweeny? – You're not Dr John's son, are you?"

"No, Father."

"Or anything to do with the milk people?"

"No, Father."

"Next." He passed on without further comment.

Twenty-five past six. Another bus turned the corner and Kevin saw his father standing on the platform. He moved forward to the stop as the bus slowed down. His father jumped lightly off and saw Kevin waiting for him. He clipped him over the head with the tightly rolled newspaper he was carrying.

"How are you big lad?"

"All right," said Kevin shivering. He humped his shoulders and set off beside his father, bumping into him uncertainly as he walked.

"How did it go today?" his father asked.

"All right." They kept silent until they reached the corner of their own street.

"What about the Latin?"

Kevin faltered, feeling a babyish desire to cry.

"How was it?"

"O.K. Fine."

"Good. I was a bit worried about it. It was done in a bit of a rush. Son, your Da's a genius." He smacked him with the paper again. Kevin laughed and slipped his hand into the warmth of his father's overcoat pocket, deep to the elbow.

THE LEFT OUTSIDE

BERYL C. LAWLEY

This story was first published around 1930 and even now, when people talk about 'a school story', this is exactly the kind of thing they have in mind – gymslips, hockey sticks and topping girls.

"**H**ULLO, JOCELYN. Heard the news?"

Aileen Golding, Head Prefect and Hockey Captain of St Monica's College for girls, hurried into the Sixth Form room on the First day of the spring term. Her chum, Jocelyn Buchanan, busily pinning time-tables on the notice board, swung round quickly.

"Cheerio, Aileen. Topping to see you again. What's the excitement?"

Dumping a pile of books on the table Aileen dropped into the nearest chair. Her brown eyes danced gleefully, and a scrap of wavy chestnut hair strayed from its place in her usually spruce shingle.

"We've two new girls in the Sixth," she announced. "A pair of cousins."

"Oh, Opal and Sybil Meredith." Jocelyn frowned, and selected another drawing-pin from the box at her elbow. "Not much reason to rejoice," she continued. "They won't be prefects, like the rest of us, and we can't treat them as if they were small fry. Fancy coming to a new school for a couple of terms! Rotten for them as well as for us."

"One of them isn't small fry," triumphed Aileen. "My sister, Joan, met Opal Meredith at the Fosters' dance. As boys were scarce they went down to supper together, and Opal talked of hockey from start to finish. Joan said she seemed a first-rate sort and knew all about the game. On the other hand, Sybil scarcely mentioned the subject, evidently she's not keen. Then I remembered that they came from Gratton Towers." Aileen paused dramatically.

"Well, what of that?" asked Jocelyn.

"Don't tell me you haven't heard of Meredith from Gratton Towers who plays in the Saxshire Junior County Eleven!" groaned Aileen.

"Gemini!" exclaimed Jocelyn, light beginning to dawn. "You don't say she's really come here?"

"Positively," nodded Aileen. "Joan put me wise. Did you ever know such luck? I've racked my brains all the hols trying to think of a fresh wing in Margaret's place. Opal mentioned to Joan that she was a forward. She's awfully modest, though; never said a word about playing for Saxshire."

"Pity she's only come for one hockey term," commented Jocelyn.

"Yes, but we'll have plenty of games between now and Easter. P'raps we'll even beat Wickley College this season. We might; our defence is splendid, and one star forward would make all the difference."

"Sybil may be good," suggested Jocelyn.

"No hope," shrugged Aileen. "She told Joan she was going to swot for matric and not trouble about games."

"Better get hold of Opal at break," advised Jocelyn. "The sooner she comes to a team practice the better. Crumbs, it's five to nine! Where's the bell?"

Seizing it from its niche Jocelyn strode into the passage ringing vigorously. From that moment until eleven o'clock she and Aileen had no further chance of conversation. During chemistry Jocelyn took in every detail of Opal's appearance. She was a tall, striking-looking girl, with copper-red hair, green eyes, and a rose-and-cream complexion. "A trifle affected," Jocelyn thought critically, and a minute afterwards decided that it was only shyness.

During an experiment Opal pulled up her jumper sleeve and Aileen noticed a heavily bandaged wrist. Directly Jocelyn had rung the eleven o'clock bell, and the Science Mistress had gone, Aileen crossed the laboratory.

"We'll be awfully bucked to have you in the Hockey Eleven," she smiled. "Turning out to practice today?"

Opal started and seemed to hesitate. "I'd love to come," she sighed, "but you see my wrist!" Holding out her arm she indicated the bandage.

"Will it keep you from playing long?" gasped Aileen, her delightful visions of at last defeating Wickley College beginning to fade.

"Don't know," said Opal doubtfully. "I sprained it in the Christmas hols. The doctor won't hear of my touching a stick for another couple of months, at least."

"How perfectly rotten!" Intense disappointment was in Aileen's voice as she gazed at Opal commiseratingly. "Was it in the Shropnor County match?"

"No, no," said Opal hastily. "Not a proper game at all. I was mucking about with my brother."

"What a shame!" sympathized Aileen. "Well, I shall have to find a temporary wing. You *will* play for us directly you're fit," she added anxiously.

"I may not be good enough," demurred Opal.

"Not good enough!" Aileen exploded. "My hat, what modesty! Sorry I must fly. Staircase duty, you know." With a parting wave she hurried into the corridor and posted herself outside the Fourth Form door.

"Opal's wrist doesn't seem to improve," remarked Jocelyn, eight weeks later, as she and Aileen walked home together one Tuesday afternoon.

"It's sickening!" groaned the Captain. "Here's the match against Wickley College next Saturday, and each left wing I try seems worse than the last."

"Opal's having massage with Miss Hatton," said Jocelyn casually. "Perhaps another four days of treatment will make a difference."

"After that it will be too late," said Aileen drearily. "No more important matches except Saturday's. It's the vilest luck! Fancy having a star turn in St Monica's and not being able to play her!"

"Have you tried Sybil?" suggested Jocelyn.

"Not an atom of good," retorted Aileen. "She hasn't practised once this term. Besides, you've only to look at her. Always has her nose in a book and is a perfect nonentity. Blessing she isn't a prefect."

"She's never had a chance," argued Jocelyn. "Nobody asks her to play. Matter of fact, she helped with the kids one afternoon when Miss Hatton had a rotten cold. I heard she had heaps of patience and they got on quite well."

"Patience with the infants doesn't make a First Eleven forward," sniffed Aileen. "As for asking her to play, I can see it's no use. She's only here to work and has no interest in anything else. Now, how's this for the team list? I've brought in Mary Thompson as the left wing."

For the next three days the reorganized eleven practised

hard, but it was evident that something was lacking. Try as they would the forwards were unable to score, even against the Second Eleven defence. Aileen, in the centre, was badly supported; her wings either passing squarely or too far ahead. By Saturday morning the Captain felt desperate.

"I'm horribly disappointed with Mary," she confided to Jocelyn. "Every day she gets worse."

"She's had a vile cold," returned her chum. "Miss Hatton said yesterday that she ought not to be playing."

The girls were sitting disconsolately in the Goldings' dining-room. Suddenly the front-door bell rang. A minute later the maid brought Aileen a note.

Tearing it open the latter gave an exclamation of disgust, and handed it to her chum.

"Phew!" groaned Jocelyn. "Mary in bed with a temperature. What's to be done?"

"Goodness knows!" snapped Aileen. "How are we to get anybody at the last minute?"

"Who's the reserve?"

"Geraldine Sutton; but she's a half."

"Get hold of Miss Hatton," advised Jocelyn. "She lives in the next road."

"So she does. I'd forgotten. Come with me."

Scrambling into coats and hats they rushed to the Games Mistress's house. Luckily she was at home, and listened to Aileen's woeful story sympathetically.

"It's very bad luck," she consoled briskly. "But why not play Opal?"

"Opal!" echoed Aileen in amazement. "But her wrist? What about that?"

"She may use it now," said Miss Hatton in surprise. "Dr Tapscott said so, yesterday. I wonder she didn't tell you the moment she knew."

"How perfectly splendid!" exulted Aileen. "Thank goodness I know!" Then her face clouded. "She lives three miles away," she ended.

"Mrs Meredith is on the telephone. Come along." Miss

Hatton pased into the hall, the girls following excitedly. "Tailton 2687."

A minute later the Games Captain was asking for Opal. But a voice at the other end of the wire informed her that the latter was out.

"What shall I do?" The usually confident Aileen turned to Miss Hatton.

"Leave a message," directed the Games Mistress. "Say it is very important, and ask the maid to write it down. If by any unlucky chance it should miss Opal, you have Geraldine Sutton as reserve."

"We can't do any more," said Aileen, resignedly hanging up the receiver. "Opal won't be home until one. Thank you so much, Miss Hatton." Together the girls left the house.

"Funny thing Opal never mentioning that her wrist was well," wondered Jocelyn.

"That's her modesty," retorted Aileen. "You don't half appreciate her. She's a jolly good sort."

"Um," grunted Jocelyn, and muttered something about playing for popularity.

"What did you say?" said Aileen sharply.

But Jocelyn refused to continue, and talked of the coming match. For the rest of the morning Aileen was on thorns, wondering whether Opal would receive the message. The Goldings were not on the telephone so it was unlikely that she would hear any news before the afternoon.

Directly dinner was over Aileen collected her hockey things and called for Jocelyn. Wickley College was in the next town, some five miles distant, and the two caught a bus that passed the field. Crossing the ground to the pavilion Aileen eagerly scanned the group of St Monica's girls already arrived. But Opal was not to be seen, and desperately she hurried to Miss Hatton.

"I've not heard a word," replied the Games Mistress, answering her query. "I should say that Opal is most certainly coming. Is Geraldine Sutton here?"

"Everyone else has arrived," said Aileen anxiously.

175

"We're all rather early," observed Miss Hatton. "It is only twenty past two."

Just then Aileen's attention was taken by the Wickley College captain. Politely she tried to listen to trivial hockey gossip, but her eyes constantly strayed to the St Monica group near the door.

"Are you all ready?" the home captain inquired at last.

"We were one player short, just now," said Aileen in worried tones. "Would you excuse me a moment? I'll see if she has arrived."

"A St Monica player has jumped off that bus!" cried Jocelyn, as Aileen joined her. "I caught a glimpse of the green and white hat-band and a hockey stick. It must be Opal."

"Good!" breathed Aileen. "Sorry, Gerry!" She threw the reserve an apologetic glance.

"That's all right," said Geraldine, who was renowned for her good nature. "Doesn't matter a bit."

"Jocelyn!" gasped Aileen, frantically clutching her chum's arm. "It's not Opal!"

"Golly, no! Who is it?"

"It's –" Words failed Aileen and she stuttered wildly. "It's – it's Sybil!"

"What!"

But it was only too true. Dressed in hockey tunic and equipped with stick, pads, and shoes, Sybil ran across the field and shyly entered the pavilion.

"Opal is terribly sorry but she can't play," she panted. "She expects you have a reserve forward but wanted me to come along in case of accidents. Left wing happens to be my place," she ended self-consciously.

Aileen gasped, looking ready to collapse, and there were one or two mild titters. Suddenly Geraldine pushed to her Captain's side.

"Play Sybil, Aileen," she whispered. "I'm not a wing, and should only make a howling mess of everything. Give her a chance."

"Wait a minute." Utterly bewildered Aileen consulted with Miss Hatton. The Games Mistress inclined to Geraldine's suggestion.

"See what Sybil can do," she advised. "Geraldine is quite right; she is certainly not a wing. It is not risking much."

"Very well, Miss Hatton," murmured Aileen, but her voice sounded rebellious. Privately, she considered that Sybil had pushed herself forward in the most brazen manner, and richly deserved a thorough snubbing. But there was not time for indignation. Winning the toss, Aileen decided to play downfield during the first half. Leading her team on to the ground she beckoned to Jocelyn.

"Sybil, left wing," she murmured. "Otherwise, left outside! Twig my meaning?"

"You really and truly don't want me to pass to her?" gasped the centre half.

"Exactly. Keep the ball on the right. She's probably no good and is better, well, left outside!" Aileen smiled at her own joke.

"What a rotten thing to do!" said Jocelyn indignantly.

Aileen flushed. "Am I captain or am I not?" she inquired heatedly.

There was silence as the teams took their places. The centre forwards bullied off, and Aileen neatly flicked the ball back to Jocelyn. With a swinging drive the centre half cleared to her right wing, who promptly flashed downfield. The College left back hesitated. Should she come out to tackle the runaway, or stay and mark the inner? Deciding on the bolder course she dashed to the side line. In a trice the wing centred, well ahead of the visiting forwards. The latter swooped onward, but the goalkeeper was too quick. Running out, she cleared upfield with a well-timed shot.

"Oh, topping!" shouted the College supporters. "Follow up, fowards!"

The scarlet-tunicked home team pressed hard. Their wings were swift and tricky, soon having the opposing defence thoroughly worried. Every time Aileen secured the ball she doggedly swung it out to her right. Sybil, on the extreme left, was thoroughly starved. Occasionally her inner flicked a pass which, however, the wing seemed disinclined to keep. Invariably she drove hard across field at once, as if realizing Aileen's mistrust.

After twenty minutes play the St Monica goalkeeper conceded a penalty corner. The home right wing sent the ball straight to her inner. Forgetting their instructions, the visiting defence instantly converged towards the danger spot. Making no attempt to shoot, the inner calmly tapped the ball across the circle to her totally unmarked left wing; who promptly opened the College score.

"Shot!" chorused the onlookers, as the players returned to the centre of the field.

"Stick to it, St Monica's!" chanted fifty voices.

Just before half-time the visiting right inner broke away. As she reached the circle she shot hard, but the goalkeeper cleared up midfield. Stopping the ball with the tip of her reversed stick, Jocelyn pushed it to her Captain. But Aileen was well marked, and flicked back to her chum as she dashed into the circle. Glancing in front for a second the centre half realized the position. Getting the head of her stick under the ball she scooped it over the mass of rival sticks and feet into the corner of the goal.

"One all!" shrieked the spectators, agog with excitement, as the whistle blew for half-time.

Standing in the centre of her team group Aileen offered some trenchant advice. When they took their places for the restart, everybody was not only determined to score at least once more, but also to keep their opponents well away from the shooting circle.

For twenty minutes play was of the humdrum order. Neither goalkeeper was seriously threatened, and the onlookers were confidently expecting a draw. Then some brilliant midfield passing by the home forwards brought their centre into a favourable position. The latter was an experienced match player and made few mistakes. Lifting her stick she drove hard, and excited cheers from the College signalled that they had, once more, taken the lead.

St Monica's struggled desperately but luck was against them. Twice Aileen hit the post, and once the right inner missed by inches. Five minutes before time the ball was sent to the halfway line, just between Sybil and her inner.

"Yours, Doris!" shouted Aileen.

But before the inner could dash to the spot Sybil had pounced. Taking no notice of her Captain's frantic injunctions to pass, she fled upfield. Flicking the ball over the defence's sticks she gained the circle; and, whilst the astonished goalkeeper was deciding what to do, flashed into the centre and equalized.

Both the St Monica's team and spectators were paralysed with amazement. Too astounded to cheer, they gaped open-mouthed as their left wing modestly returned to her place. Collecting her wits Aileen realized that here was their only chance. Three more minutes' play and Jocelyn had the ball.

"Pass left!" she called frantically.

Promptly the centre half obeyed, sending the ball well ahead. Sybil, securing it, pelted upfield. As the defence bore down on her, she centred. Aileen shot, but the goalkeeper cleared.

"Quickly!" implored St Monica's Captain, as Sybil retrieved the ball. "Shoot!"

There was a sharp crack, and the goalkeeper lunged to her right. Sybil had entered the circle and her aim was deadly. An uproar of cheering, positively drowning the final whistle, announced that at last St Monica's had broken their unfortunate record and beaten the College.

"You are lucky to have a Junior County player," said the home Captain enviously to Aileen, as they crossed to the pavilion.

"She isn't playing," the latter explained.

"Not playing!" ejaculated the College Captain. "She's just shot two goals!"

"Sybil Meredith!" gasped Aileen, her mind in a whirl.

"That's the name. Surely you knew," the Colleger eyed her curiously.

"I've made an awful mistake," groaned Aileen. "Sybil." Grasping the left wing's wrist she poured out a string of eager questions.

"I do play for Saxshire," Sybil admitted. "And as I wasn't asked to school practices, I've been turning out for the Wickley Ladies on Saturday afternoons."

"Opal actually let me think that she was the County player," said Aileen indignantly.

"Don't be hard on her," pleaded Sybil. "It's been her great ambition to shine at hockey and she hated to disillusion you. When the maid gave her the phone message, this morning, she was in a terrible stew. Miss Hatton knew her wrist had recovered so the game was up. I tried to keep the ball away from myself, today, just to make you think I couldn't play; but when the position was so critical I simply had to butt in."

"Jolly glad you did," said Aileen fervently. "Frightfully sporting, after I'd perfectly starved you."

"I scarcely expected passes," answered Sybil, her eyes twinkling. "As it happens I've very sharp ears." Then she added humorously. "Don't you think, though, that it's really rather funny two goals being scored by an absolutely 'left outside'?"

A SCHOOL STORY

M. R. JAMES

Two MEN in a smoking-room were talking of their private-school days. "At *our* school," said A., "we had a ghost's footmark on the staircase. What was it like? Oh, very unconvincing. Just the shape of a shoe, with a square toe, if I remember right. The staircase was a stone one. I never heard any story about the thing. That seems odd, when you come to think of it. Why didn't somebody invent one, I wonder?"

"You never can tell with little boys. They have a mythology of their own. There's a subject for you, by the way – 'The Folklore of Private Schools'."

"Yes; the crop is rather scanty, though. I imagine, if you were to investigate the cycle of ghost stories, for instance, which the boys at private schools tell each other, they would all turn out to be highly-compressed versions of stories out of books."

"Nowadays the *Strand* and *Pearson's*, and so on, would be extensively drawn upon."

"No doubt: they weren't born or thought of in *my* time. Let's see. I wonder if I can remember the staple ones that I was told. First, there was the house with a room in which a series of people insisted on passing a night; and each of them in the morning was found kneeling in a corner, and had just time to say, 'I've seen it', and died."

"Wasn't that the house in Berkeley Square?"

"I dare say it was. Then there was the man who heard a noise in the passage at night, opened his door, and saw someone crawling towards him on all fours with his eye hanging out on his cheek. There was besides, let me think – Yes! the room where a man was found dead in bed with a horseshoe mark on his forehead, and the floor under the bed was covered with marks of horseshoes also; I don't know why. Also there was the lady who, on locking her bedroom door in a strange house, heard a thin voice among the bed curtains say, 'Now we're shut in for the night.' None of those had any explanation or sequel. I wonder if they go on still, those stories."

"Oh, likely enough – with additions from the magazines, as I said. You never heard, did you, of a real ghost at a private school? I thought not; nobody has that ever I came across."

"From the way in which you said that, I gather that *you* have."

"I really don't know; but this is what was in my mind. It happened at my private school thirty odd years ago, and I haven't any explanation of it.

"The school I mean was near London. It was established in a large and fairly old house – a great white building with very fine grounds about it; there were large cedars in the garden, as there are in so many of the older gardens in the. Thames valley, and ancient elms in the three or four fields which we used for our games. I think probably it was quite an attractive place, but boys seldom allow that their schools possess any tolerable features.

"I came to the school in a September, soon after the year 1870; and among the boys who arrived on the same day was one whom I took to: a Highland boy, whom I will call McLeod. I needn't spend time in describing him: the main thing is that I got to know him very well. He was not an exceptional boy in any way – not particularly good at books or games – but he suited me.

"The school was a large one: there must have been from 120 to 130 boys there as a rule, and so a considerable staff of masters was required, and there were rather frequent changes among them.

"One term – perhaps it was my third or fourth – a new master made his appearance. His name was Sampson. He was a tallish, stoutish, pale, black-bearded man. I think we liked him: he had travelled a good deal, and had stories which amused us on our school walks, so that there was some competition among us to get within earshot of him. I remember too – dear me, I have hardly thought of it since then! – that he had a charm on his watch-chain that attracted my attention one day, and he let me examine it. It was, I now suppose, a gold Byzantine coin; there was an effigy of some absurd emperor on one side; the other side had been worn practically smooth, and he had had cut on it – rather barbarously – his own initials, G.W.S., and a date, 24 July, 1865. Yes, I can see it now: he told me he had picked it up in Constantinople: it was about the size of a florin, perhaps rather smaller.

"Well, the first odd thing that happened was this. Sampson was doing Latin grammar with us. One of his favourite methods – perhaps it is rather a good one – was to make us construct sentences out of our own heads to illustrate the rules he was trying to make us learn. Of course that is a thing which gives a silly boy a chance of being impertinent: there are lots of school stories in which that happens – or anyhow there might be. But Sampson was too good a disciplinarian for us to think of trying that on with him. Now, on this occasion he was telling us how to express *remembering* in Latin: and he ordered us each to make a sentence bringing in the verb *memini*, 'I remember'. Well, most of us made up some ordinary sentence such as 'I remember my father', or 'He remembers his book', or something equally uninteresting: and I dare say a good many put down *memino librum meum*, and so forth: but the boy I mentioned – McLeod – was evidently thinking of something more elaborate than that. The rest of us wanted to have our sentences passed, and get on to something else, so some kicked him under the desk, and I, who was next to him, poked him and whispered to him to look sharp. But he didn't seem to attend. I looked at his paper and saw he had put down nothing at all. So I jogged him again harder than before and upbraided him sharply for keeping us all waiting. That did have some effect. He started and seemed to wake up, and then very quickly he scribbled about a couple of lines on his paper, and showed it up with the rest. As it was the last, or nearly the last, to come in, and as Sampson had a good deal to say to the boys who had written *meminiscimus patri meo* and the rest of it, it turned out that the clock struck twelve before he had got to McLeod, and McLeod had to wait afterwards to have his sentence corrected. There was nothing much going on outside when I got out, so I waited for him to come. He came very slowly when he did arrive, and I guessed there had been some sort of trouble. 'Well,' I said, 'what did you get?' 'Oh, I don't know,' said McLeod, 'nothing much: but I think Sampson's rather sick with me.' 'Why, did you show him up some rot?' 'No fear,' he said. 'It was all right as far as I could see: it was like this: *Memento* – that's right enough for remember, and it takes a genitive – *memento putei inter quattuor taxos.*' 'What silly rot!' I said. 'What made you shove that down? What does it mean?' 'That's the funny part,' said McLeod. 'I'm not quite sure what it does mean. All I know is, it just came into my head and I corked it down. I know what I *think* it means, because just before I wrote it down I had a sort of picture of it in my head: I believe it means "Remember the well among the four" – what are those dark sort of trees that have red berries on them?' 'Mountain ashes, I s'pose you mean.' 'I never heard of them,' said McLeod; 'no, I'll tell you – yews.' 'Well, and what did Sampson say?' 'Why, he was jolly odd about it. When he read it he got up and went to the mantelpiece and stopped quite a long time without saying anything, with his back to me. And then he said, without turning round, and rather quiet, "What do you suppose that means?" I told him what I thought; only I couldn't remember the name of the silly tree: and then he wanted to know why I put it down, and I had to say something or other. And after that he left off talking about it, and asked me how long I'd been here, and where my people lived, and things like that: and then I came away: but he wasn't looking a bit well.'

"I don't remember any more that was said by either of us about this. Next day McLeod took to his bed with a chill or something of the kind, and it was a week or more before he was in school again. And as much as a month went by without anything happening that was noticeable. Whether or not Mr Sampson was really startled, as McLeod had thought, he didn't show it. I am pretty sure, of course, now, that there was something very curious in his past history, but I'm not going to pretend that we boys were sharp enough to guess any such thing.

"There was one other incident of the same kind as the last which I told you. Several times since that day we had had to make up examples in school to illustrate different rules, but there had never been any row except when we did them wrong. At last there came a day when we were going through those dismal things which people call Conditional Sentences, and we were told to make a conditional sentence, expressing a future consequence. We did it, right or wrong, and showed up our bits of paper, and Sampson began looking through them. All at once he got up, made some odd sort of noise in his throat, and rushed out by a door that was just by his desk. We sat there for a minute or two, and then – I suppose it was incorrect – but we went up, I and one or two others, to look at the papers on his desk. Of course I thought someone must have put down some nonsense or other, and Sampson had gone off to report him. All the same, I noticed that he hadn't taken any of the

papers with him when he ran out. Well, the top paper on the desk was written in red ink – which no one used – and it wasn't in anyone's hand who was in the class. They all looked at it – McLeod and all – and took their dying oaths that it wasn't theirs. Then I thought of counting the bits of paper. And of this I made quite certain: that there were seventeen bits of paper on the desk, and sixteen boys in the form. Well, I bagged the extra paper, and kept it, and I believe I have it now. And now you will want to know what was written on it. It was simple enough, and harmless enough, I should have said.

" '*Si tu non veneris ad me, ego veniam ad te*', which means, I suppose, 'If you don't come to me, I'll come to you.' "

"Could you show me the paper?" interrupted the listener.

"Yes, I could: but there's another odd thing about it. That same afternoon I took it out of my locker – I know for certain it was the same bit, for I made a finger-mark on it – and no single trace of writing of any kind was there on it. I kept it, as I said, and since that time I have tried various experiments to see whether sympathetic ink had been used, but absolutely without result.

"So much for that. After about half an hour Sampson looked in again, said he had felt very unwell, and told us we might go. He came rather gingerly to his desk, and gave just one look at the uppermost paper: and I suppose he thought he must have been dreaming: anyhow, he asked no questions.

"That day was a half-holiday, and next day Sampson was in school again, much as usual. That night the third and last incident in my story happened.

"We – McLeod and I – slept in a dormitory at right angles to the main building. Sampson slept in the main building on the first floor. There was a very bright full moon. At an hour which I can't tell exactly, but some time between one and two, I was woken up by somebody shaking me. It was McLeod; and a nice state of mind he seemed to be in. 'Come,' he said – 'come! there's a burglar getting in through Sampson's window.' As soon as I could speak, I said, 'Well, why not call out and wake everybody up?' 'No, no,' he said, 'I'm not sure who it is: don't make a row: come and look.' Naturally I came and looked, and naturally there was no one there. I was cross enough, and should have called McLeod plenty of names: only – I couldn't tell why – it seemed to me that there *was* something wrong – something that made me very glad I wasn't alone to face it. We were still at the window looking out, and as soon as I could, I asked him what he had heard or seen. 'I didn't *hear* anything at all,' he said, 'but about five minutes before I woke you, I found myself looking out of this window here, and there was a man sitting or kneeling on Sampson's window-sill, and looking in, and I thought he was beckoning.' 'What sort of man?' McLeod wriggled. 'I don't know,' he said, 'but I can tell you one thing – he was beastly thin: and he looked as if he was wet all over: and,' he said, looking round and whispering as if he hardly liked to hear himself, 'I'm not at all sure that he was alive.'

"We went on talking in whispers some time longer, and eventually crept back to bed. No one else in the room woke or stirred the whole time. I believe we did sleep a bit afterwards, but we were very cheap next day.

"And next day Mr Sampson was gone: not to be found: and I believe no trace of him has ever come to light since. In thinking it over, one of the oddest things about it all has seemed to me to be the fact that neither McLeod nor I ever mentioned what we had seen to any third person whatever. Of course no questions were asked on the subject, and if they had been, I am inclined to believe that we could not have made any answer: we seemed unable to speak about it.

"That is my story," said the narrator. "The only approach to a ghost story connected with a school that I know, but still, I think, an approach to such a thing."

The sequel to this may perhaps be reckoned highly conventional; but a sequel there is, and so it must be produced. There had been more than one listener to the story, and, in the latter part of that same year, or of the next, one such listener was staying at a country house in Ireland.

One evening his host was turning over a drawer full of odds and ends in the smoking-room. Suddenly he put his hand upon a little box. "Now," he said, "you know about old things; tell me what that is." My friend opened the little box, and found in it a thin gold chain with an object attached to it. He glanced at the object and then took off his spectacles to examine it more narrowly. "What's the history of this?" he asked. "Odd enough," was the answer. "You know the yew thicket in the shrubbery: well, a year or two back we were cleaning out the old well that used to be in the clearing here, and what do you suppose we found?"

"Is it possible that you found a body?" said the visitor, with an odd feeling of nervousness.

"We did that: but what's more, in every sense of the word, we found two."

"Good Heavens! Two? Was there anything to show how they got there? Was this thing found with them?"

"It was. Amongst the rags of the clothes that were on one of the bodies. A bad business, whatever the story of it may have been. One body had the arms tight round the other. They must have been there thirty years or more – long enough before we came to this place. You may judge we filled the well up fast enough. Do you make anything of what's cut on that gold coin you have there?"

"I think I can," said my friend, holding it to the light (but he read it without much difficulty); "it seems to be G.W.S., 24 July, 1865."

A NEW BOY

TALBOT BAINES REED

from The Fifth Form At St Dominic's

Written over a hundred years ago, the first real school story is still one of the best. Oliver Greenfield is already a senior boy at St Dominic's, but soon after the opening of the book his younger brother Stephen joins the Fourth Form. School is not quite what he was expecting.

"Good Bye, my boy; God bless you! and don't forget to tell the housekeeper about airing your flannel vests."

With this final benediction ringing in his ears, the train which was to carry Master Stephen Greenfield from London to St Dominic's steamed slowly out of the station, leaving his widowed mother to return lonely and sorrowful to the home from which, before this day, her youngest son had never wandered far without her.

Stephen, if the truth must be told, was hardly as affected by the parting as his poor mother. Not that he was not sorry to leave home, or that he did not love her he left behind; but with all the world before him, he was at present far too excited to think of anything rationally. Besides, that last remark about the flannel vests had greatly disturbed him. The carriage was full of people, who must have heard it, and would be sure to set him down as no end of a milksop and mollycoddle.

He blushed to the roots of his hair as he pulled up the window and sat down in his corner, feeling quite certain every one of his fellow-travellers must be secretly smiling at his expense. He wished his mother would have whispered that last sentence. It wasn't fair to him. In short, Stephen felt a trifle aggrieved; and, with a view to manifesting his hardihood, and dispelling all false impressions caused by the maternal injunction, he let down the window and put his bare head out of it for about a quarter of an hour, until a speck of dust settled in his eye and drove him back to his seat.

It is decidedly awkward to get dust in your eye when you want to figure as a hero, for the eyes will water, and must be wiped, and that looks particularly like weeping. Stephen refrained from using his handkerchief as long as he could; but it was no use; he must wipe his eye in the presence of his fellow-passengers. However, if he whistled a tune while doing so, no one could suspect him of real tears; so he struck up, 'Glide along, my bonny boat', as cheerfully as he could, and mopped his smarting eye at the same time. Alas! the dust only got farther in, and the music, after half an hour's heroic perseverance, flagged altogether. It was no use trying to appear heroic any longer, so, what with pain and a dawning sense of loneliness and home-sickness, Stephen shed a few real tears into his handkerchief, an indulgence which did him good in every way, for it not only relieved his drooping spirits, but washed that wretched piece of dust fairly out of its hiding-place.

This relief, with the aid of a bun and a bottle of ginger-beer at one of the stations, set him, so to speak, on his feet again, and he was able to occupy the rest of his journey very pleasantly in drumming his heels on the floor, and imagining to himself all the marvellous exploits which were to mark his career at St Dominic's. He was to be a prodigy in his new school from the very first; in a few terms he was to be captain of the cricket club, and meanwhile was to gain the favour of the Sixth by helping them regularly in their lessons, and fighting any one against whom a special champion should be requisite. He was, indeed, just being invited to dinner with the Doctor, who was about to consult him concerning some points of school management, when the train suddenly pulled up at Maltby, and his brother Oliver's head looked in at the window with a "Hullo! here you are! Tumble out!"

Oliver and Stephen were Mrs Greenfield's only children. Their father had died twelve years ago, when Stephen was a baby, and the two boys had been left in charge of an uncle, who had carefully watched over their education, and persuaded his sister to allow her elder boy to go to a public school. Mrs Greenfield had consented, with many tremblings, and Oliver had, four years ago, been sent to St Dominic's, where he was now one of the head boys in the Fifth Form. Only a few weeks before the opening of this story the boys' uncle had died, leaving in his will a provision for sending Stephen to the same school as his brother, or any other his mother might select. The poor widow, loth to give up her boy, yet fain to accept the offer held out, chose to send Stephen to St Dominic's too, and this was the reason of that young gentleman's present appearance on the stage at that centre of learning.

"I'll send up your traps by the carter; we can walk," said Oliver, taking his young brother into charge.

Stephen was only too glad, as it gave him time to breathe before plunging at once into the scene of his future exploits. "Is it far?" he asked.

"Only a mile," said Oliver; "come on. Hullo, Rick, where have you been to?"

This was addressed to Ricketts, whom they met just outside the station.

"Oh! to Sherren's about my togs. I wanted them for the match tomorrow, you know. I've told him if he doesn't send them up in time we'll all get our things made in London, so I guess he'll hurry himself for once. Oh, look here! did you get a paper with the result of the American match? Bother! Here, you kid, what's your name, cut back to the station and get a daily. Look sharp! Bring it to me in my room. Come on, Greenfield."

Master Stephen looked so astonished at this cool request from a total stranger that both the elder boys laughed.

"This is my young brother, Rick, just come –"

"Oh, I beg your pardon," said Mr Ricketts, blushing, "I'll go –"

"No, I'll go," said Stephen, darting off, and expending a penny of his own to get this magnifico of the Fifth his paper.

This little incident served to break the ice for the new boy, who felt highly honoured when Ricketts said he was 'much obliged to him'.

"By the way," said Oliver, suddenly, "I ought to get my togs up too. Bother that Sherren! I say, Rick, see my young brother up to the school, will you? while I cut back; he can wait in my study."

Stephen felt very desolate to be left thus alone the moment after his arrival, and it did not add to his pleasure to observe that Ricketts by no means appeared to look upon the task of seeing him to St Dominic's as a privilege. They walked on in silence for about half a mile, and then encountered several groups of boys strolling out along the road. Ricketts stopped to talk to several of them, and was very nearly going off with one of the party, when he suddenly remembered his charge. It was rather humiliating this, for Stephen; and already his triumphal entry into St Dominic's was beginning to be shorn of some of its glory. No one noticed him; and the only one that paid him the least attention appeared to look upon him as a nuisance.

"Here, Tony," suddenly shouted Ricketts to Pembury, who was jogging along on his crutches a little way ahead, towards the school; "do you mind showing this kid the way up? I have to go back with Wren. There's a good fellow."

"Well, that's cool," replied Master Pembury; "I'm not a

kid-conductor! Come on, youngster; I suppose you haven't got a name, have you?"

"Yes, Stephen Greenfield."

"Oh, brother of our dear friend Oliver; I hope you'll turn out a better boy than him, he's a shocking character."

Stephen looked concerned. "I'm sure he doesn't mean to do what's wrong," began he, apologetically.

"That's just it, my boy. If he doesn't mean to do it, why on earth does he do it? I shall be sorry if he's expelled, very sorry. But come on; don't mind if I walk too fast," added he, hobbling along by Stephen's side.

Stephen did not know what to think. If Ricketts had not addressed his companion as 'Tony' he would have fancied he was one of the masters, he spoke with such an air of condescension. Stephen felt very uncomfortable, too, to hear what had been told him about Oliver. If he had not been told, he could not have believed his brother was anything but perfection.

"I'm lame, you see," said Pembury, presently. "You are quite sure you see? Look at my left leg."

"I see," said Stephen, blushing; "I – I hope it doesn't hurt."

"Only when I wash my face. But never mind that; Vulcan was lame too, but then he never washed. You know who Vulcan was, of course?"

"No, I don't think so," faltered Stephen, beginning to feel very uneasy and ignorant.

"Not know Vulcan? My eye! where have you been brought up? Then of course you don't know anything about the Tenth Fiji War? No? I thought not. Dreadful! We shall have to see what you do know. Come on."

Stephen entered St Dominic's thoroughly crestfallen, and fully convinced he was the most ignorant boy that ever entered a public school. The crowds of boys in the playground frightened him, and even the little boys inspired him with awe. *They*, at any rate, had heard of Vulcan, and knew about the Tenth Fiji War!

"Here," said Anthony, "is your brother's study. Sit here till he returns, and make the most of your time, for you'll have to put your best foot foremost tomorrow in the Doctor's exam."

So saying, he left abruptly, and the poor lad found himself alone, in about as miserable a frame of mind as a new boy would wish to be in.

He looked about the study; there were some shelves with books on them. There was a little bed let into the wall on one side; there was an easy-chair, and what professed to be a sofa; and there was a pile of miscellanies, consisting of bats and boots and collars and papers, heaped up in the corner, which appeared to be the most abundantly furnished portion of the little room. Stephen sat there, very dismal, and wishing himself home again once more, when the door suddenly opened and a small boy of his own age appeared.

"Hullo! What do you want?" demanded this hero.

"I'm waiting for my brother."

"Who's your brother?"

"Oliver Greenfield."

"Oh, all right! you can get his tea as well as I can; you'll find all the things in the cupboard there. And look here, tell him Bullinger wants to know if he can lend him some jam – about half a pint, tell him."

Poor Stephen! even the small boys ordered him about, and regarded him as nobody. He would fain have inquired of this young gentleman something about Vulcan, and have had the advantage of his experience in the preparation of his brother's tea; but the youth seemed pressed for time, and vanished.

As well as he could, Stephen extricated the paraphernalia of his brother's tea-table from the cupboard, and set it out in order on the table, making the tea as well as profound inexperience of the mystery and a kettle full of lukewarm water would permit. Then he sat and waited.

Before Oliver arrived, four visitors broke in upon Stephen's vigil. The first came 'to borrow' some tea, and helped himself coolly to two teaspoonfuls out of Oliver's canister. Stephen stood by aghast and speechless.

"Tell him I'll owe it him," calmly remarked the young gentleman, as he departed with his booty, whistling a cheerful ditty.

Then a fag came in and took a spoon, and after him another fag, with a mug, into which he poured half of the contents of Oliver's milk-jug; and finally a big fellow rushed in in a desperate hurry and snatched up a chair and made off with it.

Stephen wondered the roof of St Dominic's did not fall in upon these shameless marauders, and was just contemplating putting the stores all back again into the cupboard to prevent further piracy, when the welcome sound of Oliver's voice in the passage put an end to further suspense.

"Well, here you are," said Oliver, entering with a friend. "Wray, this is my young brother, just turned up."

"How are you?" said Wraysford, in a voice which won over Stephen at once; "I heard you were coming. Have you –"

"Oh!" suddenly ejaculated Oliver, lifting up the lid of his teapot. "If that young wretch Paul hasn't been and made my tea with coal-dust and cold water! I'd like to scrag him! And – upon my word – oh, this is too much! – just look, Wray, how he's laid the table out! Those Guinea-pigs are beyond all patience. Where *is* the beggar?"

"Oh!" exclaimed Stephen, starting up, very red in the face, as his brother went to the door; "it wasn't him. I made the tea. The boy told me to, and I didn't know the way. I had to guess."

Oliver and Wraysford both burst out laughing.

"A pretty good guess, too, youngster," said Wraysford. "When you come and fag for me I'll give you a few lessons to begin with."

"Oh! by the way, Wray," said Oliver, "that's all knocked on the head. Loman makes out the captain promised him the first new boy that came. I'm awfully sorry."

"Just like Loman's cheek. I believe he did it on purpose to spite me or you. I say, Greenfield, I'd kick up a row about it if I were you."

"What's the use, if the captain says so?" answered Oliver. "Besides, Loman's a monitor, bad luck to him!"

"Loman's a fellow I don't take a great fancy to," said Wraysford. "I wouldn't care for a young brother of mine to fag to him."

"You are prejudiced, old man," said Oliver. "But I wish all the same Stephen was to fag for you. It's a pity, but it can't be helped."

"I'll speak to the captain, anyhow," growled Wraysford, sitting down to his tea.

All this was not very pleasant for Stephen, who gathered that he was destined to serve a not very desirable personage in the capacity of fag, instead of, as he would have liked, his brother's friend Wraysford.

However, he did justice to the tea, bad as it was, and the sardines Oliver had brought from Maltby. He was relieved, too, to find that his brother was not greatly exasperated on hearing of the various raids which had been made on his provisions, or greatly disconcerted at Mr Bullinger's modest request for half a pint of jam.

Then, as the talk fell upon home, and cricket, and other cheerful topics, the small boy gradually forgot his troubles, even down to the Fiji War, and finished up his first evening at St Dominic's in a good deal more cheerful frame of mind than that in which he had begun it.

It so happened that on the day following Stephen Greenfield's arrival at St Dominic's, the head master, Dr Senior, was absent.

This circumstance gave great satisfaction to the new boy when his brother told him of it, as it put off for another twenty-four hours the awful moment when he would be forced to expose his ignorance before that terrible personage.

"You'd better stick about in my room while I'm in school," said Oliver, "and then you can come down to the cricket-field and see the practice. By the way, some of the fellows may be in to bag my ink; they always run short on Friday; but don't let them take it, for I shall want it tonight. Ta, ta; give my love to the *mater* if you're writing home. I'll be back for you after the twelve bell."

And off he went, leaving Stephen to follow his own sweet devices for three hours.

That young gentleman was at no loss how to occupy part of the time. He must write home. So after much searching he unearthed a crumpled sheet of note-paper from one of the drawers, and set himself to his task. As he wrote, and his thoughts flew back to the home and the mother he had left only yesterday, his spirits fell, and the home-sickness came over him worse than ever. What would he not give to change places with this very letter, and go back home!

Here, no one cared for him, every one seemed to despise him. He wasn't used to those rough public schools, and would never get on at St Dominic's. Ah! that wretched Tenth Fiji War. What *would* become of him tomorrow when the Doctor would be back? There was no one to help him. Even Oliver seemed determined to let him fight his own battles.

Poor boy! He sat back in his chair and let his mind wander once more back to the snug little home he had left. And, as he did so, his eyes unconsciously filled with tears, and he felt as if he would give anything to escape from St Dominic's.

At this moment the door opened and a small boy entered.

He did not seem to expect to find any one in the room, for he uttered a hurried "Hullo!" as he caught sight of Stephen.

Stephen quickly dashed away a tear and looked up.

"Where's Greenfield?" demanded the small boy.

"He's in school," replied Stephen.

"Hullo! what are you blubbering at?" cried the small boy, growing very bold and patronizing all of a sudden, "eh?"

Stephen did not answer this home question.

"I suppose you are a new kid, just left your mammy?" observed the other, with the air of a man of forty; "what's your name, young 'un?"

"Stephen Greenfield."

"Oh, my! is it? What form are you in?"

"I don't know yet."

"Haven't you been examined?"

"No, not yet."

"Oh, of course; old Senior's away. Never mind, you'll catch it tomorrow, blub-baby!"

This last epithet was thrown in in such a very gratuitous and offensive way, that Stephen did not exactly like it.

The small youth, however, finding himself in a bantering mood, pursued his questions with increasing venom.

"I suppose they call you Steenie at home?" he observed, with a sneer that was meant to be quite annihilating.

"No, they don't," replied Stephen; "mother calls me Steevie."

"Oh, Steevie, does she? Well, Steevie, were you ever licked over the knuckles with a ruler?"

"No," replied Stephen; "why?"

"Because you will be – I know who'll do it, too, and kick you on the shins, too, if you're cheeky!"

Stephen was quite at a loss whether to receive this piece of news in the light of information or a threat. He was inclined to believe it the latter; and as he was a rash youth, he somewhat tartly replied,

"*You* won't!"

The small boy looked astounded – not that he ever contemplated attempting the chastisement about which he had talked; but the idea of a new boy defying *him*, one of the chosen leaders of the Tadpoles, who had been at St Dominic's two years, was amazing. He glared at the rash Stephen for half a minute, and then broke out,

"Won't I? that's all! you see, you pretty little blubber boy! Yow-ow-ow! little sneak! why don't you cut behind your mammy's skirt, if you're afraid? I would cry if I were you. Where's his bottle? Poor infant! Yow-ow-boo-boo!"

This tornado, delivered with increasing vehemence and offensiveness, quite overpowered Stephen, who stared at the boy as if he had been a talking frog.

That youth evidently seemed to expect that his speech would produce a far deeper impression than it did, for he looked quite angry when Stephen made no reply.

"Wretched little sneak!" the amiable one continued; "I suppose he'll go peaching to his big brother. Never mind, *we'll* pay you out, see if we don't! Go and kiss your mammy, and tell your big brother what they did to little duckie Steevie, did they then? they shouldn't! Give him a suck of his bottle! oh, my!" and he finished up with a most withering laugh. Then, suddenly remembering his errand, he walked up to the table, and said,

"I want that inkpot!"

Now was Stephen's time. He was just in the humour for an argument with this young Philistine.

"What for?"

"What's that to you? Give it up!"

"I sha'n't give it up; Oliver said it was not to be taken."

"What do you say?" yelled the small boy, almost beside himself with rage and astonishment.

"It's my brother's ink, and I'm not to give it up," said Stephen, shutting the top and keeping his hand on it.

It was enough! The patriarch of the Tadpoles knew his strong point was in words rather than action; but this could not be endured. At whatever risk, the dignity of his order must be maintained, and this insolent, mad new boy must be – kicked.

THE CHOICE IS YOURS

JAN MARK

THE MUSIC ROOM was on one side of the quadrangle and the Changing Room faced it on the other. They were linked by a corridor that made up the third side, and the fourth was the view across the playing-fields. In the Music Room Miss Helen Francis sat at the piano, head bent over the keyboard as her fingers tittuped from note to note, and swaying back and forth like a snake charming itself. At the top of the Changing Room steps Miss Marion Taylor stood, sportively poised with one hand on the doorknob and a whistle dangling on a string from the other; quivering with eagerness to be out on the field and inhaling fresh air. They could see each other. Brenda, standing in the doorway of the Music Room, could see them both.

"Well, come in, child," said Miss Francis. "Don't *haver*. If you must haver, don't do it in the doorway. Other people are trying to come in."

Brenda moved to one side to make way for the other people, members of the choir who would normally have shoved her out of the way and pushed past. Here they shed their school manners in the corridor and queued in attitudes of excruciated patience. Miss Helen Francis favoured the noiseless approach. Across the quadrangle the Under-Thirteen Hockey XI roistered, and Miss Marion Taylor failed to intervene. Miss Francis observed all this with misty disapproval and looked away again.

"Brenda dear, are you coming in, or going out, or putting down roots?"

The rest of the choir was by now seated; first sopranos on the right, second sopranos on the left, thirds across one end and Miss Humphry, who was billed as an alto but sang tenor, at the other. They all sat up straight, as trained by Miss Francis, and looked curiously at Brenda who should have been seated too, among the first sopranos. Her empty chair was in the front row, with the music stacked on it, all ready. Miss Francis cocked her head to one side like a budgerigar that sees a millet spray in the offing.

"Have you a message for us, dear? From above?" She meant the headmistress, but by her tone it could have been God and his angels.

"No, Miss Francis."

"From *beyond*?"

"Miss Francis, can I ask – ?"

"You *may* ask, Brenda. Whether or not you *can* is beyond my powers of divination."

Brenda saw that the time for havering was at an end.

"Please, Miss Francis, may I be excused from choir?"

The budgie instantly turned into a marabou stork.

"Excused, Brenda? Do you have a pain?"

"There's a hockey practice, Miss Francis."

"I am aware of that." Miss Francis cast a look, over her shoulder and across the quadrangle, that should have turned Miss Taylor to stone, and the Under-Thirteen XI with her. "How does it concern you, Brenda? How does it concern me?"

"I'm in the team, Miss Francis, and there's a match on Saturday," said Brenda.

"But, my dear," Miss Francis smiled at her with surpassing sweetness. "I think my mind must be going." She lifted limp fingers from the keyboard and touched them to her forehead, as if to arrest the absconding mind.

"Hockey practices are on Tuesdays and Fridays. Choir practices are on Mondays and Thursdays. It was ever thus. Today is Thursday. Everyone else thinks it's Thursday, otherwise they wouldn't be here." She swept out a spare arm that encompassed the waiting choir, and asked helplessly, "It *is* Thursday, isn't it? You all think it's Thursday? It's not just me having a little brainstorm?"

The choir tittered, *sotto voce*, to assure Miss Francis that it was indeed Thursday, and to express its mass contempt for anyone who was fool enough to get caught in the cross-fire between Miss Francis and Miss Taylor.

"It's a match against the High School, Miss Francis. Miss Taylor called a special practice," said Brenda, hoping that her mention of the High School might save her, for if Miss Francis loathed anyone more than she loathed Miss Taylor, it was the music mistress at the High School. If the match had been against the High School choir, it might have been a different matter, and Miss Francis might have been out on the side-lines chanting with the rest of them: "Two – four – six – eight, who – do – we – hate?"

Miss Francis, however, was not to be deflected. "You know that I do not allow any absence from choir without a very good reason. Now, will you sit down, please?" She turned gaily to face the room. "I think we'll begin with the Schubert."

"Please. May I go and tell Miss Taylor that I can't come?"

Miss Francis sighed a sigh that turned a page on the music stand.

"Two minutes, Brenda. We'll wait," she said venomously, and set the metronome ticking on the piano so that they might all count the two minutes, second by second.

Miss Taylor still stood upon the steps of the Changing Room. While they were all counting, they could turn round and watch Brenda tell Miss Taylor that she was not allowed to attend hockey practice.

Tock.

Tock.

Tock.

Brenda closed the door on the ticking and began to run. She would have to run to be there and back in two minutes, and running in the corridors was forbidden.

Miss Taylor had legs like bath loofahs stuffed into long, hairy grey socks, that were held up by tourniquets of narrow elastic. When she put on her stockings after school and mounted her bicycle to pedal strenuously home up East Hill, you could still see the twin red marks, like the rubber seals on Kilner jars. The loofahs were the first thing that Brenda saw as she mounted the steps, and the grey socks bristled with impatience.

"Practice begins at twelve fifty," said Miss Taylor. "I suppose you were thinking of joining us?"

Brenda began to cringe all over again.

"Please, Miss Taylor, Miss Francis says I can't come."

"Does she? And what's it got to do with Miss Francis? Are you in detention?"

"No, Miss Taylor. I'm in choir."

"You may only be the goalkeeper, Brenda, but we still expect you to turn out for practices. You'll have to explain to Miss Francis that she must manage without you for once. I don't imagine that the choir will collapse if you're missing."

"No, Miss Taylor."

"Go on, then. At the double. We'll wait."

Brenda ran down the steps, aware of the Music Room windows but not looking at them, and back into the corridor. Halfway along it she was halted by a shout from behind.

"*What* do you think you're doing?"

Brenda turned and saw the Head Girl, Gill Rogers, who was also the school hockey captain and had the sense not to try and sing as well.

"Running, Gill. Sorry, Gill."

"Running's forbidden. You know that. Go back and walk."

"Miss Taylor told me to run."

"It's no good trying to blame Miss Taylor; I'm sure she didn't tell you to run."

"She said at the double," said Brenda.

"That's not the same thing at all. Go back and *walk*."

Brenda went back and walked.

"Two minutes and fifteen seconds," said Miss Francis, reaching for the metronome, when Brenda finally got back to the Music Room. "Sit down quickly, Brenda. Now then – I said sit down, Brenda."

"Please, Miss Francis – "

A look of dire agony appeared on Miss Francis's face – it could have been wind so soon after lunch – and she held the metronome in a strangler's grip.

"I think you've delayed us long enough, Brenda."

"Miss Taylor said couldn't you please excuse me from choir just this once as it's such an important match," said Brenda, improvising rapidly, since Miss Taylor had said nothing of the sort. Miss Francis raised a claw.

"I believe I made myself perfectly clear the first time. Now, sit down, please."

"But they're all waiting for me."

"So are we, Brenda. I must remind you that it is not common practice in this school to postpone activities for the sake of Second Year girls. What position do you occupy in the team? First bat?" Miss Francis knew quite well that there are no bats required in a hockey game, but her ignorance suggested that she was above such things.

"Goalkeeper, Miss Francis."

"Goalkeeper? From the fuss certain persons are making, I imagined that you must be at least a fast bowler. Is there no one else in the lower school to rival your undoubted excellence at keeping goal?"

"I *did* get chosen for the team, Miss Francis."

"Clearly you have no equal, Brenda. That being the case, you hardly need to practise, do you?"

"Miss Taylor thinks I do," said Brenda.

"Well, I'm afraid I don't. I would never, for one moment, keep you from a match, my dear, but a practice on a *Thursday* is an entirely different matter. Sit down."

Brenda, panicking, pointed to the window. "But she won't start without me."

"Neither will I. You may return very quickly and tell Miss Taylor so. At once."

Brenda set off along the corridor, expecting to hear the first notes of 'An die Musik' break out behind her. There was only silence. They were still waiting.

"Now run and get changed," said Miss Taylor, swinging her whistle, as Brenda came up the steps again. "We've waited long enough for you, my girl."

"Miss Francis says I can't come," Brenda said, baldly.

"Does she, now?"

"I've got to go back." A scarcely suppressed jeer rose from the rest of the team, assembled in the Changing Room.

"Brenda, this is the Under-Thirteen Eleven, not the Under-Thirteen Ten. There must be at least sixty of you in that choir. Are you really telling me that your absence will be noticed?"

"Miss Francis'll notice it," said Brenda.

"Then she'll just have to notice it," said Miss Taylor under her breath, but loudly enough for Brenda to hear and appreciate. "Go and tell Miss Francis that I insist you attend this practice."

"Couldn't you give me a note, please?" said Brenda. Miss Taylor must know that any message sent via Brenda would be heavily edited before it reached its destination. She could be as insulting as she pleased in a note.

"A note?" Brenda might have suggested a dozen red roses thrown in with it. "I don't see any reason to send a note. Simply tell Miss Francis that on this occasion she must let you go."

Brenda knew that it was impossible to tell Miss Francis that she must do anything, and Miss Taylor knew it too. Brenda put in a final plea for mercy.

"Couldn't you tell her?"

"We've already wasted ten minutes, Brenda, while you make up your mind."

"You needn't wait – "

"When I field a team, I field a team, not ten-elevenths of a team." She turned and addressed the said team. "It seems we'll have to stay here a little longer," her eyes strayed to the Music Room windows, "while Brenda arrives at her momentous decision."

Brenda turned and went down the steps again.

"Hurry UP, girl."

Miss Taylor's huge voice echoed dreadfully round the confining walls. She could have been in the choir herself, singing bass to Miss Humphry's tenor. Brenda began to run, and like a cuckoo from a clock, Gill Rogers sprang out of the cloakroom as she cantered past.

"Is that you again?"

Brenda side-stepped briskly and fled towards the Music Room, where she was met by the same ominous silence that had seen her off. The choir, cowed and bowed, crouched over the open music sheets and before them, wearing for some reason her *indomitable* expression, sat Miss Francis, tense as an overwound clockwork mouse and ready for action.

"At last. Really, Brenda, the suspense may prove too much for me. I thought you were never coming back." She lifted her hands and brought them down sharply on the keys. The choir jerked to attention. An over-eager soprano chimed in and then subsided as Miss Francis raised her hands again and looked round. Brenda was still standing in the doorway.

"Please sit down, Brenda."

Brenda clung to the door-post and looked hopelessly at Miss Francis. She would have gone down on her knees if there had been the slightest chance that Miss Francis would be moved.

"Well?"

"Please, Miss Francis, Miss Taylor says I *must* go to the practice." She wished devoutly that she were at home where, should rage break out on this scale, someone would have thrown something. If only Miss Francis would throw something; the metronome, perhaps, through the window.

Tock . . . tock . . . tock . . . *CRASH!* Tinkle tinkle.

But Miss Francis was a lady. With tight restraint she closed the lid of the piano.

"It seems," she said, in a bitter little voice, "that we are to have no music today. A hockey game is to take precedence over a choir practice."

"It's *not* a game," said Brenda. "It's a practice, for a match. Just this once . . .?" she said, and was disgusted to find a tear boiling up under her eyelid. "Please, Miss Francis."

"No, Brenda. I do not know why we are enduring this ridiculous debate (Neither do I, Miss Francis) but I thought I had made myself quite clear the first time you asked. You will not miss a scheduled choir practice for an unscheduled hockey practice. Did you not explain to Miss Taylor?"

"Yes I did!" Brenda cried. "And she said you wouldn't miss me."

Miss Francis turned all reasonable. "Miss you? But my

dear child, of course we wouldn't miss you. No one would miss you. You are not altogether indispensable, are you?"

"No, Miss Francis."

"It's a matter of principle. I would not dream of abstracting a girl from a hockey team, or a netball team or even, heaven preserve us, from a shove-ha'penny team, and by the same token I will not allow other members of staff to disrupt my choir practices. Is that clear?"

"Yes, Miss Francis."

"Go and tell Miss Taylor. I'm sure she'll see my point."

"Yes, Miss Francis." Brenda turned to leave, praying that the practice would at last begin without her, but the lid of the piano remained shut.

This time the Head Girl was waiting for her and had her head round the cloakroom door before Brenda was fairly on her way down the corridor.

"Why didn't you come back when I called you, just now?"

Brenda leaned against the wall and let the tear escape, followed by two or three others.

"Are you crying because you've broken rules," Gill demanded, "or because you got caught? I'll see you outside the Sixth-Form Room at four o'clock."

"It's not my fault."

"Of course it's your fault. No one forced you to run."

"They're making me," said Brenda, pointing two-handed in either direction, towards the Music Room and the Changing Room.

"I daresay you asked for it," said Gill. "Four o'clock, please," and she went back into the Senior cloakroom in the hope of catching some malefactor fiddling with the locks on the lavatory doors.

This last injustice gave Brenda a jolt that she might otherwise have missed, and the tears of self-pity turned hot with anger. She trudged along to the Changing Room.

"You don't exactly hurry yourself, do you?" said Miss Taylor. "Well?"

"Miss Francis says I can't come to hockey, Miss Taylor."

210

Miss Taylor looked round at the restive members of the Under-Thirteen XI and knew that for the good of the game it was time to make a stand.

"Very well, Brenda, I must leave it to you to make up your mind. Either you turn out now for the practice or you forfeit your place in the team. Which is it to be?"

Brenda looked at Miss Taylor, at the Music Room windows, and back to Miss Taylor.

"If I leave now, can I join again later?"

"Good Lord. Is there no end to this girl's cheek? Certainly not. This is your last chance, Brenda."

It would have to be the choir. She could not bear to hear the singing and never again be part of it, Thursday after Monday, term after term. If you missed a choir practice without permission, you were ejected from the choir. There was no appeal. There would be no permission.

"I'll leave the team, Miss Taylor."

She saw at once that Miss Taylor had not been expecting this. Her healthy face turned an alarming colour, like Lifebuoy kitchen soap.

"Then there's nothing more to say, is there? This will go on your report, you understand. I cannot be bothered with people who don't take things seriously."

She turned her back on Brenda and blew the whistle at last, releasing the pent-up team from the Changing Room. They were followed, Brenda noticed, by Pat Stevens, the reserve, who had prudently put on the shin-pads in advance.

Brenda returned to the Music Room. The lid of the piano was still down and Miss Francis's brittle elbow pinned it.

"The prodigal returns," she announced to the choir as Brenda entered, having seen her approach down the corridor. "It is now one fifteen. May we begin, dear?"

"Yes, Miss Francis."

"You finally persuaded Miss Taylor to see reason?"

"I told her what you said."

"And?"

"She said I could choose between missing the choir practice and leaving the team."

Miss Francis was transformed into an angular little effigy of triumph.

"I see you chose wisely, Brenda."

"Miss Francis?"

"By coming back to the choir."

"No, Miss Francis . . ." Brenda began to move towards the door, not trusting herself to come any closer to the piano. "I'm going to miss choir practice. I came back to tell you."

"Then you will leave the choir, Brenda. I hope you understand that."

"Yes, Miss Francis."

She stepped out of the room for the last time and closed the door. After a long while she heard the first notes of the piano, and the choir finally began to sing. Above the muted voices a whistle shrilled, out on the playing-field. Brenda went and sat in the Junior cloakroom, which was forbidden in lunch hour, and cried. There was no rule against that.

212

THE FALL OF THE IDOL

RICHMAL CROMPTON

WILLIAM WAS BORED. He sat at his desk in the sunny schoolroom and gazed dispassionately at a row of figures on the blackboard.

"It isn't *sense*," he murmured scornfully.

Miss Drew was also bored, but, unlike William, she tried to hide the fact.

"If the interest on a hundred pounds for one year is five pounds," she said wearily, then, "William Brown, do sit up and don't look so stupid!"

William changed his position from that of lolling over one side of his desk to that of lolling over the other, and began to justify himself.

"Well, I can't unner*stand* any of it. It's enough to make anyone look stupid when he can't unner*stand* any of it. I can't think why people go on givin' people bits of money for givin' 'em lots of money and go on an' on doin' it. It dun't seem sense. Anyone's a mug for givin' anyone a hundred pounds just 'cause he says he'll go on givin' him five pounds and go on stickin' to his hundred pounds. How's he to *know* he will? Well," he warmed to his subject, "what's to stop him not givin' any five pounds once he's got hold of the hundred pounds an' goin' on stickin' to the hundred pounds – "

213

Miss Drew checked him by a slim, upraised hand.

"William," she said patiently, "just listen to me. Now suppose," her eyes roved round the room and settled on a small red-haired boy, "suppose that Eric wanted a hundred pounds for something and you lent it to him – "

"I wun't lend Eric a hundred pounds," he said firmly, "'cause I ha'n't got it. I've only got 3½d., an' I wun't lend that to Eric, 'cause I'm not such a mug, 'cause I lent him my mouth-organ once an' he bit a bit off an' – "

Miss Drew interrupted sharply. Teaching on a hot afternoon is rather trying.

"You'd better stay in after school, William, and I'll explain."

William scowled, emitted his monosyllable of scornful disdain "Huh!" and relapsed into gloom.

He brightened, however, on remembering a lizard he had caught on the way to school, and drew it from its hiding-place in his pocket. But the lizard had abandoned the unequal struggle for existence among the stones, top, penknife, bits of putty, and other small objects that inhabited William's pocket. The housing problem had been too much for it.

William in disgust shrouded the remains in blotting-paper, and disposed of it in his neighbour's inkpot. The neighbour protested and an enlivening scrimmage ensued.

Finally the lizard was dropped down the neck of an inveterate enemy of William's in the next row, and was extracted only with the help of obliging friends. Threats of vengeance followed, couched in blood-curdling terms, and written on blotting-paper.

Meanwhile Miss Drew explained Simple Practice to a small but earnest coterie of admirers in the front row. And William, in the back row, whiled away the hours for which his father paid the education authorities a substantial sum.

But his turn was to come.

At the end of afternoon school one by one the class departed, leaving William only nonchalantly chewing an india-rubber and glaring at Miss Drew.

"Now, William."

Miss Drew was severely patient.

William went up to the platform and stood by her desk.

"You see, if someone borrows a hundred pounds from someone else – "

She wrote down the figures on a piece of paper, bending low over her desk. The sun poured in through the window, showing the little golden curls in the nape of her neck. She lifted to William eyes that were stern and frowning, but blue as blue above flushed cheeks.

"Don't you *see*, William?" she said.

There was a faint perfume about her, and William the devil-may-care pirate and robber-chief, the stern despiser of all things effeminate, felt the first dart of the malicious blind god. He blushed and simpered.

"Yes, I see all about it now," he assured her. "You've explained it all plain now. I cudn't unner*stand* it before. It's a bit soft – in't it – anyway, to go lending hundred pounds about just 'cause someone says they'll give you five pounds next year. Some folks is mugs. But I do unner*stand* now. I cudn't unnerstand it before."

"You'd have found it simpler if you hadn't played with dead lizards all the time," she said wearily, closing her books.

William gasped.

He went home her devoted slave. Certain members of the class always deposited dainty bouquets on her desk in the morning. William was determined to outshine the rest. He went into the garden with a large basket and a pair of scissors the next morning before he set out for school.

It happened that no one was about. He went first to the hothouse. It was a riot of colour. He worked there with a thoroughness and concentration worthy of a nobler cause. He came out staggering beneath a piled-up basket of hothouse blooms. The hothouse itself was bare and desolate.

Hearing a sound in the back garden he hastily decided to delay no longer, but to set out to school at once. He set out as unostentatiously as possible.

Miss Drew, entering her class-room, was aghast to see instead of the usual small array of buttonholes on her desk, a mass of already withering hothouse flowers completely covering her desk and chair.

William was a boy who never did things by halves.

"Good Heavens!" she cried in consternation.

216

William blushed with pleasure.

He changed his seat to one in the front row. All that morning he sat, his eyes fized on her earnestly, dreaming of moments in which he rescued her from robbers and pirates (here he was somewhat inconsistent with his own favourite *rôle* of robber-chief and pirate), and bore her fainting in his strong arms to safety. Then she clung to him in love and gratitude, and they were married at once by the Archbishops of Canterbury and York.

William would have no half-measures. They were to be married by the Archbishops of Canterbury and York, or else the Pope. He wasn't sure that he wouldn't rather have the Pope. He would wear his black pirate suit with the skull and crossbones. No, that would not do –

"What have I just been saying, William?" said Miss Drew.

William coughed and gazed at her soulfully.

"'Bout lendin' money?" he said, hopefully.

"William!" she snapped. "This isn't an arithmetic lesson. I'm trying to teach you about the Armada."

"Oh, *that!*" said William brightly and ingratiatingly. "Oh, yes."

"Tell me something about it."

"I don't *know* anything – not jus' yet – "

"I've been *telling* you about it. I do wish you'd listen," she said despairingly.

William relapsed into silence, nonplussed, but by no means cowed.

When he reached home that evening he found that the garden was the scene of excitement and hubbub. One policeman was measuring the panes of glass in the conservatory door, and another was on his knees examining the beds near. His grown-up sister, Ethel, was standing at the front door.

"Every single flower has been stolen from the conservatory some time this morning," she said excitedly. "We've only just been able to get the police. William, did you see anyone about when you went to school this morning?"

William pondered deeply. His most guileless and innocent expression came to his face.

"No," he said at last. "No, Ethel, I didn't see anybody."

William coughed and discreetly withdrew.

That evening he settled down at the library table, spreading out his books around him, a determined frown upon his small face.

His father was sitting in an armchair by the window reading the evening paper.

"Father," said William suddenly, "s'pose I came to you an' said you was to give me a hundred pounds an' I'd give you five pounds next year an' so on, would you give it me?"

"I should not, my son," said his father firmly.

William sighed.

"I knew there was something wrong with it," he said.

Mr Brown returned to the leading article, but not for long.

"Father, what was the date of the Armada?"

"Good Heavens! How should I know? I wasn't there."

William sighed.

"Well, I'm tryin' to write about it and why it failed an' – why did it fail?"

Mr Brown groaned, gathered up his paper, and retired to the dining-room.

He had almost finished the leading article when William appeared, his arms full of books, and sat down quietly at the table.

"Father, what's the French for 'my aunt is walking in the garden'?"

"What on earth are you doing?" said Mr Brown irritably.

"I'm doing my home-lessons," said William virtuously.

"I never even knew you had the things to do."

"No," William admitted gently, "I don't generally take much bother over them, but I'm goin' to now – 'cause Miss Drew" – he blushed slightly and paused – "'cause Miss Drew" – he blushed more deeply and began to stammer, "'c – cause Miss Drew" – he was almost apoplectic.

Mr Brown quietly gathered up his paper and crept out

to the verandah, where his wife sat with the week's mending.

"William's gone raving mad in the dining-room," he said pleasantly, as he sat down. "Takes the form of a wild thirst for knowledge, and a babbling of a Miss Drawing, or Drew, or something. He's best left alone."

Mrs Brown merely smiled placidly over the mending.

Mr Brown had finished one leading article and begun another before William appeared again. He stood in the doorway frowning and stern.

"Father, what's the capital of Holland?"

"Good Heavens!" said his father. "Buy him an encyclopedia. Anything, anything. What does he think I am? What – "

"I'd better set apart a special room for his homework," said Mrs Brown soothingly, "now that he's beginning to take such an interest."

"A room!" echoed his father bitterly. "He wants a whole house."

Miss Drew was surprised and touched by William's earnestness and attention the next day. At the end of the afternoon school he kindly offered to carry her books home for her. He waved aside all protests. He marched home by her side discoursing pleasantly, his small freckled face beaming devotion.

"I like pirates, don't you, Miss Drew? An' robbers an' things like that? Miss Drew, would you like to be married to a robber?"

He was trying to reconcile his old beloved dream of his future estate with the new one of becoming Miss Drew's husband.

"No," she said firmly.

His heart sank.

"Nor a pirate?" he said sadly.

"No."

"They're quite nice really – pirates," he assured her.

"I think not."

219

"Well," he said resignedly, "we'll jus' have to go huntin' wild animals and things. That'll be all right."

"Who?" she said, bewildered.

"Well – jus' you wait," he said darkly.

Then: "Would you rather be married by the Archbishop of York or the Pope?"

"The Archbishop, I think," she said gravely.

He nodded.

"All right."

She was distinctly amused. She was less amused the next evening. Miss Drew had a male cousin – a very nice-looking male cousin, with whom she often went for walks in the evening. This evening, by chance, they passed William's house, and William, who was in the garden, threw aside his temporary *rôle* of pirate and joined them. He trotted happily on the other side of Miss Drew. He entirely monopolized the conversation. The male cousin seemed to encourage him, and this annoyed Miss Drew. He refused to depart in spite of Miss Drew's strong hints. He had various items of interest to impart, and he imparted them with the air of one assured of an appreciative hearing. He had found a dead rat the day before and given it to his dog, but his dog didn't like 'em dead and neither did the ole cat, so he'd buried it. Did Miss Drew like all those flowers he'd got her the other day? He was afraid that he cudn't bring any more like that jus' yet. Were there pirates now? Well, what would folks do to one if there was one? He din't see why there shun't be pirates now. He thought he'd start it, anyway. He'd like to shoot a lion. He was goin' to one day. He'd shoot a lion an' a tiger. He'd bring the skin home to Miss Drew, if she liked. He grew recklessly generous. He'd bring home lots of skins of all sorts of animals for Miss Drew.

"Don't you think you ought to be going home, William?" said Miss Drew coldly.

William hastened to reassure her.

"Oh, no – not for ever so long yet," he said.

"Isn't it your bed-time?"

220

"Oh, no – not yet – not for ever so long."

The male cousin was giving William his whole attention.

"What does Miss Drew teach you at school, William?" he said.

"Oh, jus' ornery things. Armadas an' things. An' 'bout lending a hundred pounds. That's a norful *soft* thing. I unner*stand* it," he added hastily, fearing further explanation, "but it's *soft*. My father thinks it is, too, an' he oughter *know*. He's bin abroad lots of times. He's bin chased by a bull, my father has – "

The shades of night were falling fast when William reached Miss Drew's house still discoursing volubly. He was drunk with success. He interpreted his idol's silence as the silence of rapt admiration.

He was passing through the gate with his two companions with the air of one assured of welcome, when Miss Drew shut the gate upon him firmly.

"You'd better go home now, William," she said.

William hesitated.

"I don't mind comin' in a bit," he said. "I'm not tired."

But Miss Drew and the male cousin were already half-way up the walk.

William turned his steps homeward. He met Ethel near the gate.

"William, where *have* you been? I've been looking for you everywhere. It's *hours* past your bed-time."

"I was goin' a walk with Miss Drew."

"But you should have come home at your bed-time."

"I don't think she wanted me to go," he said with dignity. "I think it wun't of bin p'lite."

William found that a new and serious element had entered his life. It was not without its disadvantages. Many had been the little diversions by which William had been wont to while away the hours of instruction. In spite of his devotion to Miss Drew, he missed the old days of care-free exuberance, but he kept his new seat in the front row, and clung to his *rôle* of earnest student. He was beginning to find also, that a conscientious performance of home lessons limited his activities after school hours, but at present he hugged his chains. Miss Drew, from her seat on the platform, found William's soulful concentrated gaze somewhat embarrassing, and his questions even more so.

As he went out of school he heard her talking to another mistress.

"I'm very fond of syringa," she was saying. "I'd love to have some."

William decided to bring her syringa, handfuls of syringa, armfuls of syringa.

He went straight home to the gardener.

"No, I ain't got no syringa. Please step off my rose-bed, Mister William. No, there ain't any syringa in this 'ere garding. I dunno for why. Please leave my 'ose pipe alone, Mister William."

"Huh!" ejaculated William, scornfully turning away.

He went round the garden. The gardener had been quite right. There were guelder roses everywhere, but no syringa.

He climbed the fence and surveyed the next garden. There were guelder roses everywhere, but no syringa. It must have been some peculiarity in the soil.

William strolled down the road, scanning the gardens as he went. All had guelder roses. None had syringa.

Suddenly he stopped.

On a table in the window of a small house at the bottom of the road was a vase of syringa. He did not know who lived there. He entered the garden cautiously. No one was about.

He looked into the room. It was empty. The window was open at the bottom.

He scrambled in, removing several layers of white paint from the window-sill as he did so. He was determined to have that syringa. He took it dripping from the vase, and was preparing to depart, when the door opened and a fat woman appeared upon the threshold. The scream that she emitted at sight of William curdled the very blood in his veins. She dashed to the window, and William, in self-defence, dodged round the table and out of the door. The back door was open, and William blindly fled by it. The fat woman did not pursue. She was leaning out of the window, and her shrieks rent the air.

"Police! Help! Murder! Robbers!"

The quiet little street rang with the raucous sounds.

William felt cold shivers creeping up and down his spine. He was in a small back garden from which he could see no exit.

Meanwhile the shrieks were redoubled.

"Help! *Help! Help!*"

Then came sounds of the front door opening and men's voices.

"Hello! Who is it? What is it?"

William glared round wildly. There was a hen-house in the corner of the garden, and into this he dashed, tearing open the door and plunging through a mass of flying feathers and angry, disturbed hens.

William crouched in a corner of the dark hen-house determinedly clutching his bunch of syringa.

Distant voices were at first all he could hear. Then they came nearer, and he heard the fat lady's voice loudly declaiming.

"He was quite a small man, but with such an evil face. I just had one glimpse of him as he dashed past me. I'm sure he'd have murdered me if I hadn't cried for help. Oh, the coward! And a poor defenceless woman! He was standing by the silver table. I disturbed him at his work of crime. I feel so upset. I shan't sleep for nights. I shall see his evil, murderous face. And a poor unarmed woman!"

"Can you give us no details, madam?" said a man's voice. "Could you recognize him again?"

"*Anywhere!*" she said firmly. "Such a criminal face. You've no idea how upset I am. I might have been a lifeless corpse now, if I hadn't had the courage to cry for help."

"We're measuring the footprints, madam. You say he went out by the front door?"

"I'm convinced he did. I'm convinced he's hiding in the bushes by the gate. Such a low face. My nerves are absolutely jarred."

"We'll search the bushes again, madam," said the other voice wearily, "but I expect he has escaped by now."

"The brute!" said the fat lady. "Oh, the *brute!* And that *face.* If I hadn't had the courage to cry out – "

The voices died away and William was left alone in a corner of the hen-house.

A white hen appeared in the little doorway, squawked at him angrily, and retired, cackling indignation. Visions of life-long penal servitude or hanging passed before William's eyes. He'd rather be executed, really. He hoped they'd execute him.

Then he heard the fat lady bidding good-bye to the policeman. Then she came to the back garden evidently with a friend, and continued to pour forth her troubles.

"And he *dashed* past me, dear. Quite a small man, but with such an evil face."

A black hen appeared in the little doorway, and with an angry squawk at William, returned to the back garden.

"I think you're *splendid*, dear," said the invisible friend. "How you had the *courage*."

The white hen gave a sardonic scream.

"You'd better come in and rest, darling," said the friend.

"I'd better," said the fat lady in a plaintive, suffering voice. "I do feel very . . . shaken . . ."

Their voices ceased, the door was closed, and all was still.

Cautiously, very cautiously, a much-dishevelled William crept from the hen-house and round the side of the house. Here he found a locked side-gate over which he climbed, and very quietly he glided down to the front gate and to the road.

"Where's William this evening?" said Mrs Brown. "I do hope he won't stay out after his bed-time."

"Oh, I've just met him," said Ethel. "He was going up to

224

his bedroom. He was covered with hen feathers and holding a bunch of syringa."

"Mad!" sighed his father. "Mad! mad! mad!"

The next morning William laid a bunch of syringa upon Miss Drew's desk. He performed the offering with an air of quiet, manly pride. Miss Drew recoiled.

"*Not* syringa, William. I simply can't *bear* the smell!"

William gazed at her in silent astonishment for a few moments.

Then: "But you *said* . . . you *said* . . . you said you were fond of syringa an' that you'd like to have them."

"Did I say syringa?" said Miss Drew vaguely. "I meant guelder roses."

William's gaze was one of stony contempt.

He went slowly back to his old seat at the back of the room.

That evening he made a bonfire with several choice friends, and played Red Indians in the garden. There was a certain thrill in returning to the old life.

"Hello!" said his father, encountering William creeping on all fours among the bushes. "I thought you did home lessons now?"

William arose to an upright position.

"I'm not goin' to take much bother over 'em now," said William. "Miss Drew, she can't talk straight. She dunno what she *means*."

"That's always the trouble with women," agreed his father. "William says his idol has feet of clay," he said to his wife, who had approached.

"I dunno as she's got feet of clay," said William, the literal. "All I say is she can't talk straight. I took no end of trouble an' she dunno what she means. I think her feet's all right. She walks all right. 'Sides, when they make folks false feet, they make 'em of wood, not clay."

JANE EYRE

CHARLOTTE BRONTË

MY FIRST QUARTER at Lowood seemed an age; and not the golden age either; it comprised an irksome struggle with difficulties in habituating myself to new rules and unwonted tasks. The fear of failure in these points harassed me worse than the physical hardships of my lot; though these were no trifles.

During January, February, and part of March, the deep snows, and, after their melting, the almost impassable roads, prevented our stirring beyond the garden walls, except to go to church; but within these limits we had to pass an hour every day in the open air. Our clothing was insufficient to protect us from the severe cold; we had no boots, the snow got into our shoes and melted there; our ungloved hands became numbed and covered with chilblains, as were our feet: I remember well the distracting irritation I endured from this cause every evening, when my feet inflamed; and the torture of thrusting the swelled, raw, and stiff toes into my shoes in the morning. Then the scanty supply of food was distressing: with the keen appetites of growing children, we had scarcely sufficient to keep alive a delicate invalid. From this deficiency of nourishment resulted an abuse, which pressed hardly on the younger pupils: whenever the famished great girls had an opportunity, they would coax or menace the little ones out of their portion. Many a time I have shared between two claimants the precious morsel of brown bread distributed at tea-time; and after relinquishing to a third, half the contents of my mug of coffee, I have swallowed the remainder with an accompaniment of secret tears, forced from me by the exigency of hunger.

Sundays were dreary days in that wintry season. We had to walk two miles to Brocklebridge Church, where our patron officiated. We set out cold, we arrived at church colder; during the morning service we became almost paralysed. It was too far to return to dinner, and an allowance of cold meat and bread, in the same penurious proportion observed in our ordinary meals, was served round between services.

At the close of the afternoon service we returned by an exposed and hilly road, where the bitter winter wind, blowing over a range of snowy summits to the north, almost flayed the skin from our faces.

I can remember Miss Temple walking lightly and rapidly along our drooping line, her plaid cloak, which the frosty wind fluttered, gathered close about her, and encouraging us, by precept, and example, to keep up our spirits, and march forward, as she said, 'like stalwart soldiers'. The other teachers, poor things, were generally themselves too much dejected to attempt the task of cheering others.

How we longed for the light and heat of a blazing fire when we got back! But, to the little ones at least, this was denied: each hearth in the school-room was immediately surrounded by a double row of great girls, and behind them the younger children crouched in groups, wrapping their starved arms in their pinafores.

A little solace came at tea-time, in the shape of a double ration of bread – a whole, instead of a half, slice – with the delicious addition of a thin scrape of butter; it was the hebdomadal treat to which we all looked forward from Sabbath to Sabbath. I generally contrived to reserve a moiety of this bounteous repast for myself; but the remainder I was invariably obliged to part with.

The Sunday evening was spent in repeating, by heart, the Church Catechism, and the fifth, sixth, and seventh chapters of St Matthew; and in listening to a long sermon, read by Miss Miller, whose irrepressible yawns attested her weariness. A frequent interlude of these performances was the enactment of the part of Eutychus by some half dozen of little girls; who, overpowered with sleep, would fall down, if not out of the third loft, yet off the fourth form, and be taken up half dead. The remedy was, to thrust them forward into the centre of the school-room, and oblige them to stand there till the sermon was finished. Sometimes, their feet failed them, and they sank together in a heap; they were then propped up with the monitors' high stools.

I have not yet alluded to the visits of Mr Brocklehurst; and indeed that gentleman was from home during the greater part of the first month after my arrival; perhaps prolonging his stay with his friend the archdeacon: his absence was a relief to me. I need not say that I had my own reasons for dreading his coming: but come he did at last.

One afternoon (I had then been three weeks at Lowood), as I was sitting with a slate in my hand, puzzling over a sum in long division, my eyes, raised in abstraction to the window, caught sight of a figure just passing: I recognized almost instinctively that gaunt outline; and when, two minutes after, all the school, teachers included, rose *en masse*, it was not necessary for me to look up in order to ascertain whose entrance they thus greeted. A long stride measured the school-room, and presently, beside Miss Temple, who herself had risen, stood the same black column which had frowned on me so ominously from the hearth-rug at Gateshead. I now glanced sideways at this piece of architecture. Yes, I was right: it was Mr Brocklehurst, buttoned up in a surtout, and looking longer, narrower, and more rigid than ever.

I had my own reasons for being dismayed at this apparition: too well I remembered the perfidious hints given by Mrs Reed about my disposition, etc.; the promise pledged by Mr Brocklehurst to apprise Miss Temple and the teachers of my vicious nature. All along I had been dreading the fulfilment of this promise, – I had been looking out daily for the 'Coming Man', whose information respecting my past life and conversation was to brand me as a bad child for ever: now there he was. He stood at Miss Temple's side; he was speaking low in her ear: I did not doubt he was making disclosures of my villainy; and I watched her eye with painful anxiety, expecting every moment to see its dark orb turn on me a glance of repugnance and contempt. I listened, too; and as I happened to be seated quite at the top of the room, I caught most of what he said: its import relieved me from immediate apprehension.

"I suppose, Miss Temple, the thread I bought at Lowton will do; it struck me that it would be just of the quality for the calico chemises, and I sorted the needles to match. You may tell Miss Smith that I forgot to make a memorandum of the darning needles, but she shall have some papers sent in next week; and she is not, on any account, to give out more than one at a time to each pupil: if they have more, they are apt to be careless and lose them. And, oh ma'am! I wish the woollen stockings were better looked to! – when I was here last, I went into the kitchen-garden and examined the clothes drying on the line; there was a quantity of black hose in a very bad state of repair: from the size of the holes in them I was sure they had not been mended from time to time."

He paused.

"Your directions shall be attended to, sir," said Miss Temple.

"And, ma'am," he continued, "the laundress tells me some of the girls have two clean tuckers in the week: it is too much; the rules limit them to one."

"I think I can explain that circumstance, sir. Agnes and

Catherine Johnstone were invited to take tea with some friends at Lowton last Thursday, and I gave them leave to put on clean tuckers for the occasion."

Mr Brocklehurst nodded.

"Well, for once, it may pass; but please not to let the circumstance occur too often. And there is another thing which surprised me: I find, in settling accounts with the housekeeper, that a lunch, consisting of bread and cheese, has twice been served out to the girls during the past fortnight. How is this? I look over the regulations, and I find no such meal as lunch mentioned. Who introduced this innovation? and by what authority?"

"I must be responsible for the circumstance, sir," replied Miss Temple: "the breakfast was so ill-prepared that the pupils could not possibly eat it; and I dared not allow them to remain fasting till dinner time."

"Madam, allow me an instant. – You are aware that my plan in bringing up these girls is, not to accustom them to habits of luxury and indulgence, but to render them hardy, patient, self-denying. Should any little accidental disappointment of the appetite occur, such as the spoiling of a meal, the under or the over dressing of a dish, the incident ought not to be neutralized by replacing with something more delicate than the comfort lost, thus pampering the body and obviating the aim of this institution; it ought to be improved to the spiritual edification of the pupils, by encouraging them to evince fortitude under the temporary privation. A brief address on those occasions would not be mistimed, wherein a judicious instructor would take the opportunity of referring to the sufferings of the primitive Christians; to the torments of martyrs; to the exhortations of our blessed Lord himself, calling upon his disciples to take up their cross and follow Him; to His warnings that man shall not live by bread alone, but by every word that proceedeth out of the mouth of God; to His divine consolations, 'if ye suffer hunger or thirst for my sake, happy are ye'. Oh, madam, when you put bread and cheese, instead of burnt porridge, into these children's mouths, you may indeed feed their vile bodies, but you little think how you starve their immortal souls!"

Mr Brocklehurst again paused – perhaps overcome by his feelings. Miss Temple had looked down when he first began to speak to her; but she now gazed straight before her, and her face, naturally pale as marble, appeared to be assuming also the coldness and fixity of that material; especially her mouth, closed as if it would have required a sculptor's chisel to open it, and her brow settled gradually into petrified severity.

Meantime, Mr Brocklehurst, standing on the hearth, with his hands behind his back, majestically surveyed the whole school. Suddenly his eye gave a blink, as if it had met something that either dazzled or shocked its pupil; turning, he said in more rapid accents than he had hitherto used: –

"Miss Temple, Miss Temple, what – *what* is that girl with curled hair? Red hair, ma'am, curled – curled all over?" And extending his cane he pointed to the awful object, his hand shaking as he did so.

"It is Julia Severn," replied Miss Temple, very quietly.

"Julia Severn, ma'am! And why has she, or any other, curled hair? Why, in defiance of every precept and principle of this house, does she conform to the world so openly – here, in an evangelical, charitable establishment – as to wear her hair one mass of curls?"

"Julia's hair curls naturally," returned Miss Temple, still more quietly.

"Naturally! Yes, but we are not to conform to nature: I wish these girls to be the children of Grace: and why that abundance? I have again and again intimated that I desire the hair to be arranged closely, modestly, plainly. Miss Temple, that girl's hair must be cut off entirely; I will send a barber tomorrow: and I see others who have far too much of the excrescence – that tall girl, tell her to turn round. Tell all the first form to rise up and direct their faces to the wall."

Miss Temple passed her handkerchief over her lips, as if

to smooth away the involuntary smile that curled them; she gave the order, however, and when the first class could take in what was required of them, they obeyed. Leaning a little back on my bench, I could see the looks and grimaces with which they commented on this manoeuvre: it was a pity Mr Brocklehurst could not see them, too; he would perhaps have felt that, whatever he might do with the outside of the cup and platter, the inside was further beyond his inter-ference than he imagined.

He scrutinized the reverse of these living models some five minutes, then pronounced sentence. These words fell like the knell of doom: –

"All those top-knots must be cut off."

Miss Temple seemed to remonstrate.

"Madame," he pursued, "I have a Master to serve whose kingdom is not of this world: my mission is to mortify in these girls the lusts of the flesh; to teach them to clothe themselves with shame-facedness and sobriety, not with braided hair and costly apparel; and each of the young persons before us has a string of hair twisted in plaits which vanity itself might have woven: these, I repeat, must be cut off; think of the time wasted, of – "

Mr Brocklehurst was here interrupted: three other visitors, ladies, now entered the room. They ought to have come a little sooner to have heard his lecture on dress, for they were splendidly attired in velvet, silk, and furs. The two younger of the trio (fine girls of sixteen and seventeen) had grey beaver hats, then in fashion, shaded with ostrich plumes, and from under the brim of this graceful head-dress fell a profusion of light tresses, elaborately curled; the elderly lady was enveloped in a costly velvet shawl, trimmed with ermine, and she wore a false front of French curls.

These ladies were deferentially received by Miss Temple, as Mrs and Misses Brocklehurst, and conducted to seats of honour at the top of the room. It seems they had come in the carriage with their reverend relative, and had been conducting a rummaging scrutiny of the rooms upstairs, while he transacted business with the housekeeper, questioned the laundress, and lectured the superintendent. They now proceeded to address divers remarks and reproofs to Miss Smith, who was charged with the care of the linen and the inspection of the dormitories: but I had no time to listen what they said; other matters called off and enchained my attention.

Hitherto, while gathering up the discourse of Mr Brocklehurst and Miss Temple, I had not, at the same time, neglected precautions to secure my personal safety; which I thought would be effected, if I could only elude observation. To this end, I had sat well back on the form, and while seeming to be busy with my sum, had held my slate in such a manner as to conceal my face: I might have escaped notice, had not my treacherous slate somehow happened to slip from my hand, and falling with an obtrusive crash, directly drawn every eye upon me; I knew it was all over now, and, as I stopped to pick up the two fragments of slate, I rallied my forces for the worst. It came.

"A careless girl!" said Mr Brocklehurst, and immediately after – "It is the new pupil, I perceive." And before I could draw breath, "I must not forget I have a word to say respecting her." Then aloud: how loud it seemed to me! "Let the child who broke her slate, come forward!"

Of my own accord, I could not have stirred; I was paralysed: but the two great girls who sat on each side of me, set me on my legs and pushed me towards the dread judge, and then Miss Temple gently assisted me to his very feet, and I caught her whispered counsel, –

"Don't be afraid, Jane, I saw it was an accident; you shall not be punished."

The kind whisper went to my heart like a dagger.

"Another minute, and she will despise me for a hypocrite," thought I; and an impulse of fury against Reed, Brocklehurst, and Co. bounded in my pulses at the conviction. I was no Helen Burns.

"Fetch that stool," said Mr Brocklehurst, pointing to a very high one from which a monitor had just risen: it was brought.

"Place the child upon it."

And I was placed there, by whom I don't know: I was in no condition to note particulars; I was only aware that they had hoisted me up to the height of Mr Brocklehurst's nose, that he was within a yard of me, and that a spread of shot orange and purple silk pelisses, and a cloud of silvery plumage extended and waved below me.

Mr Brocklehurst hemmed.

"Ladies," said he, turning to his family; "Miss Temple, teachers, and children, you all see this girl?"

Of course they did; for I felt their eyes directed like burning-glasses against my scorched skin.

"You see she is yet young; you observe she possesses the ordinary form of childhood; God has graciously given her the shape that He has given to all of us; no signal deformity points her out as a marked character. Who would think that the Evil One had already found a servant and agent in her? Yet such, I grieve to say, is the case."

A pause – in which I began to steady the palsy of my nerves, and to feel that the Rubicon was passed; and that the trial, no longer to be shirked, must be firmly sustained.

"My dear children," pursued the black marble clergyman, with pathos, "this is a sad, a melancholy occasion; for it becomes my duty to warn you that this girl, who might be one of God's own lambs, is a little castaway: not a member of the true flock, but evidently an interloper and an alien. You must be on your guard against her; you must shun her example: if necessary, avoid her company, exclude her from your sports, and shut her out from your converse. Teachers! you must watch her: keep your eyes on her movements, weigh well her words, scrutinize her actions, punish her body to save her soul: if, indeed, such salvation be possible, for (my tongue falters while I tell it) this girl, this child, the native of a Christian land, worse than many a little heathen who says its prayers to Brahma and kneels before Juggernaut – this child is – a liar!"

Now came a pause of ten minutes; during which I, by this time in perfect possession of my wits, observed all the female Brocklehursts produce their pocket-handkerchiefs and apply them to their optics, while the elderly lady swayed herself to and fro, and the two younger ones whispered, "How shocking!"

Mr Brocklehurst resumed.

"This I learned from her benefactress; from the pious and charitable lady who adopted her in her orphan state, reared her as her own daughter, and whose kindness, whose generosity the unhappy girl repaid by an ingratitude so bad, so dreadful, that at last her excellent patroness was obliged to separate her from her own young ones, fearful lest her vicious example should contaminate their purity: she has sent her here to be healed, even as the Jews of old sent their diseased to the troubled pool of Bethesda; and teachers! superintendent! I beg of you not to allow the waters to stagnate round her."

With this sublime conclusion, Mr Brocklehurst adjusted the top button of his surtout, muttered something to his family, who rose, bowed to Miss Temple, and then all the great people sailed in state from the room. Turning at the door, my judge said: –

"Let her stand half an hour longer on that stool, and let no one speak to her during the remainder of the day."

There was I, then, mounted aloft: I, who had said I could not bear the shame of standing up on my natural feet in the middle of the room, was now exposed to general view on a pedestal of infamy. What my sensations were, no language can describe; but just as they all rose, stifling my breath and constricting my throat, a girl came up and passed me: in passing, she lifted her eyes. What a strange light inspired them! What an extraordinary sensation that ray sent through me! How the new feeling bore me up! It was as if a martyr, a hero, had passed a slave or victim, and imparted strength in the transit. I mastered the rising hysteria, lifted up my head, and took a firm stand on the stool. Helen Burns asked some slight question about her work of Miss Smith, was chidden for the triviality of the inquiry, returned to her place, and smiled at me as she again went by. What a smile! I remember it now, and I know that it was the effluence of fine intellect, of true courage; it lit up her marked lineaments, her thin face, her sunken grey eyes, like a reflection from the aspect of an angel. Yet at that moment Helen Burns wore on her arm 'the untidy badge'; scarcely an hour ago I had heard her condemned by Miss Scatcherd to a dinner of bread and water on the morrow, because she had blotted an exercise in copying it out. Such is the imperfect nature of man! such spots are there on the disc of the clearest planet; and eyes like Miss Scatcherd's can only see those minute defects, and are blind to the full brightness of the orb.

TOM SAWYER

MARK TWAIN

THERE WAS SOMETHING about Aunt Polly's manner when she kissed Tom, that swept away his low spirits and made him light-hearted and happy again. He started to school, and had the luck of coming upon Becky Thatcher at the head of Meadow Lane. His mood always determined his manner. Without a moment's hesitation he ran to her and said:

"I acted mighty mean today, Becky, and I'm so sorry. I won't ever, ever do it that way again as long as ever I live – please make up, won't you?"

The girl stopped and looked him scornfully in the face.

"I'll thank you to keep yourself *to* yourself, Mr Thomas Sawyer. I'll never speak to you again."

She tossed her head and passed on. Tom was so stunned that he had not even presence of mind enough to say "Who cares, Miss Smarty?" until the right time to say it had gone by. So he said nothing. But he was in a fine rage, nevertheless. He moped into the school-yard wishing she were a boy, and imagining how he would trounce her if she were. He presently encountered her and delivered a stinging remark as he passed. She hurled one in return, and the angry breach was complete. It seemed to Becky, in her

237

hot resentment, that she could hardly wait for school to 'take in', she was so impatient to see Tom flogged for the injured spelling-book. If she had had any lingering notion of exposing Alfred Temple, Tom's offensive fling had driven it entirely away.

Poor girl, she did not know how fast she was nearing trouble herself. The master, Mr Dobbins, had reached middle age with an unsatisfied ambition. The darling of his desires was to be a doctor, but poverty had decreed that he should be nothing higher than a village schoolmaster. Every day he took a mysterious book out of his desk, and absorbed himself in it at times when no classes were reciting. He kept that book under lock and key. There was not an urchin in school but was perishing to have a glimpse of it, but the chance never came. Every boy and girl had a theory about the nature of that book; but no two theories were alike, and there was no way of getting at the facts in the case. Now as Becky was passing by the desk, which stood near the door, she noticed that the key was in the lock! It was a precious moment. She glanced around; found herself alone, and the next instant she had the book in her hands. The title-page – Professor somebody's *Anatomy* – carried no information to her mind; so she began to turn the leaves. She came at once upon a handsomely engraved and coloured frontispiece – a human figure. At that moment a shadow fell on the page, and Tom Sawyer stepped in at the door and caught a glimpse of the picture. Becky snatched at the book to close it, and had the hard luck to tear the pictured page half down the middle. She thrust the volume into the desk, turned the key, and burst out crying with shame and vexation:

"Tom Sawyer, you are just as mean as you can be, to sneak up on a person and look at what they're looking at."

"How could *I* know you was looking at anything?"

"You ought to be ashamed of yourself, Tom Sawyer; you know you're going to tell on me; and, oh, what shall I do, what shall I do? I'll be whipped, and I never was whipped in school."

Then she stamped her little foot and said:

"*Be* so mean if you want to! *I* know something that's going to happen. You just wait, and you'll see! Hateful, hateful, hateful!" – and she flung out of the house with a new explosion of crying.

Tom stood still, rather flustered by this onslaught. Presently he said to himself:

"What a curious kind of a fool a girl is. Never been licked in school! Shucks, what's a licking! That's just like a girl – they're so thin-skinned and chicken-hearted. Well, of course *I* ain't going to tell old Dobbins on this little fool, because there's other ways of getting even on her that ain't so mean; but what of it? Old Dobbins will ask who it was tore his book. Nobody'll answer. Then he'll do just the way he always does – ask first one and then t'other, and when he comes to the right girl he'll know it, without any telling.

239

Girls' faces always tell on them. They ain't got any backbone. She'll get licked. Well, it's a kind of a tight place for Becky Thatcher, because there ain't any way out of it." Tom conned the thing a moment longer, and then added: "All right, though; she'd like to see me in just such a fix – let her sweat it out!"

Tom joined the mob of skylarking scholars outside. In a few moments the master arrived and school 'took in'. Tom did not feel a strong interest in his studies. Every time he stole a glance at the girls' side of the room, Becky's face troubled him. Considering all things, he did not want to pity her, and yet it was all he could do to help it. He could get up no exultation that was really worth the name. Presently the spelling-book discovery was made, and Tom's mind was entirely full of his own matters for a while after that. Becky roused up from her lethargy of distress, and showed good interest in the proceedings. She did not expect that Tom could get out of his trouble by denying that he spilt the ink on the book himself; and she was right. The denial only seemed to make the thing worse for Tom. Becky supposed she would be glad of that, and she tried to believe she was glad of it, but she found she was not certain. When the worst came to the worst, she had an impulse to get up and tell on Alfred Temple, but she made an effort and forced herself to keep still, because, said she to herself, "he'll tell about me tearing the picture, sure. I wouldn't say a word, not to save his life!"

Tom took his whipping and went back to his seat not at all broken-hearted, for he thought it was possible that he had unknowingly upset the ink on the spelling-book himself, in some skylarking bout – he had denied it for form's sake and because it was custom, and had stuck to the denial from principle.

A whole hour drifted by; the master sat nodding in his throne, the air was drowsy with the hum of study. By-and-by Mr Dobbins straightened himself up, yawned, then unlocked his desk, and reached for his book, but seemed undecided whether to take it out or leave it. Most of the pupils glanced up languidly, but there were two among them that watched his movements with intent eyes. Mr Dobbins fingered his book absently for a while, then took it out, and settled himself in his chair to read.

Tom shot a glance at Becky. He had seen a hunted and helpless rabbit look as she did, with a gun levelled at its head. Instantly he forgot his quarrel with her. Quick, something must be done! done in a flash, too! But the very imminence of the emergency paralysed his invention. Good! he had an inspiration! He would run and snatch the book, spring through the door and fly! but his resolution shook for one little instant, and the chance was lost – the master opened the volume. If Tom only had the wasted opportunity back again! Too late; there was no help for Becky now, he said. The next moment the master faced the school. Every eye sank under his gaze; there was that in it which smote even the innocent with fear. There was silence while one might count ten; the master was gathering his wrath. Then he spoke:

"Who tore this book?"

There was not a sound. One could have heard a pin drop. The stillness continued; the master searched face after face for signs of guilt.

"Benjamin Rogers, did you tear this book?"

A denial. Another pause.

"Joseph Harper, did you?"

Another denial. Tom's uneasiness grew more and more intense under the slow torture of these proceedings. The master scanned the ranks of boys, considered a while, then turned to the girls:

"Amy Lawrence?"

A shake of the head.

"Gracie Miller?"

The same sign.

"Susan Harper, did you do this?"

Another negative. The next girl was Becky Thatcher. Tom

241

was trembling from head to foot with excitement, and a sense of the hopelessness of the situation.

"Rebecca Thatcher" – (Tom glanced at her face; it was white with terror) – "did you tear – no, look me in the face" – (her hands rose in appeal) – "did you tear this book?"

A thought shot like lightning through Tom's brain. He sprang to his feet and shouted:

"*I* done it!"

The school stared in perplexity at this incredible folly. Tom stood a moment to gather his dismembered faculties; and when he stepped forward to go to his punishment, the surprise, the gratitude, the adoration that shone upon him out of poor Becky's eyes seemed pay enough for a hundred floggings. Inspired by the splendour of his own act, he took without an outcry the most merciless flogging that even Mr Dobbins had ever administered; and also received with indifference the added cruelty of a command to remain two hours after school should be dismissed – for he knew who would wait for him outside till his captivity was done, and not count the tedious time as loss either.

Tom went to bed that night planning vengeance against Alfred Temple; for with shame and repentance Becky had told him all, not forgetting her own treachery; but even the longing for vengeance had to give way soon to pleasanter musings, and he fell asleep at last with Becky's latest words lingering dreamily in his ear:

"Tom, how *could* you be so noble!"

I AM GOING TO BE GOOD

GEOFFREY WILLANS

HERE WE GO AGANE!

O WILD WEST wind thou breath of autumns being thou from whose unseen presence the leaves dead are driven like gostes from an enchanter fleeing. Posh, eh? i bet you 6d. it fooled you. "molesworth at his rolling best. Sonorus and sublime" i expect you said. Aktually it is not me it is a weed called shelley and i copied it from the peotry book.

"Why?" sa molesworth 2 who zoom up like the wet he is. "Why copy peotry when you mite be buzzing bricks, conking me on the napper or braking windows with yore air pistol go on tell me o you mite."

"Becos," i tell him, "it is autumn and the long hols are nearly over. Soon we shall be back at SKOOL."

At these words he burst out blubbing and will not be comforted. i confess there hav been many times when the thort of GRIMES, the master, the bullies cads, snekes wets and weeds would hav depressed me too. But not this time.

I AM GOING TO BE GOOD THIS TERM.

i will tell you how this happened. The other day i am fed up with toughing up molesworth 2 and am stooging about saing wot shall i do mum wot shall i do eh?

To this she gives various replies i.e.

(a) *go for a walk.*
(b) *pla with your toys.*
(c) *watch t.v. childrens hour ect.*

none of these are acceptable to me so in the end she make a suggestion so rude hem-hem i canot print it here. It is thus i find myself locked in the atick until teatime chiz chiz chiz and find gran's old book called chaterbox 1896. There is 0 to do so i turn its weedy pages and read the story of wee tim:

> *"wee tim is riding in his grandpater's cariage as staunch and sturdy a little felow as ever you would wish to see. Sudenly he see an old lady who is carying a heavy basket and he clutch his grandpater's knee. 'Granpa granpa,' he sa, 'can we not let this pore old lady ride in our cariage, eh? She is so weak and frale.' Wot a good kind thort! His fierce grandpa sa 'O.K. tim even though i am an earl let us take her for a ride . . .' "*

(molesworth thinks: this is where the story get craking. Now wee tim will hit her with a COSH and pinch wot is in the basket while boris the foul coachman look on with a cruel grin. But no!)

> *"Will you ride with us, old lady?" sa tim and wot a pikture he looked with his long golden curls! "Thank you young sir," she sa. "But i canot ride in the cariage of an earl." "He is a good earl," sa tim, "even though he look like that." "And i," she sa, "am really a rich old lady and becos you hav been good and gentle i will leave you my fortune when i die . . ."*

Coo ur gosh i mean to sa if that is wot you get for being good it is worth it it is easier than the pools. I look back on my condukt in the hols. Hav it been all it should be?

scene: the molesworth brekfast table.

ME: gosh chiz kippers again this is worse than skool.

FATHEFUL NAN: get on, nigel, you are ungrateful. The pore boys would be glad to have nice kippers for brekfast.

MOLESWORTH 2: Yar boo and sucks molesworth 1 hav a face like a flea.

ME: Et tu, weed, thrice over and no returns.

(A kipper fly through the air).

FATHEFUL NAN: No little gentleman thro kippers, nigel.

MOLESWORTH 1: Then i will thro korn flakes instead. Ha ha ha witty boy ha ha ha ect. . . .

i blush with shame at the memory of this unsavoury incident and *let's face it, my dears*, it was only one of many. Would wee tim hav thrown a kipper at molesworth 2? Would he hav been cheeky to fatheful nan? I doubt it very much. He would hav given his kipper to the pore boys . . . O woe i am a weed chiz! Next term i will alter my ways. Already i can pikture the scene at st custard's:

a thortful figure is walking among the dead beetles crushed biskuits and old buns which litter the skool passage. He is reading a peotry book.

MOLESWORTH 1: The asyrian came down like a wolf on the fold ect. . . . Wot a luvley poem! To think that even a term ago i drew tadpoles all over it and wrote "turn to page 103 if my name ect!" How can i hav done such a thing? The asyrian came down . . .

At this moment a huge mob of cads, snekes, oiks, tuoughs, oafs and skool dogs charge ta-ran-ta-rah like the light brigade all covered with marmalade in my direction.

MOLESWORTH 1: Silence! *(There is a hush.)* Boys, this is foul condukt. You are ragging in the passage an offence under section 88888/b/107 of the skool rules. Go back to yore desks and be good in future. *(They slink awa with bowed heads.)*

GRIMES the headmaster hav been silently observing this good DEED and he pat me on the head make me head of the skool instead of grabber and give me mrs joyful prize for rafia work.

But, you kno, wot will really hapen? It wil be quite different i am afraid and will go like this.

Scene: The klassroom. Enter master for lat. lesson. molesworth 1 hav all his books out, pencils sharp, AND BUNGY at the ready.

ME: Good morning, dere sir. i hope you slept well?

BEAK: (*thinks*) A trap! (*He aim a vicious blow*) Take that, you dolt. Do you think you can rag me, the scurge of the skool?

ME: i forgive you, sir. You look pale you have drunk BEER last night. May i get you a pil?

BEAK: Stand on yore chair, molesworth. Any more and you will get 6!

ME: Do not open that desk, sir, it is full of old cucumbers put there by i kno not whom.

BEAK: Enuff! Wate for me outside.
(A vale is drawn over the foul proceedings.)

Am i rite in this foul proffecy? Shall it alter my determination to be like wee tim? Shall i shake in my resolution? onley time will revele all – wate fellow-weeds, with baited breath, and you mite catch a wopper, ha ha.

THE GRATE MASTER TRAP

Hay ho! Hullo birds! Hullo clouds! Hullo, skool dog! Hullo, sirup of figgs! Hullo, potts and pilcher fr. primer!

Who is this who skip weedily along the skool passage and out towards the den of ye olde skoole pigge? One would really hav thort it was fotherington-tomas so gay is he, so lite-harted. There, dere reader, you make a big mistake as c. dickens (auther of d. Coperfield the book of the film) would sa. No, dere, gentle reader who may chance to con these pages with so much sympathy ect, you make one helluva big mistake. You are way, way out, coyottes. It is i, n. molesworth, the ex-curse of st custards, who skip weedily, who cry hay-ho, hay-ho ect. And wot hav i been doing, eh?

FLASHBACK! 2 minits ago.

N. MOLESWORTH: Matronne, i have brought you this pressed leaf. May i do yore flowers?

MATRONNE: *(reaching for her gat)* Scram, scruff! Or i will do you!

N. MOLESWORTH: i forgive you, matronne, for those uncouth words. A still tongue in a wise head.

MATRONNE: Git!

N. MOLESWORTH: i will, indeed. A rolling stone gathers no moss. Likewise, procrastination is the thief of time.

MATRONNE: *YAR!*

N. MOLESWORTH: As you plese. An empty barrel makes the most noise.

(exit with a courteous bow.)

It is a strange, lonely world when you are GOOD. Is it my fault that i hav been practising my handwriting in the copy books? Now i kno wot pore, pore basil fotherington-tomas, that wet and weed, hav gone through. People seme to avoid me – no friendly hale of darts and inkpots comes my way. Even molesworth 2 refuses my buble-gum and masters pat me on the head.

YET i MUST KEPE TO MY CHOSEN ROAD.

But, soft, wot is this? It is peason, my grate frend, who worketh upon some strange contraption near the pigge den. Wot mischief can he be up to?

"Hullo, peason," i sa. "The devil finds work for idle hands. Wot is that?"

"Nothing," he repli.

"if't be nothing, yet 'tis something, for nothing is not but wot something semes (shakespere)" i riposte, litely. "Yet if't be something –" He buzz a brick at me. No matter, i try agane.

"Go on, peason, you mite tell me go on, o you mite the same to you and no returns."

"you would not be interested," he grate, turning a nut with his spanner. "Nowadays you are a weed, a wet and uterly wormlike. Gone are the days when we invented the molesworth/peason lines machine together."

"It hav a good streme-line effect and neat basket work. i like the way the electronick brane give easy control and at the same time there is wide vision and plenty of lugage space. Good points are – "

He buzz another brick and, sorowfully, i depart. Ah me, where is there to go? Who else luv me but my old frende the skool pigge, who hav never let me down? Hurrah, hurrah, he leap to greet me and place his piggy paws on the sty wall. He take my buble-gum graciously and lick my hand. i recite a poem i hav written e.g.

> *O pigge, you are so beautiful!*
> *I luve yore snouty nose!*
> *ect.*

n.b. pigs are the cleanest animals in the world, although i sometimes think there are exceptions.

And so, refreshed and strengthened, i return once agane into the wicked world of st custard's where peason is still at work. Wot can it be?

Is it:

An atommic fast-bowling machine?

An automatick golekeeper?

A loudspeker for calling 'Fire!' in the middle of maths lessons?

A measles-rash injector?

Curiosity overcome me and i return.

"No honestly, peason, word of honour cross my hart fingers uncrossed and pax tell me, rat, wot it is or i will utterly ruough you up."

"That is better, clot. Now i will tell you – it is a MASTER TRAP."

Hurrah! Hurrah! A trap for beaks! Wot a wizard wheeze! Gosh, absolutely super and smashing! Good show! Charge ta-ran-ta-rah! Dozens of masters – lat. masters fr. geom. algy. div masters all caught and eliminated. And it work for mistresses, too! But chiz wot am i saing? For a moment i thort the world mite be safe in future for children – i must be careful.

"Kindly explane," i sa, a triffel stiffly (but no enuff to make him withdraw into the silence usuhually so alien to him).

He tell me all. There is a bait of lat. books. Attracted iresistibly the beak creep stealthily in through the door and before he can get to ex.1. the trap hav closed. A see-saw tip him into a cold bath and an endless belt take him to a third chamber where he get six from the automatick caning machine.

"Yes, yes," i sa, excitedly. "Wot then! Wot devilish fate waits for them then?"

"They die sloly on a diet of skool food!"

"Gosh, yes! Or you mite hang a skool sossage eternally out of reach."

"That would be no punishment, oaf. And you are lucky. i am going to make my first experiment with *YOU!*"

Too late i see the plot, chiz! A dozen hands with beetles and earwigs drawn on them scrag me. The leader is grabber, the tete de la skool. "Make haste slowly," i yell. "Too many cooks spoil the broth; Help; Rescue." But whereas in the old days fifty trusty boys would hav leaped from the thickets at the sound – today none come. None at all. And robin hood had better take note of it. i am pushed towards the infernal trap and my DOOM IS SEALED.

But wot is this? My trusty frende the skool pigge hav got there first. Before they can stop him he is inside: he eat the lat. books: enjoy the bath, the caning machine tickle him litely, he wolf the skool food and with one heave of his mitey flanks he knock the whole machine for SIX! Cheers, cheers, cheers i am saved. But wot a narow shave, eh? That nite i rite carefully in my dere copy book

Virtue is its own reward

"You're so right," sa fotherington-tomas. "So true, so true! Hullo, clouds! Hullo sky!"

This all needs a lot of thort.

SO FAR SO GOOD

It is evening after prep at st custard's. The curtanes hav been drawn, the gas lites are popping merrily and the crow hav long since gone to its nest, tho where else it could go to i do not kno. In every nook and crany, knee-deep in blotch pelets, bits of bungy, old lines and pages of deten the gay little chaps enjoy there freedom. Some toste sossages over the gas mantle, others, more adventurous, swing upside down on the chandeleres. The air echo with cries of *pax*, *unpax*, *fains*, *roter*, *shutup*, and *the same to you with no returns*. WOW-EEEEEE sa molesworth 2 zooming past as a jet bomber.

But who is this quiet student who reads The book of berds and there eggs, eh? It is me, molesworth 1 believe it or not, for i hav determined to be GOOD and it is easy pappy and absolutely 0 to it at all. E.g. soon i put down my book, mark the place with an old pressed leaf, put it in my tidy desk and make my way quietly to the study of GRIMES the headmaster. *Knock tap tap tap!*

Wot is it, molesworth? sa GRIMES, looking up from his pools.

i hav been reading a most interesting book, sir. It is called berds and there eggs. Take the jackdaw, sir. It frequents parks, old buildings and often perform aerial acrobaticks. It hav a propensity for hiding food and other objects. Eggs ushually 4 to 6.

yes, yes, molesworth, indeed? Thank you for the information. Now –

Sometimes, however, sir, only 2 eggs are to be found. The linet, on the other hand – shall i tell you about the linet?

Some other time, molesworth. i am very busy now. times are hard how about 5 bob till tuesday?

(Thinks: it is worth a try. A mug is born every minit.)

Here is a pound, sir, i sa, o forget yore gratitude it would be a pore hart who did not aid an old frend in distress. It is a gift. If you want any good deed done agane just let me kno.

(GRIMES thinks: stone the crows who would hav thort it? A hem-hem plaster saint. No need to take out the old whelk stall this week now.)

And so it go on. That is just one example. Another thing i hav become a swot and a brane. I am top in lat, hist, algy, geom, div. ect.

Brave, proud and fearless molesworth 1 can face the world safe in the knoledge that SWOTING ALWAYS PAYS.

Scene: a t.v. studio, poorly furnished, a table with three legs, lit by a candle in a botle. An interviewer in rags come forward.

Interviewer: This is the 960 million quid programme. Who is the next contestant wot subjeckt do you choose?

St. M. it is i. wigan, lancs. i certainly do. i would. me and the wife will certainly hope to. History.

Interviewer: Half a mo. Wate for me to ask the q's. Who burned the cakes?

St. M. Who pinched the cakes, you mean. molesworth 2, of corse.

Interviewer: You hav won 6000 quid would you car to go for the jakpot? Go into the box can you hear me ect. Now for 960 quid wot berd frequents parks, does aerial acrobaticks, hides food and usually lay 4 to 6 eggs, eh?

St. M. The – um – o gosh it's ur-er choke gosh garble.

Interviewer: i'm sorry. i'm very sorry. i'm very sorry indeed. The answer was – A JACKDAW!

(Exit st. m. blubbing on the arm of a beautiful GURL.)

Well, there you are. Being GOOD is pappay. Try it. Try it toda. Try it brighter, try it whiter, try it with or without a hole in the family size. But wot is this? As i walk upon my pious way i come upon a MASTER who bendeth over. He is a sitting target. Wot a chance! With foot drawn back molesworth bare his fangs. Will he sukumb to temptation?

(see another daring, palpittating instalment in our next issue.)

THE KARACKTER KUP

"Boys," sa GRIMES, the headmaster, smiling horibly, "the time have come to present the scrimgeour kup for good karackter. This is never an easy kup to award" (of course not, it is ushually at the pornbrokers) "becos there must be no doubt either in my mind or those of the staff" – he give an even more horible smile at the thugs seated around – "that the winner is WORTHY of this supreme honor. The choice hav to be a most careful one ect."

Aktually i do not see the dificulty. If you look at the 56 gallant little pupils of st custards, each with his own peculiar ways, it is easy, pappy to devise a SYSTEM. You simply get rid of them in this way i.e. there are: 5 squits, 9 snekes, 19 cribbers, 2 maniaks, 3 bookmakers, 4 swots, 11 cig. smokers. Total 53.

Chiz this leaves only one pupil to whom the kup can possibly be awarded. Well, you kno, i mean to sa, i hav been joly GOOD lately and sucking up to the beaks. Obviously this fakt hav been noted. GRIMES continue:

"The boy who win this kup must be noble, upright, brave, fearless, intreppid and honnest. He must not have been afrade to stick up for wot he kno to be right. He must protekt the weak. He must luv the highest when he see it."

Oh come on, gosh chiz this is going a bit far. i blush to the roots.

"Every boy at st custard's," continue GRIMES, "must search himself to see if he comes up to these high standards and if he do not the pot is not his. Hav he been a help to the masters?"

Well, that one is easy. Look wot hapened only yesterday.

Scene: Klassroom of 3B, early dawn. A pupil stands on guard with a sten gun, the rest snore at their desks. Outside a burd sings sweetly.

A beak drags himself in to his desk.

BEAK: Gosh blime, i feel terible.

MOLESWORTH: Pore sir, you have missed brekfast. Let me get you some skool fish or a nice runny egg.

(Takt, but the beak do not seme to fancy my sugestion. He shudereth and groweth pale.)

BEAK: Ugh. Wot lesson is it? I thort you was all due for woodwork in the carpentry shed. You can go along there if you like.

MOLESWORTH: Oh, no, sir. We prefer to stay with you and do our peotry.

BEAK: i was afraid of it. Gillibrand, say yore prep.

GILLIBRAND: Who, sir, wot me, sir.

BEAK: Wot was the name of the famous peom of which you were required to learn 24 lines?

GILLIBRAND: Search me, sir.

BEAK: *(some of his old fire reviving)* i do not wish to search you, gillibrand, i mite be appaled at wot i should find.

(Ha-ha-ha-ha-ha-ha-ha-ha from all, gillibrand struggle to his feet, his mouth open like a fish, he stare, he stammer, he scratcheth his head and the ushual shower of beetles fall out.)

You seme nonplussed, gillibrand. Can it be that you were drawing H-bombs during prep? TAKE A DETEN. Now which of you scum can sa the peom?

MOLESWORTH: *(flipping his fingers like bullet shots, dancing on the points of his tiny toes.)* Oh, gosh, sir. Please, sir. Gosh, sir, can i, sir?

BEAK: Ah, molesworth. i had not thort of you heretofore as one keen on the arts. Let us see. Sa prep.

(molesworth stand to attention, fingers in line with the seam of his trousis, eyes straight ahead.)

MOLESWORTH: "THE SAND OF DEE BY C. KINGSLEY."
O Mary, go and call the catle home.
  And call the catle home.
  And call the catle home,
Across the sands o' dee.
The western wind was wild –
BEAK: *(hastily)* That's enuff, molesworth. v.g.v.g., indeed.
MOLESWORTH: – and dank wi fome,
  And all alone went she.
The creeping tide came up along the sand,
  and o'er and o'er –
BEAK: well done molesworth joly good ten out of ten you can stop now.
MOLESWORTH: – the sand,
  And round and round the sand,
As far as eye could see:
The blinding mist came down and hid the land,
  And never home came she.
(fotherington-tomas burst out blubbing)
O, is it weed, or fish, or floating hair? –
BEAK: Thank you, molesworth, thank you. excellent.

(But nothing can stop me. i continue to the end of the peom despite a hale of ink darts. At the conclusion i bow low and strike my nose upon the desk. All look at me as if amazed.)

Yes, i think i may sa i hav been a help to the masters the kup is as good as mine. Wot else? GRIMES looks around.

"Hav he been a help to the other members of the huge staff to whom i owe so much? (i.e. about 9 million quid back wages.) Hav he helped our very overworked skool gardener? And matron – how do he and she get on?"

All too well, old top, if you are thinking of PRUDENCE ENTWHISTLE, the glamorous under-matron. But it must be MATRON herself, who look like a gunman's moll in a gangster pikture. But even here my record is good –

Scene: Matronne's room, the doors of ye olde physick cupboard are open.

MOLESWORTH: i hav been reading of the labours of hercules, matronne, may i clean out yore cupboard? . . . Wot hav we here in the syrup of figgs bot? It smell like G-I-N . . . and wot can these BEER bottles be doing, as if hidden behind the radio-malt? . . . I will arrange them neatly in the front row . . . And wot is this which look like the skeleton of a boy chained to the wall . . . ect. O.K. there, you see. Now for the Kup.

"The winner must be of excellent repute, (o come, sire). Talented, (o fie!). Inspired." (Enuff. You sla me.)

"And so," sa Grimes smiling more horibly than ever, "i hav no hesitation in awarding the kup to GRABBER."

Well its the old story. A fat cheque and you can fix anything but right, i suppose, will triumph in the end. In the meantime o mary go and call the catle home ect, or go and do something, i am fed up.